WE ARE MAYHEM

BECK ROURKE-MOONEY

FEIWEL AND FRIENDS

NEW YORK

A Feiwel and Friends Book
An imprint of Macmillan Publishing Group, LLC
120 Broadway, New York, NY 10271 • fiercereads.com

Our books may be purchased in bulk for promotional, educational, or
business use. Please contact your local bookseller or the Macmillan
Corporate and Premium Sales Department at (800) 221-7945 ext. 5442
or by email at MacmillanSpecialMarkets@macmillan.com.

Library of Congress Cataloging-in-Publication Data is available.

First edition, 2024
Book design by Julia Bianchi
Feiwel and Friends logo designed by Filomena Tuosto
Printed in the United States of America

ISBN 978-1-250-83659-5 (hardcover)
10   9   8   7   6   5   4   3   2   1

To Chris: the best there is, the best there was,
the best there ever will be

You set a generation of freaks free with your persona
With your rubber banded face and your rubber banded beard

You gave a lot of kids permission to let out their inner weird

So here's to you, Captain Lou yeah, I love you yeah
Captain Lou, Captain Lou yeah, I love you yeah

—KIMYA DAWSON

CHAPTER 1

The Deep Lagoon is an evergreen paradise where the creek bends and the earth rises behind it, creating a wide, full belly of a pool. A rope swing hangs from a tree limb high above the river's edge, and if I let go at exactly the right spot, I can flip and land in the deepest part.

George stands near the water, angling her phone to catch the best selfie light. In her bikini top and cutoff shorts, a crystal pendant tangled in her wavy hair, my sister fully embodies the latest incarnation of her brand, George of the Wild. Back to nature, but like . . . with crystals and astrology memes. Her previous fashion project, Specs and the City, featured "hot girls wearing glasses in Brooklyn"—the actual tagline.

I'm pretty sure George only came to the Deep Lagoon because she needs me to take pictures of her looking hot in the woods. You've heard of the Instagram boyfriend? Meet me: the Instagram sister.

I used to feel like, if I watched George closely enough and

tried my hardest to be just like her, someday I actually might be. But George is so George—and I'm still just so . . . me.

"Still rocking the boy shorts, huh, Bird?" George says, and I look down at my favorite swimsuit.

It feels like she's calling me a little kid and I try not to let it show.

"I know, I know. I should switch to a string bikini so I, too, can constantly pick my own wedgie while I swim," I say. But inside, I'm already shopping for something more grown-up. Less *me*. And then cringing at the thought of wearing it.

Boy shorts is a stupid name, anyway, for something girls wear.

George always jokes that Mom and Dad's entire plan—naming her George, dressing her in a whole lot of yellow, trying to delay the inevitable onslaught of the world shoving what it means to be a girl down her throat—backfired. Instead, she became obsessed with all things pink and sparkly. She swears that's why they gave up by the time I was born.

And it's true. George, through all her many incarnations, is a legit femme icon. You'd think it'd rub off on me by proxy, and believe me, I've tried to absorb it. I spent the first two years of middle school trying to reinvent myself as George, but every time I curled my long hair or put on lip gloss, I felt like a kid in a costume, not a grown-up version of myself.

No matter what makeup I play with, or which outfits I try on: Inside, I'm still George's tomboy (also kind of a stupid name for girls) kid sister. Which is why it's ridiculous that I've let Lexie talk me into trying out for cheerleading.

The creek is so cold my breath catches, but I wade into the current and plunge my head under. The water smells like rocks, like snowmelt from the mountain, and it wakes me up the same way it does every summer we come to visit my grandparents. Only now, thanks to Mom's midlife crisis, I live here.

I snake around the riverbank, up to where the rope hangs, and it feels like stepping back inside my skin, dripping in the warm summer air. My bare feet press into years of soft orange-brown pine needles layered over the cool soil, grounding me.

My best memories are tucked here in these mountains. Hiking Overlook, swimming anywhere the water's deep and clear. The smell of evergreens stretching for miles. Fireflies floating like flickering lanterns. Campfires and s'mores. Spinning our names in sparkler script across the night sky, chins sticky with watermelon and river water.

I grip the rope and inhale the familiar mix of sap and needles, bark and forest floor, the water calling to me. I take a few steps back from the edge to get a running start. When I launch off the cliff and swing out, I recognize the familiar arc. I feel for it, the *exact* moment where the rope is at the perfect angle for release, and then—let go—I fly free, tuck my knees to my chest, and roll back, spinning.

I crash soles-first into the pool and come up for air, joy lighting up my cells like a full body smile.

"I got the best video of that," George says. "And . . . uploaded." I step out of the water and grab my towel, hardly believing.

She holds it up for me to see.

The post is titled POETRY IN MOTION: the video of me with an unattributed Keats quote—*Beauty is truth, truth beauty. The Deep Lagoon.* If ten years from now the internet misattributes the Keats line to a beauty influencer named George, I know why.

"There's nothing more beautiful than someone doing what

they're meant to do," George says. "I know you think Mom's full of crap right now, but she's right. It really is the privilege of a lifetime to be who you are."

I shake my wet hair like a dog coming out of the water. I don't need to hear any more about Mom's midlife crisis. How her sudden need to *find her bliss* means we have to live here, now.

My entire life used to be gymnastics, and since I quit, I've had one focus. Not friends. Not fun. Not some cliché list of how to seize the day before graduation.

I focus on my future. Which, for the record, has more to do with how many AP classes I ace, how many competitive internships I rack up, and how often and impressively I volunteer. All of which are harder to do out here in the middle of nowhere.

I don't get into it, but what George says hurts more than it helps. Flying through the air and nailing a complicated move *is* my bliss. Not that gymnastics always felt that way. It was all-consuming. Painful. Incredibly hard. And then over.

A hundred and fifty pounds of pure, unadulterated muscle, I used to boast. Back before Coach told me that with my body growing as it was—taller, thicker, wider—my shot at making it from Level 10 to Elite was shrinking. That it didn't matter how many twenty-hour weeks I put in. How hard I trained to be the best. I grew too big. Coach said it like he was doing me a favor.

It's nothing personal, he said. As if there's anything more personal than your body.

"Some things never change," George says, looking around as we leave the Deep Lagoon, and I want to believe that's true. Even though all signs currently point to the fact that it's definitely not.

CHAPTER 2

I'm sitting shotgun on my way to cheerleading tryouts in Lexie's beloved ride, Ted—named for the used car salesman she bought him from, the one who told her *cars deserve pretty names like pretty girls*. It feels like I'm being held hostage, even though no one is making me do this. I have actual glitter in my hair courtesy of the palmful Lexie blew at me when I got into the car. With her work visor hanging from the rearview mirror, Ted smells like the inside of a Stewart's Shop: coffee, ice cream, and apple fritters.

I text George: *Remind me again why I'm doing this*, even though I know exactly what she's going to write.

"You guys are so lucky your mom had a nervous breakdown," Lexie says, riding the air with her palm out the window. "My migratory summer Birdie, finally here forever."

"Hardly," I say. "It's the summer before senior year, so unless I fail out of life, forever's kind of a stretch." *Even if my parents have sabotaged my future by dragging me to this Podunk town*, I think.

To bloom where you're planted, George writes back. It's her mantra every time I complain about moving and having to be here now. Apparently blooming where I'm planted has something to do with a face full of glitter and a stomach knotted with dread.

I love Lexie, but it's different up here in the mountains. At my high school back in New Jersey, all anyone talked about last semester was their SAT scores and what internships they wanted to get this summer so they could go to Yale instead of Penn. Lexie and her friends don't worry about any of that.

Lexie's trying out for cheer for the first time because she loves making TikTok dance videos with her cheerleader best friend, and she works as many shifts at Stewart's as she can. Unless I never want to see her once school starts—and she's literally my only friend, here or otherwise—I've got to make the squad, too. I haven't had any real friends since I quit gymnastics and lost all of mine. It'd be kind of nice to start the year on a team.

The thing is, even though I can knock out a floor routine in gymnastics, I couldn't be less . . . cheerleader-y. I mean, I admire them. All that pep. The unfailing, season-long, outcome-independent optimism. The wholehearted embrace of all things glitter.

I even actually really *like* glitter. It's just, when you put all those pieces together, I can't do it. I know there's not one right way to be a girl. But sometimes it feels like the world thinks there is, and I'm not it. Cheerleaders, though? They nail it.

We pull into the parking lot and the knot in my stomach burns. Kayleigh, Lexie's best friend, who's vying for captain, spots us and runs over, her curled and glitter-sprayed pigtails trailing behind her like handlebar streamers. I've never felt so unprepared for anything in my life.

"Are we ready for this or what, bitches?" Kayleigh shakes her pom-poms in the air and executes a perfect double cross, a term I just learned.

Lexie bounds out of the car, beaming. "I practiced only a million times more when I got home last night, and I finally nailed that eight-count I've been stumbling on."

"Shut up! Seriously?" Kayleigh shoves her the way only friends can without consequence, and I wonder if there's a maximum capacity for loneliness, or if it's the kind of thing that can keep expanding forever until it's completely overtaken all other feelings. Like an invasive species.

"I just want tryouts to be over so my mom will chill the F out," Kayleigh says. "She's obsessed with me being named captain. She's such a dance mom."

"Like they'd choose anyone else," Lexie says, shooting a dismissive glance at the other girls in the lot.

At the door to the gym, we're greeted by a petite woman with pink lipstick. Her brown hair is pulled into a ponytail, the collar of her polo shirt popped around her tanned neck.

"Welcome, ladies!" she calls out, her voice huskier than I expected. "New faces!"

"These strays are with me, Mo," Kayleigh says, and it's a relief the way she claims me as her own.

"What's Creepy doing here?" Lexie nudges Kayleigh in the ribs and points to the back hallway door of the gymnasium. A girl in hole-ridden black jeans, wearing intense eyeliner, leans against the wall, notebook and pen in hand. Her hair is dyed black, with two chunks of bright purple framing her face, and her shirt is homespun—a white T-shirt with BOW TO THE QUEEN written in Sharpie.

"Probably trying to poach our talent for her family's freak show," Kayleigh says.

"Or she's come to harvest bodies for the bone store?" Lexie says, and they both laugh.

"Seriously?" I whisper to Lexie.

"Once upon a time, she was halfway normal," Kayleigh says.

When she stares at the girl against the wall, the girl stares back. She doesn't even blink.

A group of guys—football players, from the look of their necks—pass by the girl, and one of them hits the notebook in her hand, knocking it to the floor. Lexie laughs and shakes her head, but the girl looks unflustered. She juts her chin out at him, like she *dares* him to try something else, and when the group disappears into the weight room, she picks up her notebook and returns her intense focus to the tryout. Like it never happened.

I blink.

Mo steps to the front and beams a quintessential cheerleader smile.

I'm not cut out for this. The girls wear so much glitter it coats the gym floor, which sparkles under fluorescent lights, and I watch them, wishing I *could* just do what George says. Bloom here—out of this rock-hard bleacher seat where I've been planted—like the flower I've always been meant to be.

But flowers need sunshine to bloom, and soil to sink roots into. They don't bloom on command in a high school gymnasium under flickering banks of fluorescent lights.

Kayleigh jumps up when she's called to the front. Two other girls flank her sides, and in unison, they chant, "Five, six, seven, eight," and then launch into dance moves.

I told myself it would all be OK. I'd impress them with my floor work. I half imagined myself bounding into the room, handspring after handspring, a human Slinky. I'd land the final flip, and a crowd would have gathered, in awe. Intimidated by the new girl.

But the only one intimidated here is me.

The dance goes as badly as I fear. Everyone else follows along—even the guys shake their hips like Shakira—and though my body is flailing its limbs in somewhat similar directions to what the choreography intends, the movements themselves can hardly be called dancing.

Mo roams the floor, making notes on her clipboard and giving suggestions, all while beaming a cheek-cramping smile. I can barely breathe when she stops at me, her head tilted.

"You're not as far off as it feels," Mo says. "Try this." She starts to sway to the beat, leading with each shoulder and then curving back on herself at the waist. The others continue around us, and I feel singled out.

If I try to do that, I won't look like she does.

"Aren't you even going to try?" The music ends and Mo's husky voice is the only sound in the gym. "It's called a *try*out for a reason."

"I am trying," I whisper, paralyzed by the spotlight suddenly on me. I look for Lexie, in the front row right behind Kayleigh, but she doesn't even meet my eyes.

"Kayleigh says you're a heck of a gymnast, so I've got high hopes for you. But you've got a lot to learn, and you're going to need to be a team player," Mo says.

Everyone else is silent and watching, catching their breath from dancing. My face grows hot. I can't do what she's asking me to do. I just can't. But maybe if I show her what I *can* do, she'll give me a shot anyway.

I spot a long clear space to take off running and launch into the opening sequence I imagined for myself. I round off into a triple back handspring and close with a backflip, sticking the landing like I never stopped training.

Blood pounds inside my ears, courses through my body, all the way to my fingertips. I'm dizzy with energy. I haven't thrown a sequence like this in over a year. I forgot how exhilarating it is. I feel alive. Unstoppable.

"You think we don't have girls who can do that?" Mo says. She nods to three girls. "Tova, Freya, Sofia. Show her."

The girls huddle together and then line up at the end of the gym. They take off running together and then, synchronized, they do four back handsprings into a backflip and cap it off with toe touches so precise their legs look like one long straight line.

"Think you're better than *that*?" Mo asks.

Wanna be the best, you gotta beat the best, Coach always said, and I feel that familiar steel confidence rise. The one I learned to turn on when Mom taught me the phrase, *Fake it until you make it*.

"I know I am," I say, desperate to prove my worth. But Mo shakes her head.

"With a cocky attitude like that, you'll be fine without us." I'm not really sure what she means, but then Mo waves me away. "You're cut."

I start toward the back door and try not to cry. I've never wanted to disappear so badly in my life. I don't want to turn around to see Lexie huddled next to Kayleigh. All of those eyes watching me through glitter-dusted lashes, wondering if I'll crack.

So I don't look back at my only friend, and I don't try to tell Mo I'm sorry or ask for a second chance. I think I just got cut for having a bad attitude, which seems worse than if I'd gotten cut because I suck. Which would also be true.

The only eyes I catch on my way out are rimmed in thick black. She's watching me, scribbling notes in her little book.

"Is this entertaining to you?" My anger oozes out, but she smiles anyway.

"You have no idea. Actually, I was hoping to talk to you. You're new here, aren't you?" the stranger says. "I've got a proposition for you, something that could change your life. This might sound crazy," she says, and so far, she's right about that, "but do you believe in fate?"

I laugh, a sharp, "Ha!" *Fate.*

I turn around to face her, but all I can see is the gym full of people staring at me. Staring at *us*. Me and this girl Lexie and Kayleigh were just moments before making fun of.

I failed. I tried to pass as a cheerleader, and I failed. What an idiot I was for even trying.

I storm down the hallway of this school I've never even been inside—which five towns and more than thirty tiny hamlets from over three hundred square miles all funnel into—and I'm almost to the outside door. My old school, with one town, had three times the student body.

But I don't feel like a big fish in a small pond up here.

I feel like a grain of sand in the ocean. A dandelion seed floating over a gorge.

"You're perfect!" the girl shouts after me, and I laugh again. But I do stop. "Your build," she says, capping her pen and tucking it into her spiral notebook. "It's perfect. For wrestling."

When I turn around, this girl I don't know holds up her phone for me to see.

"I've had an epically shitty day," I say.

"Fuck that dance shit." Her lip curls in dismissive disgust, and she holds up her phone with a picture of a woman with bright orange hair who looks like she could definitely kick my ass. Anyone's ass. Her T-shirt reads THE MAN in block letters, and she's got not one but two heavyweight belts slung over her shoulders.

The kind of bling that makes an Olympic medal almost look dinky.

"Do you know who she is?" she asks, and I'm about to lose my patience and snap at this stranger who won't take a hint.

I manage a "No" through closed teeth.

"That's Becky Lynch. The Man. What're you? Five seven?" It's unnerving, but she's right on the money and knows it.

"Is this a carnival booth?" I say. "Are you going to guess my weight next?"

She nods like my being this size is some plan she orchestrated in advance.

"Your muscle mass is impressive," she says, stepping back like she's judging a cow at the county fair. "You look like you could throw someone out of the ring."

I laugh through my nose. "That's the weirdest thing anyone's ever said to me."

I'm used to strangers saying what they want to me about my muscles. It's better than when they actually touch me. But this girl is bringing some next-level strange to the table.

"You've got the right build, and with that aerial talent?" She looks me straight in the eyes. "You could be huge."

"I don't want to be huge," I say, never surer of anything.

When I was twelve, this jerk at Splash Castle, who was running the scary slide that goes straight down, told me I had dude arms. I was *so* angry, but I just stood there. Silent.

It was ironic, him calling out the size of my arms, me feeling smaller and smaller each second. Lexie told him off, but that's Lex. She does what she wants and gets away with it.

People—mostly cis male people—are always commenting on my "guns," backing up with their hands raised, begging me not to hurt them. As if strong arms, by virtue of being on a girl, are a threat to their masculinity.

In elementary school, I was faster than all the boys until they hit their growth spurts in fourth grade. After that, I was only faster than most of them. But there was usually at least one sore loser who would insinuate that my strength and speed meant I wasn't a girl. As if speed and strength somehow belonged to boys, and girls, by definition, were weak and slow. That being "like a boy" or "like a girl" was a concrete set of characteristics to begin with, which never made sense to me at all.

This should feel like the same thing. This stranger commenting on my body. Showing me that picture of Becky Lynch, The Man. But there's something about the look on her face as she sizes me up.

"I'm sorry, but who are you?" I ask, even though I should keep walking.

Getting cut from cheerleading is bad enough; talking to this social pariah is an additional hazard to my reputation.

"Don't be sorry. Abigail Rose Mayer," she says, hand out to shake without skipping a beat. "Granddaughter of Mad Mabel, the Mother of Mayhem, and rightful—if currently thwarted— heir to the Throne of Mayhem. Someday CEO of the Future of Mayhem." Abigail Rose rattles it off like a tagline she's written for a character she plays. "Which brings me to your mission, should you choose to accept it."

"Listen, Abigail Rose, thwarted heir to Grandma whatever.

I have no idea what any of that means. Or why you're so convinced that I have something to do with it, but believe me"—I open the door to step outside—"I don't."

"Don't you believe in destiny?" Abigail Rose calls after me.

I shout, "No!" without looking back, and head through the door.

"It's the opportunity of a lifetime!" She's like a carnival barker trying to coax tickets out of my hand. She holds the door open after me and shouts, "At least check out my website! It's called *Real to Me!*"

I can't believe I talked to her for as long as I did. I came here with one goal today: to blend in well enough to make the squad and not find myself the odd one out in Lexie's world. I failed at my only hope of normalcy *and* got recruited for the town freak show.

I storm straight through the parking lot and keep walking down the rural highway, drowning in a homesickness so thick I swear it has a smell.

I choke back tears and try to clear the lump in my throat as I text George.

> Tried to bloom, got cut.

She writes back immediately: *That always happens to flowers.*

I start to type, "I'm so bad at being a girl tho," but delete it and keep walking.

There's a Chinese restaurant, an IGA grocery, and a Dollar General, and then there's nothing but me and trees and an occasional car speeding by at sixty mph. It's a fifteen-minute drive to get here from my house, so I keep walking.

Sometimes I wish Mom and Dad had named me George instead. Birdie makes me sound like one of those tiny, delicate girls, who "eats like a bird" or has dainty "winglike" bony arms. I kind of actually like Bird, which is technically my given name, but everyone's called me Birdie since I was a baby.

About a half hour later, Ted pulls into the breakdown lane in front of me, and Lexie rolls down the window and tells me to get in. I climb into the passenger seat.

"Mo says you can have a second chance," Lexie says, but I'm too upset to respond, so we ride in silence.

"What'd Abigail Rose want?" Lexie asks as she pulls up my driveway, smiling that mean smile again.

"She showed me some picture."

"Watch out, or she'll recruit you for the freak show." Lexie laughs under her breath.

"What is it? That pathetic fake wrestling crap?"

I've never watched professional wrestling, but I think I get the gist from pop culture references and the couple of episodes of *GLOW* I watched on Netflix with my mom. Violence between scantily clad racist and sexist caricatures who tussle onstage for people who eat corn dogs and pump equal parts nacho cheese and shitty beer into their veins.

"Her grandmother was famous or something. Her cousins are obsessed with it. They have this no-budget show on the public access channel once a month. It's a total joke."

"Don't worry," I say. "I won't embarrass you by joining the local lowbrow wrestling show." We both laugh. There's no one less likely to go Beast Mode in some wrestling ring than me:

the good girl gymnast, overachiever, hell-bent on being Ivy League–bound.

"Of course not," Lexie says. "You'll be busy with cheer. Mo said there wasn't a big enough turnout to cut anyone." She says it like it's a done deal. And I guess it should be.

I want people to like me. Not talk about me behind my back, like Abigail Rose.

So why, when I should be rehearsing my apology to Mo and watching YouTube videos on cheer dance, do I keep hearing Abigail Rose say *Fuck that dance shit* in my head?

I spend the night googling "becky lynch the man" instead.

CHAPTER 3

The Fort is *the* local hangout spot: a bare-bones structure in the woods, built by a group of cousins on their family compound a few miles down a dirt road, with a firepit nearby. The night air is humid, thick with a mix of woodsmoke, Off!, and AXE, and country music streams through a phone in a nearby plastic cup.

I sip my warm beer and tug at a loose thread on the pocket of my unzipped hoodie, wishing I'd stayed home.

"Your stomach is an actual slab of shale," Lexie says. "Seriously, feel this!" She grabs Kayleigh's hand and makes her feel my stomach, like I'm pregnant and they're waiting for a kick. "Right?"

Kayleigh shrugs and rolls her eyes. "I guess?" The way Kayleigh says it, I wish I hadn't come. It's bad enough that I embarrassed myself on her turf at tryouts the other day. Now I'm at this party she didn't expect me to be at, and I feel as welcome as the mosquitoes.

"You're my sturdiest friend," Lexie says as her tank strap falls from her slim shoulder, and I resist the urge to say how much muscle I've lost since I quit gymnastics. How soft and useless I feel. "Remember when you thought you had a superhuman pain tolerance because of your hair?"

Kayleigh spits out her beer, laughing. "Ginger powers?"

"Seriously," Lexie says. "George used to pull your hair until you admitted it hurt."

"Thanks for the reminder." There used to be a widely held belief, even among doctors, that redheads have higher pain tolerances, which isn't *exactly* true. We may experience pain differently—they think it has something to do with sunburns—and we may require more anesthesia—though not, as it was theorized, because we're "fiery" and "more emotional"—but the studies contradict each other, often. For years, I took it as a simple fact, which, no doubt, made me tolerate more pain. Like it was just part of who I was.

Zeke, bass player for the local band the Bedwetters, and Lexie's almost-official boyfriend, throws his head back, downs the rest of his beer, and holds up the empty Genesee can. "Who wants?" He pops up to standing. "New Girl?"

"Birdie's not really new," Lexie says. They're talking about me like I'm not here, but it's somewhat of a relief to hear Lexie defend me from total outsider status. "They moved into her grandparents' house."

"Let me guess." Zeke flicks the flame of his Zippo and closes it on itself. "Your parents are on some HGTV country home renovation kick."

"You know how it is when rich city people reno," Kayleigh says, not even looking at me. "They're probably turning the barn into a guest house to put up on Airbnb."

"No," I say. "The garage." I give a half smile, and even Kayleigh laughs at that. "My dad's from here," I say, defending our move, which, for the record, I find indefensible.

"You're more like one-season locals turned residents." Lexie says it like a conclusion, and the others seem to take it as one. These things matter around here, where they think of me as "that city girl," or worse, as a *citiot*—a "city idiot." It doesn't matter if you're from the actual city (one of the boroughs of NYC) or even *an* actual city. It's the local word for tourist. Weekender. Outsider come to buy the cottage where your great-grandma gave birth to all six children and turn it into an eco-chic Airbnb.

"Someone wants to meet you." Kayleigh nudges me.

Lexie's eyes glint with mischief. She cranes her head to look toward a group of guys.

"You gonna stand there staring all night, Darren, or come introduce yourself?"

"Oh!" Darren's friends shout in chorus. They laugh and punch him, and one guy leans forward and says something behind the cover of his hand. Darren heads our way.

"Remember Birdie from the goats?" Lexie asks before he gets to us. "Darren's Reilly's youngest brother," she says. When we were little, Lexie's mom used to take us to her friend Reilly's farm.

"*That's* who you are! You guys used to feed the crap out of those goats!" Darren says, and I recognize the small white scar cutting into his eyebrow. The one from his dog.

Darren takes a swig from a metal flask. The night is hotter than I expected, so I'm sliding out of my hoodie when Darren wraps his hand around my bicep, startling me.

"Whoa, those're some serious guns you got under there."

I rip my arm free from his grasp. I feel like I should shout or swear or just say anything at all, but only manage to scrunch my face in disgust.

Darren raises his hands, smiling as if to say *I didn't do it,* and laughs, wrapping his arm around Kayleigh's shoulder. I can smell the whiskey on his breath.

"Your friend all right? Seems jumpy," he says.

"Maybe not everyone wants your grubby hands on their body," Kayleigh says, wriggling out from his arm, and for a moment, I like her.

"Oh, snap. Sorry," Darren says. "It's just . . . we were talking over there, and we noticed you look strong. Like, stronger than most of us." I look back at Darren's scrawny friend group and assess that he's probably right. "And then Mikey O, that lumpy-looking sack right there"—he points to a really short guy whose body type most resembles a Dairy Queen cone—"said he'd put fifty dollars of his hard-earned landscaping earnings down to bet on any one of us in an arm-wrestling match against you."

"Not interested," I say, and Darren opens his mouth to say something, but Lexie cuts him off.

"She's not going to arm-wrestle you like the strong woman in the freak show," she says, and I'm relieved. But also . . . *strong woman in the freak show*?

Lexie smacks the cracked screen of her phone with her palm.

"That monster is at it again!" She holds the phone up to show Kayleigh. "Zeke has so many fangirls," Lexie says. "But this one's the worst."

"You guys need to define the relationship. Because clearly his fans"—Kayleigh nods toward the phone—"don't think you matter."

Lexie holds the phone out for me to see, but it's dark, so I pull it closer to see the video.

Zeke's fangirl bounces on a bed in her underwear and a T-shirt, on which she's scrawled WILL CHANGE ZEKE'S SHEETS.

"Oh, I get it," I say finally. "Because they're the *Bed*wetters." I almost laugh, but stop myself.

"What if we send her a message?" Kayleigh says, and Lexie rips her gaze from the magnetic girl on the screen.

"We couldn't do that." Lexie shakes her head. "But . . . like . . . what are you thinking?"

"What if we break into the bone store to steal a cursed monkey hand or something? We can leave it in her bed." Kayleigh jumps when she says it.

Lexie nods, like this is a perfectly sane idea. Obvious, even.

"You are the best friend in the entire universe," Lexie says, and it's a punch to the gut.

Kayleigh looks at me. "You in? This is your friend she's messing with."

I'm creeped out enough in the middle of the woods at night here without stealing a cursed anything from something called the bone store.

"Sounds kind of risky," I say.

Kayleigh sighs, annoyed.

"It's girl code," she says, like it shouldn't have to be explained.

"Girl code is stealing cursed bones to bully people?" I shake my head, confused.

"But she deserves it," Lexie says.

Does she? I think, but I arch an eyebrow.

"Anyone who messes with my best bitch deserves whatever comes back to her. Zeke!" Kayleigh shouts into the Fort. "Get your skinny butt out here!" I don't want to be a bad friend to Lexie. Definitely not a worse friend than Kayleigh.

"What?" Zeke comes out of the Fort, both hands raised.

"Your girlfriend is distraught because your groupie's posting thirst traps again."

Zeke groans and throws his head back in frustration.

"Why are you still hate-following her?" He looks at Lexie, but she won't even meet his eyes she's so pissed. She looks like she's about to cry.

"Don't pivot," Kayleigh says. "You should spend more time thinking about why the entire internet doesn't know you have an amazing girlfriend. Before you lose her."

Zeke puts his arm around Lexie.

"I'm sorry, babe," he says. "What do you want me to do?"

Lexie turns her head away. "I want everyone to know we're together, and I want the fangirls to back off."

"A cursed bone in her bed ought to make that clear as day," Kayleigh says.

"From the bone store?" Zeke asks with a laugh, like she's being ridiculous.

"I dare you," Lexie says, and Zeke shakes his head, then takes her face with both hands and kisses her.

"You want to steal a bone from crazy-ass Mabel," Zeke says. Lexie smiles coyly, literally batting her eyelashes. "That's going to get you off my case about this?" She nods.

"The fangirls won't get off your case unless they know your relationship status," Kayleigh says.

"Which is?" Lexie asks.

"Hanging out? Seeing each other? Dating?" Kayleigh presses. "Are you a couple?"

Zeke looks at Kayleigh. "Am I in a relationship with you or Lexie?"

"Currently, neither."

"We're in a relationship!" he shouts, exasperated. "We're a freaking couple!"

"Good for you," some guy says as he passes, to make sure Zeke knows no one else cares.

Lexie looks at me, the only one not signed on for tonight's cursed bone heist.

"I dare you," she says, nestling under Zeke's arm.

I take one look at Lexie and know that if I don't come on this escapade, I'll never live it down. I'll be worse than a *citiot*. I'll be boring. And a bad friend.

If I sit this one out, I'll be forever marked as an outsider—even more than I already am.

Still, I don't want to break into a creepy store to steal bones in the dead of night. Definitely not to harass some superhot girl I don't know. But my head tells me to be cool. If Lexie doesn't think it's a big deal, it's probably not.

"How will we know what's cursed?" I ask, and Lexie's eyes spark at the question.

"They're bones. They're all fucking cursed." Zeke burps loudly. "Who's driving the Nifty?" He dangles his key in front of us.

We're about to play a game of impaired driving roulette. I can only imagine what they'd think of me if I called my parents right now. I consider texting George, but she's spending the night at a friend's house.

"Aren't you all wasted?" They look at me, glassy-eyed.

"New Girl, you drive!" Zeke presses the key to his F-150 into my palm.

"I've never driven a truck," I say.

Zeke points to his bumper sticker, which reads, unintelligibly, DILLIGAF.

"Do I Look Like I Give an F?" he translates.

The key is light in my hand. Just one key on a key chain depicting Calvin pissing on a Chevy logo. Zeke's family probably doesn't even lock their house.

"You *guys*," I say, searching my mind for a better excuse.

They all point at the bumper sticker.

The thing is: I would never drive slightly buzzed with a car full of wasted copilots through what feels like the deepest part of the forest I've ever been to in the middle of the night. Not to break into something called the *bone* store.

I would never.

Which is why I find myself stepping up into the driver's seat and starting the engine to a truck with a DILLIGAF bumper sticker.

Three of us ride up front: Zeke next to me, Kayleigh with her head out the window, alternating threats every few miles that she's either going to puke or "get that bitch."

"She was a professional wrestler back in the day. A total freak, my mom said," Lexie says from the flip-down seat in the back of the cab. On the way to the bone store, they tell me everything they've ever heard about Mad Mabel, the Mother of Mayhem, owner of Mostly Bones. Abigail Rose's grandmother.

"You're going so *slow*." Zeke groans like an irritable toddler when he says it, like it physically pains him to be moving at this speed.

But I have no idea what the speed limit is because there hasn't been a single sign the entire drive. Out here, if you don't know where you are, it's your own damned problem.

"All these wrestling fans come here every summer," Kayleigh says, picking up where Lexie leaves off. "It's a weirdo pilgrimage or something."

"She eats the animals, then uses their bones to make her

stuff," Zeke says, and Kayleigh gags. "It's how she got her strength for the ring, and she figured out how to make a living off it after she was too old to wrestle."

Lexie groans from the back. "That's such a crock of—"

"No, it's not! My cousin said he once saw her cooking a raccoon, right through her upstairs window, and then the next week there was a raccoon skeleton chandelier in the front window of the shop."

I take a left onto the main road through the village, which is desolate.

"Creepy came to tryouts today," Kayleigh tells Zeke.

"Why?" He flicks his Zippo and waves his hand over the flame.

"The usual harvesting of souls," Lexie chimes in from the back.

"You used to be like best friends with her, didn't you?" Zeke asks Kayleigh.

"Not *best* friends."

"Matching purple outfits in Ms. Lopez's class picture kinda friends," Lexie says.

"Everyone's friends in first grade," Kayleigh says, and maybe it's the alcohol, but she sounds sad.

When we're finally onto the main road through town, Zeke directs me to an empty dirt lot next to the village cemetery. I park and am buzzing with adrenaline.

"Who's up for a heist?" I ask, but they're all fading. Kayleigh opens the truck door and throws up, and then uses her perfect hair to wipe her mouth.

"Zeke, you do it," Lexie says, crawling out of the back seat.

"I would, babe, I swear, but I promised the band I wouldn't get in trouble again," he says. "Last time I got busted my parents didn't let us practice in the garage for three months. I can't compromise my art like that again."

"Your band is called the Bedwetters," Kayleigh says, like a rebuttal. She sips from a water bottle and swishes it around before spitting it out. Then she looks at me, her eyes wide. "Birdie should do it! Even if the nutjob has security cameras, no one will know who she is."

"Ohhhh!" Lexie cries out, and then covers her mouth like she hopes no one heard. Then, slurring, "You should totally do it! I double dare you."

I should say no, but I don't right away and—for the first moment since I moved here—Kayleigh and Zeke seem surprised. Like they can't believe there's a chance I might actually be fun.

Besides, Lexie double dared me.

Mostly Bones looks mostly normal from the outside. A wooden sign signals a path off the road, down by the creek that runs through town. The route is lit by a far-off streetlight, and the only sound, other than our footsteps, is creek water moving over rocks. And Zeke's burps.

I creep toward the window and press my face to the glass.

Knives with leg bone handles, a two-headed fluffy yellow chick under a glass dome, a deer-antler candelabra. If it wasn't the dead of night and I wasn't so scared, it might be all kinds of interesting, like jarred specimens in the biology lab.

I turn to see the three of them, far behind me, huddled together.

"This is creepy, let's get out of here," Lexie whispers.

"Not without a curse." Kayleigh eyes me.

I've never broken into a building, but these old windows look like the first-floor ones at Grandma and Grandpa's. The kind that miss the latch if the metal piece goes in front of the hook instead of behind it. Old, swollen windows don't line up perfectly, especially in the summer.

I try to pry the front windows open with my fingertips, but they hold firm.

I'm about to give up when the first window I try on the side slides up with a squawk.

They wave frantically for me to climb in, so I hoist myself up until my torso is above the frame, like I'm on the uneven bars, and swing my leg inside and duck through the window.

The shop is dark and silent. With both feet finally on the floor, I freeze, afraid to take a step and wanting to make each one count. No one told me exactly what to steal, and I don't want to spend time choosing.

Zeke said, *They're all cursed.* I want to grab the first thing I see and get the hell out of here, but the candle section I've entered smells warm and sweet. They don't want just anything. Lexie and Kayleigh are hangry for bones.

I creak across the old thin floorboards, and the smell changes. There's a faint aroma of something I know from the woods, and what I can only describe as carcass. Not the pungency of actively rotting animal flesh, but the soft mineral decay of bone picked clean, the must of feathers and fur.

I reach a table with what look like chicken feet wrapped around large marbles, like something a witch would use to cast a spell, so I grab one and book it to the window.

I tuck it under my bra strap and get my leg over the threshold. I've got both legs out, my torso still hanging over the frame, when the lights shoot on and my breathing definitely stops, maybe even my heart. Startled, I launch myself out the window and crash to the ground, my ribs sore from scraping the frame.

I see the barrel of her shotgun before I see her face. In that moment I understand the rumors because I'm not sure which scares me more.

Mad Mabel, the Mother of Mayhem, has a broad circular face, sagging jowls framing her puffy lips. Unless she wears a full face of makeup in the middle of the night with her pajamas, it looks like it's tattooed on: bright blue eye shadow the color of mountain bluebird feathers, thick black eyeliner. I squint through the dark, into the backlit window, and make out the universal sign for woman—a circle with a cross underneath it— tattooed on her forehead, the circle centered like a third eye, the cross dangling down between her brows and touching the bridge of her nose.

I could almost mistake her for an old lady who just came from church on Ash Wednesday, if it weren't for the cigarette hanging out of the side of her mouth like a B-movie bad guy.

"If you move, I got every right to shoot ya," she says, so I don't move. I don't even breathe.

I'm frozen to the ground like a stick in winter when Mabel says to stay put, she'll be right outside. I wonder for a split second if I should run for my life, but reason it's safer to do as I'm told.

When she gets to me, she's no longer holding the shotgun, and I inhale sharply.

"You scared me," Mabel says, and I just nod. My heart races. I can hear the creek water moving. A branch crunches in some leaves and I wonder if that's Lexie—if she's nearby, watching to make sure I'm OK. I want to scream for help, but worry I'll get us all in trouble. "Style points for sticking it under your bra strap," she says, which seems like it should lighten the mood.

Only, up close, Mabel is just as terrifying, even without her shotgun.

"Hand it over," she says, but I'm still frozen. "The talonsman."

Mabel reaches her hand toward me, and I flinch. Then I grab the talon from where it presses just above my heart, dragging its nails across my bare skin, and hold it out to her, my fist clenched. She has to tug twice before my hand softens its grip and releases.

"Coming here in the middle of the night to steal from me," Mabel says, clearly familiar with her own reputation. "You must be either incredibly stupid or incredibly brave." She eyes me. "Which one is it?"

I try to answer, but a ragged inhale is all that comes, and Mabel's eyes shift. Soften.

She knows what I am. I'm incredibly scared.

"You got good taste, kid." She reaches a hand down to pull me up.

Standing, my head reaches Mabel's shoulder. She smells like incense and candles mixed with a home-cooked meal. Her eyebrows knit together, swallowing part of her tattoo.

"You live nearby?" she asks, and I shake my head. Her voice is deep, with the husk of a longtime smoker. "I'll get my keys." Mabel ducks inside and I search the tree line for Lexie, but I can't see or hear anything. Texts pour into my phone. I'm too scared to cry.

Mabel could have shot me. Who knows what kind of trouble I'm going to be in? With my parents. With the police. Mabel comes back outside and waves me over.

"Let's get you home," she says, and then I almost do cry in relief.

When we walk around front, the fear in my veins is tempered by the sight of Mabel's majestic hot-pink car. Tonight has felt like a dream—like something I'm watching myself live, instead of something I'm actually living—but getting into this car with Mabel is odd enough to be a hallucination.

"Can't get you home if you don't get in," she says, nodding to the door. "It doesn't bite."

Soon I'm flying along the unlit rural highway in the passenger seat of a 1963 Ford Thunderbird driven by Mad Mabel, the Mother of Mayhem, feeling lucky she's taking me home and not straight to the police. Feeling lucky to still be alive.

"Just 'cause I'm not calling the cops doesn't mean you're off the hook," Mabel says, holding up the bird foot. "That's breaking and entering. You've got to make that right."

"How?"

"The good news, like I said, is that you have good taste," Mabel says. "Which is also the bad news. That talonsman was the most expensive of the bunch. Australian black opal. Asking price is twelve hundred. That's grand larceny."

"Twelve hundred dollars!" I fight back my tears. I never realized a dead animal foot and a rock could be so expensive. "What is it?"

"A Mostly Bones original. Talismans made from talons."

"Like . . . for magic?"

"If you believe in that kind of thing," Mabel says. "Either way, it's bad energy stealing something like that. But work it off, and you'll have straightened out the cosmic fabric."

I search her face for signs that she's joking, but this lady's for real. Cosmic fabric and all.

"Work for you?" I ask.

Mabel says she'll count each hour as fifteen dollars under the table, which means I need to work eighty hours to make it to twelve hundred. That's twenty four-hour shifts, which at five shifts a week clocks off in four weeks. One month of indentured servitude in this giant lady's creepy bone store.

I steal a look at Mabel and, as she blinks, the tattooed flicker of blue above her eyelid flashes in the dark like a bird darting through the woods.

"Are you going to tell my parents?" I ask.

"That'd be up to you." Mabel turns on the radio to a hard rock station. "I got a granddaughter about your age, and I'd both want to kill her for doing what you did, and also wring my neck for pulling a gun on you, even if I had every legal right. I'm sorry about that."

"I'm sorry, too."

My phone pulses like Lexie thinks if she sends enough texts, I might get her message through notification Morse code.

Somewhere on the drive, right around the geodesic dome house George and I always used to say we were going to buy and live in together, Mabel breaks the tension with a story from her years in the ring, about a time she wrestled one of the longest-reigning champions of all time.

"And I said to her, I'll never forget this, the crowd went absolutely bonkers, I said, 'I don't care if you're the Fabulous Moolah or the Gal with the Marvelous Hoo-Ha,'" Mabel says, giving the huge steering wheel a smack with her palm. "'I'm gonna splatter you all over that ring from here to Kalamazoo-la!' Hit her with a dropkick she never saw coming."

Her laugh is loud—hearty and unrestrained—and she coughs a little, then rolls down her window to hock a loogie. Mabel is a lot to take in. She's the most unusual person I've ever met.

"But . . ." I pause, not sure if I should even ask, but wanting to know.

"But what?"

"Isn't wrestling fake?"

"Fake? No. It's fixed," Mabel says, like there's an obvious difference.

"So didn't she see the dropkick coming?"

"The ending is what's fixed," she says. "The key to most of my success was natural reaction. There's nothing like a crowd thinking something's going one way until, suddenly"—she snaps—"it changes on a dime."

My parents think I'm sleeping over at Lexie's, so when we pull up the driveway, the house lights are off. I open the heavy door of the car, its chrome gleaming in the motion-activated porch light.

"Well, I thought so before, but in that light it's clear as day," Mabel says, lighting a cigarette with a match she blows out and then touches to her tongue. "You got yourself a set of goddess arms." Through the clouds of smoke from her pink car, Mabel says, "Just don't go thinking that means you gotta carry the whole damn world on your shoulders."

Then she actually winks at me and peels out, laughing the kind of laugh that comes from deep down as she tears up the driveway, spraying gravel in her wake.

CHAPTER 4

I wake up with an adrenaline hangover buzzing in my ears and images from the night before swirling in my mind.

I couldn't sleep when I got home last night, so I looked her up.

I didn't find any videos of Mabel herself, but I found one with the lady she mentioned, the Fabulous Moolah. It was a fan video: a slideshow of events leading up to a match known as the Original Screwjob, in which a masked Fabulous Moolah—wrestling as the Spider Lady—defeated a rising young star named Wendi Richter.

Before the Screwjob, there was *The Brawl to End It All*, a match so huge it was broadcast live on MTV. The brawl was the culmination of a feud that started with popstar Cyndi Lauper's "Girls Just Want To Have Fun" music video, in which Captain Lou Albano—a guy with rubber bands dangling from piercings in both his cheek and his ear, and one looped around his long beard—plays her controlling father. In scripted wrestling matches that followed, Captain Lou played the Kanye to Cyndi Lauper's Taylor Swift. He claimed he was responsible for her success, and even went so far as to suggest he wrote the lyrics to the song. Cyndi Lauper flipped a table and bashed Captain Lou over the head with her purse, but when it came time to escalate the feud, they each chose someone else to represent them in the ring.

Lauper chose Richter to represent her, and Captain Lou chose the Fabulous Moolah. When Wendi Richter defeated the Moolah, she ended the *longest championship reign in wrestling history*. It was the most-watched show in the history of MTV. But no matter how popular Wendi Richter became—she was a household name—the company wouldn't pay her as much as they paid the men. In the end, over a supposed contract dispute, they set up Wendi to lose to the Spider Lady in the Original Screwjob. They stripped her of her power to show her they could, and in the end, she walked away.

The whole wrestling thing was way more entertaining than I thought it would be. Dramatic. Wild. Intense. *Funny*. But the story of Wendi Richter was heartbreaking.

I head downstairs for breakfast and pour myself a cup of coffee despite Dad's side-eye, while I consider what to tell my parents about my new job. I've decided against the truth. They can't handle the truth. Not the part about me breaking into Mabel's on a drunken dare. Or the part about her shotgun.

Dad plops down a plate of pancakes so hot the steam's still rising, and I read Lexie's texts while I dig in. Dad didn't always know how to cook, but after years of editing food shows and docusoaps, I'd put money on my dad making it to round three of *Chopped*. He's always worked from home, so in a way, his life is the least changed by our move. He begged Mom for years to quit her job and move here, where he grew up. But when

Grandma and Grandpa announced they were selling the house and moving to Taos, New Mexico, Mom surprised us all by finally agreeing.

It's weird to be here without them, but Grandpa's breathing better in the dry air and Grandma still sends us photocopies of her handwritten poems through the postal service.

"I thought you were staying over at Lexie's last night?" Dad asks.

"She took an extra shift at Stewart's this morning, so I had Zeke drop me off." The lie rolls off my tongue.

"Tell Zeke he could use some sandbags in his truck bed." Dad flips another pancake. "Quite the peel-out," he says, and I almost laugh, picturing Mabel as she sped off.

Mom slides past him to the coffee machine, slapping his butt on her way. My parents are mortifyingly in love.

"Where are you off to so early?" Mom asks.

"I got hired at a boutique," I say.

"Look at you, finding your niche here already," she says.

Dad asks if I'm sure this is how I want to spend my summer before flipping the last pancake and heading upstairs to finish the postproduction on a particularly chaotic fight scene between two flamboyantly violent mob-connected women. He showed me some of the raw footage, and let's just say, it's got the makings of a Must-See TV Event.

As I'm heading out, I see George sitting in the most beautiful patch of morning light that has ever shone. Either that or that's just the effect George has on morning light.

"I came home the other morning around this time, and the light here was *un*real. Now the mountain laurel blossoms are at peak, and it's the perfect time to shoot my video for the Natural Beauty Challenge," George says when I'm within earshot.

I soak in the scene: My sister, whose hair and makeup take her a combined two hours each morning and probably around $300 in highly synthesized products, thinks this is "natural beauty" because she's sitting on a wool blanket in front of a bush.

"Could you shoot it for me?" she asks, and I'm running early, so I say yes.

I shoot the video for her—starting over seven times until we have the perfect angle—and I have to admit, George is good at this. She knows an almost clinical amount of information about skincare and rattles off the names of synthetic chemical compounds, enzymes, and antioxidants as if they're normal words.

We watch the final video, huddled together in a patch of shadow on the blanket, birdsong floating through the forest around us. On the screen, my sister is a radiant, natural beauty, sun-dappled amid a parasol of pale pink blossoms.

No wonder I used to want to be her. Somehow, my sister has yet to go to college or get a real job since graduating. She tells Mom and Dad she needs time to *find herself* but her only goal so far is to be a full-time influencer. She had over seventy-five thousand followers last I checked, so who am I to crush her dream?

"If you don't win this contest, they're nuts," I tell her.

"It's not about winning," George says, and I roll my eyes.

"Life is literally one giant competition."

George shakes her head. "It's more like, we're all boats on the same sea, and a rising tide lifts us all." She leans back to move the screen into shadow. "I've just got to keep my boat in the water." George pauses, smiling as light dances across her face, and presses replay. "But you're right," she says. "They'd be nuts to pick anyone else."

When Mabel opens the door and flips the sign to OPEN, I'm standing outside.

"Thanks for coming back again during store hours," she says, like I'm a customer who came at closing yesterday. I step inside and she hands me a corn muffin, still warm from the oven. "We'll be right down."

That salty animal musk mingles in the air with the muffin, and I understand why she sells candles and incense to cover the aroma of decay. Sometimes people describe things as "acquired tastes." Mostly Bones is an acquired smell, at best.

"This story keeps getting better, Mabel!" The voice coming down the stairs is familiar.

"Keep your nose in your own business, Abigail Roosevelt Mayer, or I'll make you solely responsible for her training," Mabel barks back, and then, there they both are, marching down the stairs toward the front of the store, looking like characters straight out of a comic book.

"It's YOU!" Abigail Rose squeals, her hands lifted trium-phantly in the air, shooting her pointer fingers up and down, chanting, "YES, YES, YES!" It's a refreshing change of pace to have someone cheer my arrival.

"I didn't think this day could get better, but once again the good Lord proves me wrong," Abigail Rose says.

"You being so wrong all the time makes that easy on Her, doesn't it?" Mabel arranges a table labeled WINERY RAT BONE CORKSCREWS and moves a SALE 10% OFF sign from the nearby rack of animal tooth jewelry sets. "Birdie McCoy, this is my granddaughter, Abigail Roosev—"

"Abigail Rose." She juts her hand out to shake mine. Her

blue-gray eyes look almost violet, and she's not wearing any eye-liner. She moves to walk around me, but I move in the same direction at the same time.

"Sorry," I say.

"Why?" Abigail Rose scrunches her face and waits for an answer.

"I was in your way?" I don't say it, I ask it.

"Maybe I was in your way." Abigail Rose taps a finger to her head like *think about it*.

"Those nitwits here already? I told them noon." Mabel starts toward the door, and she looks like a boulder come to life. A boulder that moves with such a light-footed grace, I some-how wouldn't be surprised if she were to pirouette out the door and down the stairs. "You better not be hauling those pelts in through the shop door!" Mabel calls to the two guys coming down the path. "At least they bagged 'em this time."

Abigail Rose leans toward me, like we're already close.

"Last time Little Mickey and Big Mickey brought the pelts through the shop door, some homeschool kid saw it on his 'home-work walk,'" Abigail Rose says. Outside, the guys approach, one very tall and wide, carrying a large canvas sack, and one average height and wiry, nearly bouncing at his side like a puppy.

"His mom, who named the kid Kale, so honestly, what're you gonna do? She said that if the town is going to have to tolerate Mabel's grotesque—that was the word she used, *grotesque*—business, the least she could do was have the decency to hide the carnage." Mabel sends the Big and Little Mickeys around to the other door.

"Where does she get these things, anyway?" I ask, remembering what Zeke said. But Mabel comes huffing through the door before Abigail Rose can answer, and a moment later, I hear the Mickeys coming down the apartment stairs.

"You're a hundred percent wrong, isn't he, Grandma?" The wiry one walks up to Mabel and gives her a kiss on the cheek. She rustles his shaggy dirty-blond hair.

"If we're talking about bringing pelts through the wrong door, you both are."

"We're talking about the undisputed heavyweight champion of the Barn of Mayhem, and whether or not he should lose the title match at Summer Splatter to the lowliest of lowly creatures, the dippiest of the dipshits, the absolutely outdated outcast Wild Boy Bill." The kid's intense, talking so fast his face is red.

"That's your cousin Billy you're talking about." Mabel fixes her eyes on Little Mickey and he straightens his spine but looks at the ground. "If I've said it once, I've said it a thousand times—"

"You'll sell the Barn if we can't find a way to work together," Little Mickey recites, shooting daggers at Abigail Rose.

"And if either of you"—Mabel points at Big and then Little Mickey—"come through the wrong door again, I'll send you *both* to Suplex City."

"She just threatened to bear-hug them and flip them over her head." Abigail Rose smiles. "Classic finisher."

"It's time for Bill to turn face. He pitched a great storyline— he's got the funniest promo already cut for it—" Big Mickey starts.

"About what a waste of space Frankie is?" Abigail Rose says, and Mabel fixes her in place with a terrifying glare.

"About how the Men of Mayhem have been holding him back," Big Mickey says. "A Stone Cold Steve Austin antihero vibe. You know, 'I'm the best thing you got around here, and screw you for not knowing it.' He's got this great rant about how the Chaos Kid doesn't care about the audience. Doesn't respect their intelligence. And then he says that Silas the Woodsman isn't the title holder"—he points at himself—"I'm a place-holder." He laughs. "I'm telling you, the kid makes a great face. And he worked out the kinks of his new finisher," he says, his voice gentle and smooth. "Seems like his turn."

"If Big Mickey doesn't want to hold the belt, why not make room for someone else who does?" Abigail Rose says, eyeing Little Mickey. "I've been trying to get Frankie to push that Robbie and Kurt backstory angle for the last three months, and he keeps saying there isn't room. This would be the perfect heel turn for Kurt with his guitar gimmick!"

"He could write heel songs to troll the audience, like Elias," Silas says, and they point at each other, eyes wide.

"That would be hilarious." Abigail Rose picks up her note-book and jots down the idea.

"Heel turn, face turn, blah blah blah," Little Mickey says. "Who cares? Big Mickey's our money man and you know it. It's only a matter of time before someone picks him up," the little guy says, but the big guy groans under his breath. "If he stopped spending so much time playing his flute like some Jethro Tull reject and got his head in the game, he'd be pulling the weight he should be pulling."

"Adapt or die, man," Abigail Rose says. "The crowd's losing interest, and the Mayhem name is losing its luster."

"Right," Little Mickey says, nodding his head but rolling his eyes. "Because 'the future' is coming for us?" He air-quotes around "the future."

"It is!" Abigail Rose shouts after him as Little Mickey heads where Mabel disappeared to, hauling the bag. Big Mickey hangs back, looking like the world's biggest teddy bear.

Everything about him—from his silky, loose curls that end at his chin, to his skin, so pale it's almost blue—is soft. Big Mickey is one of those guys who's so big you can't tell if they're a giant mass of muscle or a beanbag chair. When he smiles, which he did when Mabel kissed his forehead, he has one deep dimple. He looks like a male version of Mabel, without all the tats.

"You're both named Mickey?" I ask.

"Neither of them, really," Abigail Rose answers for him. "Their dad's Mickey, and when they were little, they looked just like him. But they're twins."

"Twins?"

"Fraternal," Big Non-Mickey says, his voice clear and smooth like a lake at dawn. Like if I could dip my toe in his voice, it would send out ripples.

"The big one's Silas. The annoying one is Walter," Abigail Rose says. She hands me a feather duster with a bone handle. Silas gives an awkward nod and then heads to the farthest corner of the store, by the antler lamps and local art framed with leg bones.

"Why don't you start over there with the carcass case?" Abigail Rose points toward a glass case of animal skeletons that at first glance makes me wonder if this whole store isn't packed with ghosts.

I'm not all that squeamish, but I don't want to show any sign of weakness. Abigail Rose already saw me have my ass handed to me on a gym floor by a cheerleading squad. I don't need to give her any reason to doubt whether I'm up to the tasks here at Mostly Bones. I don't even want her to tell Mabel about the tryout. From what I can tell, and for reasons I can't begin to fathom, I think Mabel kind of likes me.

Halfway into my shift, Mabel tells me to take a fifteen-minute break.

I head outside for some air without the lingering stench of death, and follow the creek to the road, debating an iced coffee from the overpriced-but-worth-it café up the block.

"New Girl!" Zeke calls from across the street, waving like he wants me to cross, so I do.

I recognize the rest of the lineup of the Bedwetters from pictures, including Harley, their guitarist, Luke the drummer, and frontwoman Indigo, whose long blue curls make her pale face glow like the moon.

"New Girl," Zeke says, introducing me to the others.

"Birdie," I say, doing the awkward wave and nod thing. Like I'm ducking.

"You should've seen Birdie last night," Zeke says. "Crawling into Mabel's window like a freaking ninja." I consider saying, *You should've seen Zeke, running away,* but stop myself.

"You're already a legend, New Girl," Luke says.

"He's right," Harley says. "People are saying you're in the witness protection program."

"Seriously?" I ask.

"No." In an oversized black T-shirt, Harley's vibe is distinctly *Does Not Care What You Think.* The knees of their black jeans are almost worn through but not ripped, and when the light hits their face, copper highlighter makes their brown skin glow.

Indigo holds her hand up. "Wait, you're the one who had the gun pulled on her?"

"The night got carried away with itself," I say, as nonchalant as I can manage. "Now I work here. There's a matter of a debt." I look at Zeke, and his eyes dart to his sneakers.

"Lexie's meeting us at the coffee shop. Come with?" Zeke says.

For a moment I wish I could say yes. I could walk down the sidewalk with this local band and meet my friend, and I could feel for the first time since coming here that I've arrived. This could really be my new life.

But Zeke can't even look me in the eyes.

I shake my head and start to say I've got to get back to work.

"Speak of the she-devil-wears-nada herself," Indigo says, and I turn to see Lexie bounding down the sidewalk toward us in hot pants and a sports bra.

"Keep the slut shaming to yourself, thanks," Lexie says. "I just changed out of my Stewart's uniform and have like ten minutes before I have to leave for cheer practice."

"It's five thousand degrees out right now," Harley says. They kiss their fist and pump it to the sky. "Thanks, climate change. Wish I was half naked."

"I love that you're so hardworking and also so hot." Zeke kisses Lexie on the cheek. "I tried to talk Birdie into coming, but she's got work."

"You got a job? Where?" Lexie asks, genuinely excited.

"Mostly Bones," I say, and Lexie chokes on her inhale, remembering.

"I'm so, I mean, we"—she waves a finger between her and Zeke—"are so sorry."

"It's OK." I brush it off, but she doesn't let me.

"It's not OK. I got so scared that I ran. It was fight-or-flight, I swear," Lexie says. "Once I could tell she wasn't going to shoot you, I watched until you got in her car."

"What if she was being abducted?" Harley asks, eyebrow raised.

"It was clearly not a hostage situation," Lexie says. "We tried to warn you when we saw a light flick on upstairs. Before you went in."

"We did!" Zeke says, and I think back to last night.

"We were waving at you to leave," Lexie says.

I thought they were waving at me to hurry up and go in. They were trying to warn me.

"Mabel didn't call the cops on your ass?" Harley says.

I shake my head. "She's letting me work off what I stole."

"You savoring every last drop of that piping-hot cup of white privilege?"

I pause, trying to find the words to respond, but Lexie does before I can.

"She has to work it off," Lexie says.

"In the dead of night, you broke into a store—someone's home, someone with a shotgun—and you stole something. Instead of being arrested, or perhaps being killed and having your death deemed justified by virtue of your actions, you were driven home. And you were offered a job," Harley says.

"When you put it like that . . ." I pause.

"Which is literally just describing what happened," Indigo says.

"That *is* pretty lucky." Lexie shrugs at me when she says it, as if the structural inequities of our white-supremacist society somehow make up for how she screwed me over last night. Which is definitely not Harley's point.

"Mm-hmm." Harley takes a picture of a little dog being pushed in a stroller as it passes on the sidewalk.

"Yet now she has to work in the dead animal store," Indigo says. "Which is kind of unlucky." I must look crestfallen because she says, "Sorry."

"It's actually kind of not terrible," I say, but instantly regret it. It's an odd thing to admit. I have no desire to be known as *that weird girl who likes to hang out with the bones*. People tend to whisper about that girl behind her back. Or, as was the case with Lexie and Kayleigh when it came to Abigail Rose, right in front of her face.

"A high tolerance for strangeness is helpful around here," Harley says.

"Like how we tolerate you," Luke says, and they punch his arm, hard.

"Come at me, bro. I'll send your colonizer ass back to where you came from." Harley stares at him, then moves to punch him again, and when Luke flinches, they both laugh.

"Remember, you promised not to embarrass me," Lexie says, and I laugh even though it's not that funny. "Mo told me to remind you the door is still open."

I know the only way to salvage my social status before the school year starts is to walk back through that door and be a cheerleader. People *like* cheerleaders.

"No worries." I raise both hands in surrender. "Not going to wrestle in the freak show." I look across the street and see Mabel down by the river, moving slowly like she's doing tai chi. In her own world. The smile lingers on my face when I turn to the group.

Harley catches my eye. "You do you, but I bet you'd be kind of badass." They hold my gaze for a moment, and I almost avert my eyes.

The Bedwetters and Lexie start down the sidewalk as a group, laughing at a joke I didn't catch, and I'm left standing on the sidewalk all alone.

I cross the street to Mostly Bones and wonder what that even means.

You do you.

I head back inside when my fifteen is up, and the Mickeys are gone. Abigail Rose and Mabel are in a heated discussion by the cash register, where Mabel tends to the drawer.

"If you don't stop this fighting with each other outside the ring, I mean it. I'll sell the Barn and shut down Mayhem for good." Mabel shakes her head. "You're supposed to lift each other up, not tear each other down."

"Frankie never likes my ideas, and ever since he got called up for NXT tryouts, you know the other guys just do what he says. They've nixed every cross-promotion I've devised with the Queen City Crew." Abigail Rose looks up to see if Mabel's still listening.

"That boy's been afraid of competition his entire life," Mabel says. "You want to convince him to share his ring with outsiders, you've got to show him what's in it for him."

"I have! The Queen City Crew has more going on in their events than Mayhem ever has. Their wardrobe and storylines. Their theme songs. We would be so much better with them, and they deserve to be in the Barn of Mayhem. They deserve the spotlight with the scouts."

"I wouldn't have brought you to their Holiday Hell-Raiser if I didn't agree," Mabel says.

"Then why isn't the Future of Mayhem here already? They're freezing me out, Mabel, and I don't like it one bit."

"Frankie Jr. told me last month he offered you the second slot for an all-female promotion," Mabel says.

"Why does it have to be all female just 'cause I'm a girl? And how am I supposed to put together an all-female roster for matches when we don't have any female fighters?"

"I suppose that would be the place to start, wouldn't it?" Mabel says, but from the look on Abigail's face, she doesn't find it helpful.

"Don't you see what he's doing? He's given me an impossible opportunity!" Abigail Rose nearly yells, stamping her boot. "He's even got you hoodwinked into thinking he's being generous," she says to Mabel, which stops her in her tracks. Mabel sets down the cow skull lamp she's holding on a table of resin spider rings. Those wolf spiders look way too big to be real.

"What do we do to the impossible when it comes knocking on our door?" Mabel asks.

"We send the impossible to Suplex City." Abigail's voice is steely, determined. Her spine lengthens like she's about to bear-hug the impossible and flip it over her head.

Mabel shakes her head and starts down the stairs with the skull lamp.

"I'm not saying it's fair that you have to prove yourself," Mabel says, "or that, being the only girl in the family, you've got to prove yourself extra."

"That's bull crap!" Abigail Rose shouts. "You, a *woman*"— she points at Mabel's tattoo—"are the only reason they have a legacy to begin with."

Mabel shakes her head. "It isn't fair, but that's the thing about life."

When Mabel heads downstairs, Abigail Rose looks dejected, like a little kid who lost their balloon at the fair.

"I'm sorry," I say when she looks my way.

"What the hell for? Why are you so sorry all the time?" she asks.

"I am *not*," I say.

"Don't take this the wrong way. I mean, you're not my type. I fall exclusively for musicians, it's a curse," she says, interrupting herself. "But you're adorable when you're angry."

I scoff in offense. There's a friend vibe between us, so we're on the same page about that. But adorable? Hardly. And angry? Not even!

"I am *not*," I say.

"Not angry? Or not adorable?"

"Neither."

"There it is again!" she says through a smile, but now I'm fuming. "Adorable."

"Now you're actually pissing me off," I say.

"I'm sorry. I'll stop. But . . ." Abigail Rose pauses, thoughtful. "How about you take all of that anger and . . . I don't know . . . do something with it?"

Abigail Rose walks over to where Mabel stationed me to take pictures of shoulder blade combs for the online inventory.

"Don't look at me like that," I say, backing up.

Her otherwise perfectly fine face is marred with a look somewhere between smarmy salesperson and unwanted advance. Thanks to her brutal honesty, I know it's not the latter. Abigail Rose frames my face with her palms, and I think I know where this is headed. Again.

"I need someone local to build my lineup around."

"No way."

"Come on! You can flip. You're strong as hell. Look at those shoulders! You could not be more genetically engineered for wrestling if you were manufactured in Vince McMahon's laboratory."

"Who?"

"Mr. McMahon." She says it in a booming, gruff voice that's part growl, part megaphone. "You have so much to learn."

"No, I don't."

"Don't you see?" Abigail Rose says. "This is divine intervention. Kismet. Fate!" She puts her arm through mine and leans in close. "You're here because this is your destiny, whether you choose to accept it or not." Her face is dead serious.

"Except it's not," I say.

"Oh, but it is." Abigail Rose picks up a shoulder blade and

balances it on the back of her hand. "Birdie McCoy, won't you help me wrestle control of Mayhem?"

She lets the comb fall and, with a flick of her wrist, grabs it a few inches beneath.

"I hope that's the cheesiest thing you've ever said." I fold my arms in front of my chest.

"Not even close," Abigail Rose says. "Wrestling is unabashedly cheesy. Like the orange goop on concession stand nachos. It doesn't even matter that it's not real cheese. It's way better than the real thing."

"Like how hot dogs are better than meat," I say.

"I'm a vegetarian," Abigail Rose says. "The closest I get to hot dogs is my undying obsession with the Fourth of July Nathan's Hot Dog Eating Contest."

I groan. "You're kidding."

"I would never joke about competitive eating."

"It's so wasteful," I start. "Mass consumption of disgusting amounts of processed, factory-farmed animal parts for competition and entertainment, while plenty of hungry people starve in a twenty-mile radius." I shake my head. "Plus, it's gross to watch."

"Counterpoint," Abigail Rose says. "It's fun."

She pops both hands out and shrugs, like maybe, in all my very thorough analysis, I'm missing the entire point.

CHAPTER 5

"**W**hat do you want your lewk to say?"

George's vanity is like a cosmetic pop-up shop, with products fastidiously organized by type and color. The exact opposite of what her school binders used to be like.

"My Luke?"

"Your lewk," she says. "It's fashion-ese. Your look, but customized to your essence."

"How about: I'm here for the nachos." I plop down on her bed to be transformed.

When George offered to do my makeup for bowling tonight, my first response was a hard no. My go-to look is a polo shirt and not trying too hard. Nothing whispers "I fit in" like a polo shirt.

But getting together with Lexie has me on edge, and I figured letting George work her magic might make me feel different somehow.

"So, like . . . bowler by night, competitive eater by day?" George says.

"Bone slinger by day, competitive nacho inhaler by night."

"But, like, coy about it?" she says, and it forces a laugh out of me.

"You get me." I'm joking, but it's true. There is no one else I would trust to do this.

"Your hair's getting so long," George says, admiring it in the mirror. Our long hair is the one characteristic we share, because it's the only successful way I've managed to copy George. I don't generally wear makeup, I have no boobs, my biceps are the size of her thighs, and I wear cargo pants. But I've got long hair. If I had short hair, that kid at the water slide park wouldn't have commented on my "dude arms." He would've just thought I was a dude.

When I was seven, I asked my hairdresser to cut my hair short enough that I didn't have to tie it back for gymnastics or soccer. I loved it, but when I got home, George didn't. She said I looked like a boy. Mom and Dad lit into her, about how hairstyles aren't for boys or girls—which, for the record, is true—but my hair has been some version of long ever since.

George runs a wide-toothed comb down the center to part it.

"I'm feeling low knots, one on each side. And is the AC still always freezing at Thunder Bowl?"

"Colder than the Rosendale ice cave," I say.

"You should borrow my bomber jacket."

"The one with the rose buttons?" I arch an eyebrow.

"It's not a big deal." George brushes it off. "It'll look cute on you." I pull away from her hands working my hair, so I can see her face.

"Why are you being so nice?"

"I'm not. When you got home from work, I said you smelled like guinea pig cage." George twists my head forward with her hands to keep working, and I let her.

"That was kind of spot-on. Not mean at all." I've kept a lot of secrets for George, so when she asked why I smelled like that and I asked her if she could keep a secret for *me*, she seemed almost . . . proud. It's not that I don't want Mom and Dad to know I work at Mostly Bones; I just don't want them to find out why I work there.

"I'm never mean to you." George pauses. "OK, I'm rarely mean to you."

I shake my head. "You once said that if I borrowed your bomber jacket you'd wait in my room until I was sleeping and exact a yet-to-be-determined revenge upon my unsuspecting body."

George puts the comb down and spins her turquoise bracelet around on her wrist.

"I just realized it's a lot, is all." George looks at me, her eyes soft, concerned. "All of this." She waves a hand around. "Moving here. Switching schools. *Mom.*" The way she says it, I know she gets it. We've texted, but we haven't really talked about it because George is always busy, while I go with the flow and try not to create my own ripples in the already-choppy water.

"I didn't think parents did stuff like this in real life," I say. "It seems like something that only happens in the movies."

George wraps her arm around my shoulder and pulls me close. She smells like jasmine and cedar, sweet and warm, like flowers in the forest. I know because I watched her video about her new perfume from the boutique in town with the felted fairy hats that look like drooping foxglove blossoms in the window.

"It's OK to be pissed, Birdie," George says. "I don't know if this will be helpful or annoying, but I think what Mom's doing is courageous." My eyes roll up to the ceiling and I let out a single, "Ha!"

Of course my sister, who graduated high school two years ago and is still a full-time influencer with no real college or career prospects, approves of Mom leaping into the void. George is a full-time citizen of the void. She never lets a plan get in the way of a good time.

"All I'm saying is, all of us are going through something, but none of us is going through exactly what the others are going through," George says. "It's OK to be angry about it. But let us help."

"Like by wearing your bomber jacket?" I ask.

"And taking this." George hands me a tube of lipstick labeled VIOLET FURY. "This purple and your cool undertones? Look out, Thunder Bowl."

"Thanks," I say, doubtful I'll wear it. "What are you doing tonight?"

George picks up her phone and starts texting. "Planning. My followers want an in-person event. A mountain glam sesh with George of the Wild kind of thing," she says.

"Do you ever feel like you have no clue who you are at all?" The words are out of my mouth before I can take them back.

"All the time," George says, taking out a pair of hoop earrings, but I push them away.

"I can't pull those off."

"Pulling something off is just giving yourself permission to look different," George says, like it's that easy. As if the only thing standing between me and any number of new versions of myself is a willingness to try something new.

I look in the mirror at my hair wrapped in two low buns, the thinnest line of black eyeliner and the deep purple mascara, and decide I don't hate the look. I maybe even kind of like it. So I put on the hoops and lean forward, pressing the tube of Violet Fury to my lips.

I don't look like I usually do. But I still look like myself.

"Damn," George says, impressed with her vision brought to life. "Text me if you need anything."

I make a scowl in the mirror and have to admit Abigail Rose might be right.

I kind of do look adorable when I'm angry.

Like most things up here, Thunder Bowl hasn't changed since the beginning of time.

The same Rip Van Winkle sign stands out front: old Rip amid Henry Hudson's men, holding frothy mugs of beer and bowling balls.

The paint of Rip's white beard is almost fully worn off by tourists, who—thanks to a listicle, the bane of every upstate secret—caught wind of the local legend that rubbing the beard grants good luck.

After "The Top 11 Places to Supercharge Your Qi Upstate" went viral (with rubbing Rip's beard clocking in at number eight), the Thunder Bowl owners added a new sign next to it: BEARD FOR PAYING BOWLERS ONLY.

Lexie and I used to race to that sign every time we got to the parking lot. Lexie would joke that I should wish to suck less at bowling, and I would joke that she better wish to beat me to the sign one day.

But when Lexie rolls Ted into the Thunder Bowl lot and parks, neither of us gets out and runs to Rip's beard, and it feels like that moment in a movie right before the breakup.

"I'm sorry we ran," she says, before I even say hello. "So sorry. I'm not going to make excuses. I got scared and ditched you."

"I get that. It's OK," I say, because now, a few days out, it is.

"Really? I thought you were never going to forgive me and run off with the wrestling freaks and I'd never see you again," Lexie says, all in one breath.

"They're not freaks," I say. "They're really fun. In kind of a weird way, but—"

Lexie's laugh cuts me off. "They're the town freaks. Trust."

I want to disagree. To say that Abigail Rose and Mabel have been nicer to me than she has. But this is Lexie's hometown. She knows who its freaks are. I don't want to be a freak by association.

Being the awkward, out-of-sync member of a cheerleading squad isn't how I was hoping to spend my senior year, but it beats teaming up with the town outcasts before school even starts, if those are my only two options. Which, currently, they are.

I stay silent and follow Lexie into the bowling alley because it's what she loves to do—it's her bliss—even though I can't remember the last time she asked me what I wanted to do.

Inside Thunder Bowl, it smells like every bowling alley everywhere. Like nacho cheese, hot dogs, and beer. Ruby, the daughter of the owners, greets Lexie with a wry disdain, like always. She and Lexie have had an archnemesis-level rivalry ever since Lexie started to bowl perfect games. Ruby's a good bowler; Lexie's a damn prodigy.

"Didn't work, huh?"

"You couldn't get rid of me if you filled my lane with rattle-snakes from Overlook Mountain," Lexie says. "Last time Ruby stuck me next to a bachelorette party. Almost lost a tricky spare to a distracting penis tiara bouncing on the head of a twerking bridesmaid in my peripheral vision." She eyes Ruby. "Your tricks don't deter me. I love a challenge."

Ruby gives us our shoes and a lane, and the pre-bowling

dread sinks in. I hate to lose, and when it comes to bowling, I always do.

"I'm seriously digging the new look tonight," Lexie says when we're settling in.

I step into the lane, the bald soles of the bowling shoes gliding along the floor.

"Really?" I roll the ball straight into the gutter, like usual.

"The hoops, the lipstick, the jacket." Lexie takes her stance in the lane. "It's a whole mood." She bowls a strike.

I laugh. "What mood is that?" I grab my ball from the return and lob it down the lane unsuccessfully.

"The 'I'm pissed at you but looking cute as hell' brand of Birdie badass."

"Why does everyone always think I'm pissed?" I look at the scoreboard.

"Because you're kind of angry most of the time?" Lexie bowls her second strike and turns around to make sure Ruby's watching. She is. "You're scowling at the scoreboard."

"This is just my face."

"Last summer you were super pissed that you were missing that—whatever that camp was for smart kids who can't wait to be adults."

"The Future Leaders Symposium."

"Exactly, whatever."

"It's not whatever." I roll my ball down the center of the lane and actually knock down four pins. "It mattered to me."

"Maybe being angry is kind of your thing? You know? Like how bowling is my thing, and being less good at bowling is Ruby's thing."

"That makes me so—"

"Angry?" Lexie laughs. I open my mouth to tell her how

I feel, but she's got her phone out, texting. "Relax, Birdie, I'm *kidding*."

I wonder if it's Zeke or Kayleigh. If she's telling them how bored she is with me.

I take my phone out and text George: *Why is it possible to feel lonely when you're not alone?*

Lexie laughs at something on her phone, and George texts back.

> Try to give people a chance to understand you instead of feeling so misunderstood.

I shoot back, *Shuddup, that was so deep*, with a vomit emoji and a skull and crossbones.

"That jacket softens your shoulders," Lexie says, and I'm not sure how to take it.

She and Kayleigh both have the kind of dainty collarbones and shoulders that make me hunch my shoulders forward to look less bulky. The kind people expect from a girl named Birdie. Instead, even the compliments I get somehow critique my femininity. Or lack of.

George's text burns in my mind.

"Last night at the party," I say, "the whole 'let's arm-wrestle the strong girl' thing sucked."

"You should be proud of how strong you are," Lexie says, but I hear her comeback to Darren in my mind. *She's not going to arm-wrestle you like the strong woman in the freak show.*

I wish it were that easy. I mean, I *am* proud of how strong I am. At least I was before Coach gave me that talk. But before that, I always knew I had to watch my weight, even when that weight was muscle. I was proud of how strong I was, but I understood it would only be tolerated to a certain extent.

Now, every time I think about how strong I am—or how strong I was, with every day that I don't train, every day that I get smaller and weaker—I'm just so *angry*.

But it's not just Coach, or gymnastics. The thought of a strong woman arm wrestling made Lexie think "freak show." I'm not making that shit up.

I brace myself to go for the truth. To try to let Lexie in.

"I hate when people say stuff like that to me. When they grab at my arms, the way Darren did." I pick up my ball to roll. "If I were a guy, no one would do that." I roll a solid gutter ball. "I wouldn't be too big to be an elite gymnast, either. Don't you hate that?"

"What?" Lexie sets up, and rolls another strike.

"How things are different for guys and girls? Like how female gymnasts have to be tiny, but male gymnasts can have huge muscles."

Lexie shrugs, thinking, and then shakes her head. "Guys and girls are just different."

I scrunch my face in confusion.

"Are they, though?"

Lexie scoffs, like it should be obvious.

"Look how it turned out when your parents tried to be all anti-gender with George," Lexie says. "They don't make them girlier than your sister."

My parents sort of named my sister after George Eliot and George Sand, famous female authors who used pen names to break through the glass ceiling of their era, but also George Washington (back when they still believed his teeth were made of wood), because Mom wanted her daughter to know she could be president. Mom's über-concerned about gender discrimination on job applications, too. Because it's real.

She wanted to name me Orlando. They're a Virginia Woolf character who starts the book as a man, and upon waking up as a woman and seeing herself, thinks: *Different sex. Same person.*

When Dad suggested Bird, Mom loved it, because nothing's freer than a bird.

Mom taught us that the entire concept of pink vs. blue for babies was a marketing ploy to get people to spend more money, and when it was introduced, the colors were reversed. In the early 1900s, pink was thought to be "a more decided and stronger color," interpreted as masculine, whereas blue was seen as prettier and more feminine. Pure as a cloudless sky. Like a virgin.

The thing is, most of what people say about boys and girls is just as arbitrary as those colors. We aren't inherently different, the world is just set up like we are. And it's not like you can escape that by acting like it's not there.

Mom once had it out with a neighborhood guy at a dinner party who said that *the problem with all of this trans stuff is how confusing it is.*

If you can't figure out how to treat someone until you know his, her, or their gender, she said, *I guess you've identified your problem.*

"Arguing for the inherent differences between men and women is just bad science," I say. "Doesn't it bother you to know that actual scientists once believed genius was a masculine trait, like a beard?" I don't finish the quote, which includes *or strong muscles.* That part always rubbed me raw.

"Beverly really did a number on you," Lexie says.

"Scientists used to think women shouldn't ride bicycles!" I say.

I know Lexie thinks I'm a broken record with this stuff, but I've never understood why these things don't bother everyone. How people could possibly still believe there are more differences than similarities between guys and girls. "*Scientific American* published an article debating whether or not women should be allowed to ride bicycles, concluding that yes, they should be *allowed*, but they must never forget that girls aren't intended by nature for that kind of exertion. And that even—"

"If they're super good at it, they should never ride as fast as a grown-ass man," Lexie says, finishing my lecture. "This is the spiel you gave me the first summer you brought your weird black bike up." Which is because it's the spiel Mom gave me when I learned how to ride.

"Want to bowl another string?" she asks. But we both already know the answer.

I tried what George said. I tried to help Lexie understand how I feel.

But how can I do that when I'm not even sure how to put it into words? When I try to put it into words and, still, she doesn't get it.

When Lexie drops me off, she reminds me again about the open door with Mo, and I tell her I'll think about it. Only every time I try to imagine myself back with the cheer squad, I feel a pit in my stomach.

Back in my room, I google "am I nonbinary or just a tomboy." Again.

I've read everything there is to read about what it means to be nonbinary. The thing is: It doesn't just describe me, it describes how I see gender. If I'm faster than a lot of guys, then isn't it objectively incorrect to say guys are faster than girls? If some guys like to wear makeup, and everyone looks good in it, then isn't it objectively incorrect to say certain fashion is masculine or feminine? And if we make statements like that, aren't we arguing for our own limitations?

Back in Shakespearean times, the guys wore tights with ribbons accessorizing their junk—that was masculine. Isn't gender always fluid, when you look at it that way?

Isn't the idea that humans can be divided into two groups and described accurately just . . . flawed?

Still, isn't it a little *extra* to have to label myself to, like . . . avoid being labeled.

But the cheerleading tryout was a version of my hell. Do I really want to subject myself to that for an entire season, so I can be better at fitting in?

I know what their uniform looks like. I'll feel like I need to *soften my shoulders*. Shrink myself. No matter how athletic the sport is, I'll be back to micromanaging my weight and muscle like I had to in gymnastics. If I need to make myself smaller, I'm probably not in the right place.

Which is exactly how I feel here, ever since we moved. Like I'm in the wrong place.

Despite what Lexie said, about how Abigail Rose and her family are all total freaks, I can't help myself.

I spend the rest of the night reading Abigail Rose's website, *Real to Me*, and watching videos of the wrestlers she writes about, wondering what it's like to go ape shit in the ring.

CHAPTER 6

"Atta girl, Ronda!" Mabel peers over my shoulder into the box. "Hooking Mabel up with those sweet, sweet femurs."

It's my third day at work, and I've come to expect two things: a muffin each morning, followed by a strange shipment from a strange person somewhere in the world. Today's is from Roadkill Ronda, out in Colorado, and so far, it's mostly possum bones and elk horns.

"Your femur choker is one of our all-time bestsellers," Abigail Rose says.

"The goths flock to my femurs," Mabel says, picking one up and kissing it.

"You know," I say, "this whole town would be a lot less afraid of you if they knew where these bones came from."

Abigail Rose scoffs. "And give up all that kayfabe gold? You gotta be kidding me."

"What gold?" I ask.

"Kayfabe," Mabel says. "Wrestling lingo for pretending the

performer and the persona are one and the same. It's the reason folks who come to the shop still call me Mad Mabel."

"And the reason you used to growl at people in the supermarket when someone recognized you from the ring," Abigail Rose says, proud.

"Hard-core make-believe," I say. "Hardly an even trade-off for the entire town thinking you eat roadkill." Mabel and Abigail Rose share a look and then a laugh.

"This town can think what they want," Mabel says. "When you look like I do, they will anyway. I'd hate to spend a second more than I have to inside other people's minds."

"Kayfabe isn't run-of-the-mill make-believe. It has the power to transform the fabric of reality," Abigail Rose says.

I want to tell her how ridiculous that sounds. How, if make-believe could transform reality, I'd be an Olympian right now. I pretended. I imagined that my dream was possible. I visualized myself on podiums, medals hanging from my neck.

The fabric of reality doesn't give a crap about anyone's dreams.

We don't get to choose who we are and play whatever character we want. The world decides who we are. Other people tell us how we can act. Everyone knows that.

Mabel asks us to walk to the art store to pick up paints because she has armadillo shells from a ranch out west that she's turning into lampshades.

Out on the town green, Silas plays his flute, and he's like nothing I've ever heard before. A small group of tourists migrates from the Trailways bus stop to listen and drop bills in the hat of this mountain of a boy who pours melodies from his breath like a waterfall.

Abigail Rose records a video on her phone.

I haven't told her yet how much time I've spent reading her website—how unexpectedly *interesting* I find it—but Unexpected and Interesting are Abigail Rose's silent middle names.

In the "About" section of her site, she calls out some old wrestling blogger guy by *name*. A real boss bitch move. Blogs are still big in the wrestling world, and Abigail Rose didn't think the most famous one did a good job reviewing women's wrestling. So she started reviewing matches herself, and it became her *raison d'etre*.

"Have you given it any thought?" Abigail Rose asks. "Wrestling?"

I shake my head like it's ridiculous, even though I have. I've given it enough thought to know, without a doubt, that it would be social suicide.

"Definitely not."

Reading her post about Nia Jax, The Irresistible Force, and how she became the first person to ever be in both the men's and women's Royal Rumble match in the same event, I actually felt inspired. There aren't many sports where male and female athletes compete against each other.

Nia's a former college athlete and a gorgeous plus-sized model. For the first time since outgrowing my gymnastics dream, looking at Nia, I thought: *I could stand to bulk up.*

"Don't you want to be a part of this exciting moment in women's history?" Abigail Rose presses.

"Is it, though?" I cock an eyebrow. Even if her blog does read like a feminist diatribe.

"Female wrestlers have been challenging gender norms since . . ." Abigail Rose pauses, trying to pinpoint it. "Since

Mabel's time and before her. Now we're in the wake of the most exciting period in history—the Women's Evolution."

I recognize the phrase from her article about how the WWE Divas evolved into the current Women's Division. Long story short, women earning less than their worth in professional wrestling didn't end with Wendi Richter walking out after the Original Screwjob. The Divas was an era in which women—sometimes poorly trained models, dancers, and cheerleaders—were used mostly for sex appeal, until the writers finally gave the women an interesting storyline between Brie Bella and Stephanie McMahon—an archetypal boss vs. worker feud—and the WWE Universe demanded more airtime for compelling women's matches. The Give Divas A Chance movement rolled right into the so-called Women's Evolution.

"I'm going to be a part of it. Don't you want to try?"

When she says it, I see Mo's face at the tryout. *Aren't you even going to try?*

"It's just . . ." I pause to find the right word. I don't want to offend Abigail Rose, but all the words coming to mind probably would. Wrestling isn't something for girls from gated communities who ate at Michelin-starred restaurants with their glass ceiling–smashing mother. That's not who I even am anymore, but still . . .

"A little what?" she presses. "Trashy? Redneck?"

I shake my head, lying to my new friend like, *I couldn't think that of you.*

"I don't think . . . I mean . . ." I pause to find the words. "It's just not for me."

"Wrestling's for everyone," Abigail Rose says. "Especially the Future of Mayhem."

She couldn't be more wrong. The last thing on earth that I would ever be caught dead doing is smashing around some wrestling ring like a steroidal prizefighter. Even if it does look fun. I'll work off my debt with Mabel and then get myself back on track. Whatever that means out here in the boondocks.

"Sorry to disappoint," I say. "But I'm really not who you think I am."

"Oh yeah?" Abigail Rose says. "Who are you?"

"I'm . . ." I start, but I have no idea how to fill in the blank.

"That's what I thought," she says. "If you ask me—and I know you didn't, but if you did—I would say who you are is less relevant in life than who you want to be."

I want so badly to believe in these things she says, even when they're categorically false.

Abigail Rose is intense and kind of abrasive, but I like her. She acts like I'm worth getting to know, and it makes me think I might be.

"Who do you want to be?" I ask her.

She runs her short, painted fingernail across her bottom lip while she thinks, then she stretches both arms in front of her and looks at them before saying, "I want to feel real."

I want to ask her what she means, but for some reason, I'm embarrassed not to know.

"Yeah, I get that."

When Silas takes a break, two older couples clap loudly for him, and he blushes. He starts toward us when he sees Abigail Rose.

"Want to come to the Queen City Crew's School's Out for Summer Spectacular tonight?" she asks both of us, and even though I don't know what that is, I nod along with Silas as he says "Hell yes" before heading back to the green to play another song.

"A live wrestling event?" Excitement flutters in my heart, like a bird.

"Indie," Abigail Rose says as we start back to the store.

"What does one wear to a wrestling event?" I ask.

"Whatever one wants." Being friends with Abigail Rose smells like adventure, feels like freedom, and sounds like a crowd chanting "Yes! Yes! Yes!" the way she greeted me that first morning in Mostly Bones. Which I now know, since she trots it out regularly, is part of an old Daniel Bryan gimmick: the Yes chant.

Turns out, this wrestling thing is pretty fun. That's kind of the entire point.

"Get ready to be bit by the beast," Abigail Rose says. "After tonight, you're going to beg me to let you be the face of the Future."

"Don't get your hopes up," I say.

"Oh, that's impossible," Abigail Rose says. "My hopes are always up."

I'm riding with Silas and Abigail Rose to the Queen City Crew event, feeling like I've been picked up by an unseen hand and dropped into a completely new life.

As we cross over the river and into Poughkeepsie, Abigail Rose looks out, her eyes wide.

"The Queen City is where it all happened," she says, looking around at the city lights. "The Civic Center here is hallowed ground. Macho Man Randy Savage debuted there. Mr. Wonderful turned on Hogan."

"Andre the Giant's in-ring haircut," Silas says.

"They recorded a lot of the WWF shows here in the eighties, and the early episodes of *Raw* in the nineties." Abigail Rose sucks in a sharp breath when she catches sight of the marquee in the distance. "They even filmed the WWF superstars' 'Land of a Thousand Dances' music video there."

"Please tell me that's on YouTube," I ask from the back.

"And forever imprinted on the folds of my brain." Abigail Rose shimmies her hands at me. "Someday we'll be throwing events for Mayhem there. One of the Queen City Crew wrestlers— Petra—someone in her family owns it now."

"No shit," Silas says, impressed.

"But tonight, we've got a different destination." Abigail Rose directs Silas to turn left.

Silas pulls into a spot under a burned-out streetlamp on an empty industrial street. We get out of the car, and I follow as they start down a nearby alley. They stop at a door, and Abigail Rose knocks four times.

The doorman isn't some big huge guy. He's about my size, maybe a hair smaller.

"Well, if it isn't Abigail Rose, thorn in the side of the status quo!" He pulls her in for a hug. "I told Cami you might come, so she saved you seats up front."

"Angel, this is Silas and Birdie. Guys, this is Angel. The wrestling trainer I told you about," Abigail Rose says to Silas.

"I don't train wrestlers," Angel says. "I train superstars." He looks straight into my eyes, and I get chills.

"Yeah, man. That's what I'm talking about," Silas says, high-fiving him.

"Birdie's Mayhem's newest recruit," Abigail Rose says, and I don't correct her.

He looks me up and down, eyes lingering on my arms, but it doesn't make me cringe.

"Fierce," he says. "You said you want to talk cross-promotion again?"

"I was thinking more like world domination," Abigail Rose says.

We head down the hallway, through a metal door marked EMPLOYEES ONLY in almost completely faded lettering, and into a cement-floor room. High-energy music pumps through the speakers at the back.

"Where are we?" I ask, and Silas says, "The old underwear factory."

A strikingly beautiful, very tall girl with a headset nestled atop her braids darts around the room, from a sound table at the back to a baby-faced guy sitting on a stool with an iPhone screwed into a tripod for recording. The crown on her purple jacket sparkles like the gold highlighter illuminating her deep brown skin. She's all business and definitely in charge.

"They produce their own theme songs." Abigail Rose puts a finger in the air.

"This?" Silas listens, impressed.

"Get why I've been trying to collab since Mabel brought me to their Holiday Hell-Raiser last year? Wait until you see their wardrobe and styling. Their storylines sizzle."

"You pitched this to Frankie?" Silas asks.

"I made a *PowerPoint*! All we have to do is share our ring and our connections."

"Ay, that's the rub," Silas says. "This an eighteen-footer?"

Abigail Rose nods.

"Why would the other guys not want that?" I ask.

Silas huffs. "The Barn of Mayhem is for the Men of Mayhem."

"Frankie's got them all convinced it's not in their interest to share the ring—or their spotlight with the scouts—with anyone," Abigail Rose says.

"Especially not anyone who makes them look bad," Silas adds.

"Do you know tarot?" she asks, and I shake my head. "Frankie's the Four of Pentacles, which means he's sitting on a pile of abundance, but he's afraid to give up any of it for fear of losing. It's a fundamental misunderstanding of how the material plane works," Abigail Rose says like she's stating the obvious, "but the Four of Pentacles is *terrified* of change." She laughs.

"That's Frankie alright," Silas says.

A couple with two small kids sits ringside across from us, a poster board resting on the floor in front of them that says, inexplicably, DO YOUR HOMEWORK. It must be gimmick-related.

Cami, the girl with the headset, spots Abigail Rose, and it's the first time I see her smile. She sprints toward us and Abigail Rose jumps up to hug her hello.

"I was starting to think we'd never see you again!" Abigail Rose's head comes to Cami's chest. She's about Silas's height. She's also the confident kind of beautiful that makes every girl either hate her, want to be her, or want to date her. I instantly want to be her friend.

"This time I'm serious," Abigail Rose says. "I can deliver on the collab."

Cami's eyes light up in response, but then her focus shifts and she presses her finger to a button on her headset.

"Tell him *I* told you to do it," she says through a clenched jaw. Then, to us, "Fifteen minutes to showtime."

"What can we do to help?" Abigail Rose asks, but Cami shakes her off and talks into her headset.

Cami starts back toward the sound table, where two guys

argue over a cable, and turns to shout, "Details on the collab. After," and Abigail Rose flashes two thumbs up.

When the seats are mostly full, the lights cut out and a spotlight shines on the ring. It feels like when a movie is about to start.

"Welcome to the Queen City Crew Saturday Showcase event," Cami's voice booms over the speakers. "School's Out for Summer!" A beat kicks in, like cheerleading music. "And now, for the night's opening match, the moment you've all been waiting for. It's time for . . ." The audience pounds their hands and feet in a drumroll without being prompted.

". . . ROLL CALL!" The whole crowd chants in unison when Cami yells it.

The song changes, and a light pops on to illuminate the entrance as a girl marches into the room like a superhero English teacher with a championship belt around her waist. The lyrics blare through the room as the audience raps along.

"It's time to DO, do do do do do do, It's time to DO your HOMEWORK!"

The wrestler has paired what my mom would call "practical slacks" with a cardigan twinset, her hair wrapped into a bun. She wears cat-eye glasses and holds one of those behemoth English class anthology textbooks that are a pain to carry but *would* make a great weapon.

She waves her finger at the audience disapprovingly and shouts over the music, "Detention! Detention!" prompting even louder boos from the crowd.

"Weighing a hundred and fifty-five pounds," Cami announces, "and here to make sure you DO YOUR HOMEWORK . . ." The audience shouts along with her. "MS. MISERY!" The audience boos.

Ms. Misery jumps up in a corner and extends her arms to

the crowd. Some audience members lift their homework-related signs and cheer. One guy boos and holds up a sign that reads BURN THOSE BOOKS in block letters that look like they're burning up in flames.

"And her opponent, a fighter whose spirit was forged in the actual fires of hell . . ." Cami pauses as the new song kicks in: heroic, like a fight song. Then it crackles out, a fuzzy voice comes through, and the audience chants with it, "BURN THOSE BOOKS."

"The Fire Chief, weighing in at a hundred and seventy pounds, and not afraid to"—Cami pauses for the audience join her—"BURN THOSE BOOKS!"

The Fire Chief flips into the ring, takes off her helmet, and swings her long black hair forward and then back so it flares out dramatically. She wears red lipstick and winged eyeliner, and her outfit can best be described as a "sexy firefighter" Halloween costume. Under her skintight Lycra shirt, her muscles ripple.

"That's Jimena," Abigail Rose says. "She and Drita"—she nods toward Ms. Misery—"have had a beef going for six months."

Someone climbs into the ring wearing a black-and-white striped referee shirt. The opponents face off in the center of the ring, circling and snarling, the moment thick with dirty, angry energy.

"The following contest is for the Queen City Crew Women's Championship belt," Cami announces, "and is scheduled for one fall."

"One fall!" the audience echoes back.

A bell sounds and the fighters lock up, grabbing one another's shoulders. As they move, I'm transfixed, with them through every exchange of power.

A young white kid seated next to us, who can't be older than twelve, screams his face off, booing and cheering depending on who's taken the lead. Elsewhere in the world, this is antisocial behavior, but here? It's part of the script.

It's like part *Rocky Horror Picture Show*, part Roman gladiators. Without the maiming and the death.

Ms. Misery picks up her anthology and smashes it into the Fire Chief's head, knocking her to the floor. Misery squeezes the chief between her legs as she arches into a full backbend, and it seems like it's over. There's no way the Fire Chief can pry herself from Ms. Misery's submission hold. But I'm holding my breath, sure she won't tap out.

I have no idea how, but as the seconds tick on, I swear the Fire Chief is going to break free and get Ms. Misery to submit.

The referee starts to pound the floor, and the audience counts, "One . . . two . . ."

"And a kick-out at three!" Cami's voice booms over the speakers as the Fire Chief breaks free, presses herself to standing, and delivers a roundhouse kick to Ms. Misery's back, laying her out next to her opened anthology. The Fire Chief climbs to the top rope.

"BURN THOSE BOOKS! BURN THOSE BOOKS!" the crowd erupts with a chant.

The Fire Chief extends her arms out to the audience and, with a bounce of the rope, launches herself into a backflip off the turnbuckle, the red of her costume like a fireball heading straight for Ms. Misery.

"Look out, Ms. Misery, here comes the Flaming Moonsault!" Cami says. The Fire Chief lands the backflip, pinning Ms. Misery.

"One . . . two . . . three!" the audience counts with the referee. The bell rings, and the Fire Chief rolls off her opponent and rises to her adoring crowd. The referee holds her fist above her head in victory and hands her what she came for: the Queen City Crew Women's Championship belt.

The Fire Chief is crying *real tears*, holding the belt above her head like it's the plate at Wimbledon. The outcome may be fixed, but the win *feels* legit.

"You de-serve it!" *Clap-clap clap-clap-clap.* "You de-serve it!"

My heart is pounding, and I'm smiling. I feel like I'm eight years old.

We spend the rest of the night chanting and booing with the crowd. In a tag-team match involving musical instruments, the smallest of the guys winds up with his head in a bass drum.

The three of us laugh so hard that at one point, Abigail Rose thinks Silas is actually choking and tries to give him the Heimlich maneuver, which only makes us laugh harder.

My ribs are sore and my abs ache from it. But it feels so good.

In front of us, a group of four young Black girls wears crowns that sparkle under the house lights. Their glitter-dusted skin glows as bright as their smiles. One girl holds a sign that reads, IT'S MY BIRTHDAY, CAMI! and when they announce the match between Cami and Best Wes-tern, who wrestles in a cowboy hat and enters the ring with one of those "guy riding a horse" costumes, the birthday group loses their minds cheering.

"Cami took Wes on after he tried to end the career of her brother," Abigail Rose explains. "Not her real brother—in the plot."

The match unfolds like the best scene in an action movie. It goes on, and on, and on, until—finally—Best Wes-tern defeats Wrestling Royalty with a dizzying move.

"A Hurricanrana!" Silas shouts, and Abigail Rose says, "Angel's trained with luchadors."

Cami names the date for the rematch—the Queen City International Heavyweight Championship—and vows to strip Best Wes-tern of his belt and become the first-ever woman to hold it above her head.

And when the audience starts to cheer "Bow to the Queen! Bow to the Queen!" I really get it.

Cami is the face that runs the place.

I've seen little girls cheer like that before, but I don't know if I've ever seen them growl like that. Rage like that. Put each other's glittered faces in headlocks and wrestle like that.

There's a flutter in my chest.

On the drive home, we're quiet.

"I freaking love wrestling," Abigail Rose says as we cross the Hudson River under the twinkling bridge lights.

"Do you think Cami's going to win the guy's belt?" I ask.

"She should. There's no sport where gender is as irrelevant as professional wrestling," Abigail Rose says, and it could be a line out of one of her posts. "Wrestling is sports entertainment, and sports entertainment is about stories. The binary is use-less, except it keeps the athletes divided into two groups, one of which they can assume is the dominant, higher-paid group, the other of which is assumed to be weaker, lesser-paid group."

"Keep talking that way," Silas says, "and I'll start to think Frankie's right about you trying to take our belt."

"Frankie's trapped in the 1950s with this Men of Mayhem bullshit and you know it." She shakes her head. "The indies are intergender AF. Candace Freaking LeRae," she says.

The binary is useless.

It settles in my brain. Right in the middle of everything Mom's taught me, every feeling I've ever had about being bad at being a girl. The ways the world puts us into categories and tells us when we cross imaginary lines. The way it feels just as weird to me when someone tells me I can't do something because I'm a girl, is surprised I can do something even though I'm a girl, or encourages me to do something because there aren't enough girls who do it. Either way, I'm being defined by a category I didn't ask to be put in. Like I don't get to just be a person.

"What if I am trying to take it?" Abigail Rose asks, and Silas stares at the road ahead. "Who says it's your belt, anyway?"

The binary is useless.

Cami's fighting to be the first woman to ever hold the Queen City Crew Championship belt, but who said it was the guy's belt to begin with? Why does everything belong to guys unless it's otherwise specifically designated for girls?

CHAPTER 7

When I find Mom, she's at the desk in Grandma's old writing room, in the glow of a laptop with uncountable tabs open, a binder with charts and articles printed up and spread out over the desk.

She's even humming her *I'm so focused I'm humming along* hum. If I didn't know better, I'd think she'd gone back to work.

"Mom?" I say, when she doesn't notice me standing in the doorway.

"Yes, honey?" She stares at her notes like her old hyper-focused self, and if she weren't so absorbed into something important, I'd hug her.

Under the heading WOMEN'S LEADERSHIP IN BUSINESS, she's scrawled notes. POWER, STRENGTH, LEADERSHIP, and AMBITION sit opposite COMPASSIONATE, CARING, BEAUTIFUL, and RESPONSIBLE.

"Dad made maple scones and is boiling a pot of chai. Want some?"

"I'm not entirely sure," she says, as if I've asked a much more complex question. I'm used to this Mom, so into her work it's like she's inhabiting a parallel universe.

"What is that?" I ask, and she holds up the paper she's reading.

"A 2018 PEW Research study that looks at what traits Americans value in men and women," she says. "Sixty-seven percent of Americans view powerful as a positive trait in men, but ninety-two percent of Americans view powerful as a negative trait in women. Still."

I pretend to stab myself in the heart.

"I know, right?" Mom says, running her hand through her hair, like if she looks hard enough at her screen, she might solve the patriarchy. Like she's just one epiphany away from cracking the gender code.

"What are you doing with all of this?"

"I don't know yet," she says. "Could you do me a favor and say that's OK?"

"That it's OK to not know yet?"

Mom nods. "Yes, please."

I almost don't want to. Mom leaning into this new, untethered approach she's taking to life? It's undone everything I took for granted. But maybe George isn't wrong. Maybe Mom is courageous to step off one path and onto another, without knowing where it leads.

It seems reckless, but I'm the one out here making friends with Mayhem.

And, apparently, thinking in wrestling puns.

"It's OK to not know yet," I say, not knowing until the words are out of my mouth how badly I need to hear them, too. But there's something else I've been wanting to ask.

"Why did you guys give up on your whole gender crusade when I was born?"

Mom sits back in her chair.

"Honestly? We realized it would only work in a vacuum. Or in a world where everything, including how we feel about words—like *caring*, and *powerful*—wasn't so saturated with the gendered gaze of the patriarchy." Mom shakes her head. "Gender is one of the primary organizing factors in the world, and once we realized George was going to be obsessed with figuring out society's rules whether we believe in them or not, we stopped trying so hard. We decided to be open and talk about things when they come up." She looks at me. "Why?"

"No reason." I shrug. "Just something Lexie said. I'll be back with the scones and tea."

"Thanks, honey," Mom says, and as I slide out the door, her familiar hum tells me she's already back to work.

I take my own tea and scone into my room and sit with everything Mom said. How gender is a cage too solidly built to escape. But then I hear Abigail Rose in my head.

The indies are intergender AF. Candace LeRae, she said. So I look her up.

Candace LeRae is an indie wrestling legend who finally got hired by the WWE, but according to the wrestling sites, people thought it would never happen because of how much intergender work she's done. Including taking a thumbtacked boot to the face in a tag-team match against the Young Bucks.

But if people were wrong about the WWE not being able to handle a wrestler like Candace because she challenges their expectations of women . . . what else might they be wrong about? Sometimes it seems like the world is a lot more flexible than it lets on, but other times, you're up against a brick wall like Frankie.

How do you know when it's time to bend, or when it's time to break through?

After my shift, Abigail Rose and I head upstairs. I'm surprised to find the second-floor apartment is totally normal. Not a bone in sight.

Lexie texted me this morning because Mo says last call for joining the team. I have to decide by tomorrow, but after watching the Queen City Crew wrestlers, I don't think I want to be a cheerleader at all. They're amazing athletes, but it's never their turn to rage out in the limelight.

Still, part of me thinks it doesn't matter if I *want* to be a cheerleader or a wrestler. Cheerleading is what I *should* do. It's what Lexie expects. And wrestling? Wrestling is *nuts*.

Abigail's room is down the hall, which is lined with family pictures. Some are action shots of the guys, older, in the ring. There are a few pictures of the other cousins and Abigail Rose through the years. One where she can't be more than three and is sitting atop a horse, a woman whose hair is braided into pigtails hugging her from behind.

At the end of the hall, like a centerpiece, hangs a picture of a man in a sequined teal suit with a rhinestone-studded white cowboy hat, whose face I recognize traces of in the kids. He's got a full mustache, and when I look closer at his smile, one of his front teeth is gold.

"This room is so you," I say.

"The walls of wrestling posters, or the princess bed?" She opens the top drawer of her dresser and takes out a T-shirt that has, inexplicably, three guys with unicorn horns surrounding a pile of pancakes above the words, IT'S A NEW DAY, YES IT IS!

"Both." She's not kidding about the bed. It's the fanciest princess bed I've ever seen, and I'm from New Jersey. The purple canopy billows from above with stars woven into the sheer fabric, strung over golden bedposts.

"I used to be afraid to sleep in my own bed," Abigail Rose says. "Mabel bribed me."

"Did it work?" I sit down on the edge of the bed and, through the soft purple frame, soak in the posters of mostly female wrestlers, like a pantheon of fierce goddesses.

"Look at that thing. I sleep like a baby." Abigail Rose opens the door to her closet.

"Is that—"

"That, right there, is John Cena," she says, pointing at the poster behind the door.

"Even I know who that is," I say. "But John Cena usually looks pretty Hollywood. Why's he rocking jean shorts and a Little League baseball cap like a giant middle schooler?"

"He's a wrestler, birdbrain," Abigail Rose says, and it doesn't sound mean when she says it. She's making fun of me like we're real friends. Like she knows me. It kind of feels like she does.

"Why isn't he out there with the others?" I ask. And then it dawns on me. "Do you have a crush on him or something?"

"The only guy I've ever crushed on is Harry Styles."

"So hot," I say.

"I just love this corny-ass wrestler," Abigail Rose says, running her fingertips along the edges of the poster. "I mean, look at me. John Cena is too sincere, too genuine, too damn serious and sappy at the same time." She grabs a pair of boots from the closet. "It's so not cool to like Cena. It's like saying your favorite ice cream is vanilla."

"But what if your favorite ice cream flavor *is* vanilla? Shouldn't you enjoy it?" I ask, even though that's not exactly how I live.

"Cena's the most requested celebrity by Make-A-Wish kids for a reason, and he's one of my heroes." Abigail Rose points to the poster, autographed *To Abigail Rose* with the phrase *Hustle, Loyalty, Respect* and then signed, *Never Give Up, John Cena.* "But if my cousins knew I was a Cena fan, they'd say that's why I shouldn't be in charge of an edgy brand like Mayhem."

"Did you write this?" I point to the handwritten poem on a piece of notebook paper taped up beside the poster.

"A few years back," Abigail Rose says.

Wrestling is a home you take wherever you go.
Wrestling is a courage you didn't yet know.
Wrestling is a hope you're too jaded to feel.
Wrestling is sudden change; from babyface to heel.
So, remember, when the odds seem stacked against you:
Odds don't define the outcome. Wrestlers make their own truth.
Wrestlers win, and wrestlers lose, but never lose their tough.
Wrestlers never ever die, because wrestlers don't give up.

"That's awesome," I say. She makes wrestling sound like it's the answer to everything.

"It's cheesy," Abigail Rose says.

"It's inspiring. Almost annoyingly so." I add the last part so she doesn't think I'm too sappy or sincere.

"Like Cena." Abigail Rose cracks a smile.

"Who's the man in the cowboy hat in the hall?"

"Grandpa Wyatt," she says. "He was a wrestling promoter and Mabel's manager. He died from an aneurysm when I was five."

"I'm sorry," I say, and this time she doesn't brush it off.

Abigail Rose pauses, like she's thinking, and then looks at me. "I got Lyme disease when I was really little. I mean, I have it. It doesn't go away."

"From a tick?"

"I guess so. They didn't know I had it until I was a lot older. I lived with my mom on and off—she's not around anymore, we don't know where she is—and it wasn't until I came to live with Mabel full-time when I was four that she took me to the doctor. The doctors thought the pain was in my mind, so it took a long time to figure out what was wrong."

"They told you that what you felt wasn't real?"

"Doctors have bigger egos than wrestlers." She shrugs. "So I have the joints of a seventy-year-old, which must be why I'm so wise." She wraps it up with a joke, so I keep it light.

"Of course. Science." We're both quiet for a beat, but somehow, it's comfortable. "Does it hurt?"

"I'm in less pain now than when I was younger. Supplements, diet, exercise, and rolling on that"—Abigail Rose points at the hard foam tube by her bed—"keep me pretty steady. But yeah, it hurts. I get brain fog, and, like, incredibly tired sometimes." She says it so matter-of-fact. "It's harder during the school year."

"Is that why you can't compete in the ring?" I ask, hoping I'm not prying.

"If it was a sport where you're not repeatedly smashing yourself against a hard surface or another person, it wouldn't be such a big deal. It would still be hard, but not impossible," Abigail Rose says. "I was twelve when Mabel told me. She hoped it would change as I got older, but the Lyme led to swelling in my spleen. It's like I have the world's longest case of mononucleosis. And I've never even kissed anyone."

"That's unfair," I say unhelpfully, but I don't know what else to say.

"Mirror, mirror, on the wall," Abigail Rose asks her reflection, touching up her black lipstick, "who's the unfairest of them all?"

"Sounds like a tagline for a wrestler," I say. "A super-cruel ruler: the Unfairest of Them All." I pause. "Sorry."

"Don't be sorry. That gimmick's got legs." She jots it in her notebook, and I feel a jolt of pride. "I can't wrestle, true. But there's never been another Abigail Roosevelt Mayer. There never will be. And this bitch?" She spins around to face me, her face done up exactly how she wants it—like a dark cloud about to rage a storm on the unicorn horns and smiling faces of her New Day wrestling tee. "She's here to change the world and have fun while she's doing it."

"No pressure," I joke.

"A grand plan is just a series of small, actionable steps, my friend." Abigail Rose grabs my hand and leads me out of her room. "First, we find Frankie."

When Abigail Rose asked if I was up for a post-work field trip, I should've asked what it was. Details are on a "need-to-know basis," and, apparently, I don't need to know yet.

Silas picks us up in his Suburban and it's a fifteen-minute drive out of town to the Barn of Mayhem, the family's training and performance facility. The one Mabel keeps threatening to sell.

"When are you going to fill me in?" I ask.

"Need-to-know basis," Abigail Rose says again.

"You're not making me an accomplice here, right?" I've had my fill of that.

"Promise."

The afternoon light spills through the large, dusty windows

of the Barn. Its peaked roof is like a church, only instead of pews and an altar, there's bleacher seating and a wrestling ring.

A few guys pump iron at the back, and Little Mickey holds a weighted bag for a tough-looking guy who's punching it like he's training for the final fight scene in a *Creed* movie. The music is so loud I can't hear what Abigail Rose says to me as she heads over to the tough guy.

Silas nods toward the ring, and I follow him. He climbs up onto the edge and reaches to pull me up, and I dip through the ropes. The floor of the ring is softish, with a layer of padding over the hard surface beneath. I grab ahold of the top rope—wrapped in thick tape—and though it's stretched taut around the ring, it has the slightest give.

A guitar solo wails through the speakers as Abigail Rose talks to Little Mickey and the tough guy, whose arms are crossed in front of his chest, his head cocked to the side.

She points toward the ring, and Silas bends to my ear and says, "I need you to do something without thinking right now." I shake my head, but he nods so slowly and surely it calms me like a Jedi mind trick. "Run at me from the other side of the ring. I'll get low and put my arm out, and you run into it and do a forward flip over it. Then kick me from behind. When I fall, lay your body across mine." What he's asking sounds weird but not impossible. I can do that. "Don't get up until Robbie pounds three times."

It's not that I want to impress Abigail Rose. Being around her makes me want to surprise myself.

I don't know if it's the music, so loud I couldn't hear myself think if I tried, or the way the tough guy is looking at me, skeptical of whatever it is Abigail Rose told him. But when Silas steps into the center of the ring and shouts, "Go," I run toward the opposite side of the ring and bounce in place a few times nervously before taking off. I pick up speed toward Silas as if I'm bounding forward in a floor routine.

Silas throws out an arm to clothesline me. "Now," he says, and I take two quick steps and then spring up and over his arm, flipping around it like an uneven bar. He drops to his knees and, when I kick him in the back, he falls, his body stiff as a felled tree, the music so loud he barely makes a sound. I scramble to get my body across his and wait, like he said.

"Not bad," Silas whispers.

Robbie scrambles into the ring and pounds his hand three times, and there're actual cheers from the back. When I stand up, Silas grabs my hand and holds it above my head, and the guys cheer louder.

"The people have spoken, Frankie," Abigail Rose says to the tough guy. The music cuts out. "Thanks for hopping in, Robbie," she says to the referee, who wears shiny American flag boxing shorts.

"So, the chick can flip," Frankie says, and the dismissive look he wears makes me want knock it off his face. "Doesn't mean she can wrestle."

"Bullshit," Abigail Rose says. "I want the August promotion. I want to script it. It's my turn, and I'm here to take it."

"Last I checked we still have free speech in this country," Frankie says, looking around at the other guys. "But I'm not looking to be MeToo'd or anything, so don't take this the wrong way. I just don't like women's wrestling. It's not my thing."

"Mayhem isn't yours to rule over like a fascist dictator," Abigail Rose says. "Mabel still owns the Barn."

"Until I buy it from her," Frankie says. "Everyone here knows I'm the promoter and the booker because I'm the only one with a real job." Frankie is the oldest and makes bank with his landscaping company, while the other guys are all still in high school. Frankie's getting older and his first shot at NXT didn't go anywhere, so even I can see, the writing's on the wall for him. "I'm in charge," Frankie says, "because I'm the alpha of the pack."

What is this guy, a furry? I bite down on the edge of my tongue to stifle my laugh and shove my hands into my pockets to resist the urge to tell him, scientifically speaking, what bull-shit that is. Alpha wolves and wolf packs? There's no dominant leader controlling the others. Packs are families. The "alphas" are in charge because they're the parents.

"By what?" Abigail Rose almost spits at him she's so angry. "Being born?"

"None of those Queen City Crew kids have earned shit here, and their trainer, what's his name? Angel?" Frankie says, like he's got no place in Mayhem. "With his tutus and shit? The guy's a joke. Now you bring this girl? This gymnast?" Frankie juts a thumb at me. "She's not even a wrestler. The whole Battle of the Sexes main event idea you've been pitching doesn't work. A girl can't hold the Mayhem Heavyweight Championship belt. Look at the size differential alone. It's not remotely believable."

He says it like it's a fact, even though an audience would have no problem believing Cami could kick *his* ass.

But I see right through this guy. Frankie's afraid to lose to a girl in front of an audience. Like, he physically can't handle it.

Robbie, the referee from earlier, looks at his cousin. "What about how it's on us to sell the story? Isn't that what you always say?"

"Candace LeRae, bro." Little Mickey puts his hands out to the sides like he's just got to throw it out there.

Abigail Rose's eyebrow twitches, but she doesn't blink. Like if she does, she might miss the most important moment of her life.

"Birdie's not much smaller than you," she says, and Frankie sneers an angry growl of a face, like a dog about to bite. "She's ready to train hard. Harder than you ever have."

I've been ruled by scowls like that my entire life. From the boys I beat in those races. From the ones who decide that my muscles being big makes them need to make me small.

But Abigail Rose doesn't even flinch.

"Those were fireworks right there," one of the other cousins says, "and Silas has been wanting to get weird. Don't get me wrong, it's different. But we're not exactly selling out our shows as it is now."

It feels like the whole barn is a balloon, filling with a vibe other than Frankie's, and for a moment, we're all about to lift off the ground with the possibility of something new.

"We haven't done it because the audience won't buy it," Frankie snaps, cutting him off. "And we're not selling out the show because we're not going hard enough."

The entire group deflates. No wonder Abigail Rose calls Frankie a *real prick*.

"We need to work smarter, not harder," Abigail Rose says.

"You heard Mabel," Silas says. "Either we figure out a way to work together, or she's going to sell the Barn anyway." He looks Frankie dead in the eyes. "She'll probably sell that apartment you rent from her out back, too."

"All right, genius." Frankie spits on the floor. "You want a new Mayhem belt? Mabel's been on my ass for the last three months about giving the chicks a chance." His tone is so dismissive, not just to Abigail Rose and to me, but to Mabel. This forgettable grandson riding her coattails.

I have the unmistakable urge to body-slam him right here, right now.

"How about a revolving-door battle royale for a women's belt?" Frankie says, like he's in charge and it's his permission to give. "That shouldn't be too technically demanding for your girls. Come out, look pretty. Get tangled in a knot. Throw each other out of the ring." He wipes his hands against each other, as if washing them clean of the situation.

"Where am I supposed to get enough girls for a rumble?" Abigail Rose asks.

"I'll make it easy," he says. "Ten total, you come up with five. We'll book the rest."

"If you want to be so badass and indie, how about an inter-gender rumble." I can tell Abigail Rose's been waiting for a moment like this for years.

"Why does everything in the goddamn world all of a sudden have to be about gender?" he asks.

"You know what your problem is, Frankie?" She stares at him.

"I've got an idea," he says, staring back like he's looking right at it.

"Frankie thinks every battle is won through dominance," Abigail Rose says, to the entire group now. "He's wrong, of course. Conflict isn't a problem to be controlled; it's an opportunity to be explored."

"AEW is where they are because they dominate. Our fathers were dominant," Frankie says, looking around at the other guys. "When the next generation looks back at us, are they going to be able to say the same?"

"AEW is where they are because they're weird as hell. And I'm as much a part of this generation as you," Abigail Rose says. "We all are." She looks around at her cousins, but only Silas meets her eyes. "But how am I supposed to train five new girls in time for an August rumble? And where will you suddenly get the other five?"

"You worry about your end of the deal. I'll worry about mine."

"If I pull this off, I want my own competing brand," Abigail Rose says. "You keep the Men of Mayhem. We'll be the Future of Mayhem."

"The Men vs. the Future?" Frankie scoffs. "You should make T-shirts."

"The Future vs. the Patriarchy," Abigail Rose says. "Men welcome. Assholes respectfully declined."

Frankie laughs. Not at the tagline—at her. But it's like Abigail Rose's unicorn wrestling T-shirt is coated with insult-repellant armor. His digs don't touch her.

I'm pretty sure every mean thing anyone's ever said to me is lodged somewhere inside my body.

"Of course I'm making T-shirts." Abigail Rose starts toward the door and doesn't look back as she calls out, "Rule number one. A wrestler is only as good as her merch."

"I'm sure all the rich tourist citiots will snatch 'em up real quick," Frankie shouts, his voice slick with sarcasm. "Oh, right." He pauses. "Rich tourist citiots don't watch wrestling."

"They will when I'm done with them." She launches it over her shoulder like a grenade.

It's like she's walking in slow motion away from a car that's about to explode while the voice-over of the trailer says, *She's mad as hell, and fresh out of fucks to give.*

"He's wrong."

"Maybe he's right," I say. "I know nothing about wrestling."

She shakes her head. "Wrong to say a girl can't hold the Mayhem belt. Wrestlers are superheroes and supervillains *pretending* to hurt each other. It's good and evil. Fuck gender."

I cock my head to the side. "You sure about that? This is fighting."

Abigail Rose grabs at the back of her neck. "I've got the worst headache."

"Let's go turn on the Suburban and sit in the AC," I say. She looks so tired. "Want a piggyback ride?" I ask, and the pain and anguish drain from her face.

She hops on and wraps her arms around my neck, and within moments we're waiting for Silas inside the chilled cabin of a running car. Abigail Rose chugs water from her metal thermos and hands it to me.

"Mabel says a great wrestler can have a meaningful match with a broom. After dinner I'll show you Kenny Omega vs. Haruka, and you'll see what I'm talking about. A grown man can have a captivating match with a nine-year-old girl, if they both know what they're doing."

"Just when I think I'm starting to understand this whole wrestling thing," I say, "you send my brain to Suplex City."

Abigail Rose smiles, proud, and holds out her notebook open to a page headed:

THE INTERGENDER WRESTLING MANIFESTO

"The Future vs. the Patriarchy has a nice ring to it," I say.

"It does. Originally, I was thinking the Future vs. the White Supremacist Capitalist Ableist Patriarchy. But that's a little long."

"For T-shirts?"

"And buttons," Abigail Rose says with a glint in her eye. "I *love* buttons." She shakes her head. "But that kid ain't right. Frankie's getting desperate, and a desperate wrestler is a dangerous wrestler, depending on how far they're willing to go to chase their dream."

"I had no idea what you guys were talking about in there," I say. "What's AEW?"

"All Elite Wrestling. Frankie's wrong about most things, but he's right about that one. All Elite Wrestling is the first significant competitor to the WWE in twenty years, and they're doing their own thing. If they have a chance, it means we have a chance. Not just to be a part of what already exists, but to make a show as wildly uncategorizable as Mabel herself."

"How do you do that?"

"By writing the best damned wrestling plots the world has ever seen." Abigail Rose sets her jaw, determined. "The Elite are best friends who travel the world together and got a TV show. I want that. I need to build a brand strong enough to attract investors."

It's funny how Frankie and Abigail Rose both want the same thing—the survival of Mayhem—but have such different visions of what it takes to get there.

Inside the Barn, an argument grows so loud we hear it through the closed windows. Both sides are shouting. We start for the doors but stop as Silas lopes back out to the Suburban and climbs in without talking. As he pulls down the driveway, Abigail Rose turns the radio on. He shuts it off, and his face is impossible to read. It feels like forever before he speaks.

"I'm defecting from the Men of Mayhem."

"Did you tell Frankie? Is that what the shouting was about?"

Silas shakes his head. "He'll find out soon enough."

"You've always been too future for the patriarchy," Abigail Rose says, mussing up his hair the way Mabel would, and kissing him on the cheek. "Way too future."

Back at Mabel's, I'm so hungry I eat two plates of pasta and three meatballs without even realizing they're textured vegetable protein balls and the pasta's made of chickpeas.

"What do you mean you're not doing it?" Abigail Rose rips off a piece of gluten-free garlic bread from the loaf and mops up the sauce on her plate. "You're definitely doing it. You loved it. It was written clear across your face. It said 'I LOVE THIS' in cursive."

"It was fun flipping over Silas," I say, "but that's not an entire match. Never mind this royal, what's it called? A revolving door of opponents? You heard Frankie—just because I can flip doesn't mean I can wrestle."

"If I could install a mute button on that boy," Mabel mutters.

"You're the face of my brand," Abigail Rose says.

"What does that even *mean*?" I ask, and Mabel laughs.

"In wrestling, you've got faces, and you've got heels. The face is the one you're supposed to cheer for; the heel's the one you boo." Abigail Rose grabs the last slice of bread.

"Who wants to get booed?" I say.

"Kurt Angle. Former Olympic champion, won a gold medal with a broken-fricken-neck." She emphasizes each word. "He beams with pride as the WWE Universe chants 'You suck' when he walks into an arena. It's pure love and respect."

"That's messed up." I take another bite.

"Imagine the freedom! Not caring what other people think of you is *big-time* goals," she says.

"And yet, also physically impossible," I say. I mean it. People always say stuff like that. *Who cares what other people think?* Answer: me. And when I think someone doesn't like me, it feels like an actual, physical ache in my ribs. Like a splinter in my brain.

"You don't have to worry about that. You'll be the face. You get one of the last slots in the rumble, which sets you up to win. It's the opportunity of a lifetime," Abigail Rose says, dead serious. "You think I'm kidding, but scouts have their eye on Silas, and there's nothing more powerful in wrestling than the attention of the WWE. This could be a big deal."

What if Abigail Rose is right? What if I could be good at this thing?

But what if I try and I suck at it? What if I look like a joke?

I'll be worse than that citiot girl with dude arms. I'll be a fool, too.

"You've been awfully quiet over there, Mabel," Abigail Rose says.

Mabel gets up to grab an album from the bookshelf and opens it to a photo of a much younger her, standing up on the ropes, her tattooed arms extended to the audience.

"I don't have much to say about it, but this gal"—Mabel points to her picture—"would've given her firstborn for a shot at a Royal Rumble."

"We can give up your firstborn's firstborn instead," Abigail Rose jokes.

I offer to do the dishes, but Mabel tells us to go hang out.

"When we watched the first Women's Royal Rumble, Mabel cried," Abigail Rose says. "Practically every month, doors are opening for women that didn't exist in her day. First women's Royal Rumble, first female Hell in a Cell, first all-female pay-per-view, first all-female WrestleMania headline," she says, a fire in her eyes. "I *see* something in you. The guys saw it, too. We can do this. You just have to seize your destiny. Help me wrestle control of Mayhem."

"That line doesn't get any less cheesy the more you use it," I say.

"Wrestling mouth," Abigail Rose says, pointing at her lips. "Now, prepare yourself for greatness. This is"—she pauses dramatically—"Kenny Omega vs. Haruka."

Silas and Abigail Rose tried to explain the match to me. Kenny Omega spent a lot of time wrestling in Japan before AEW, sometimes with Dramatic Dream Team, a promotion known for over-the-top matches, like wrestling against dolls.

Haruka was the youngest student at a girls' school the DDT collaborated with, and she was sad that only the older girls were called up for matches, because she knew she was the biggest wrestling fan. So, Kenny Omega agreed to battle her.

The match is way more interesting than I expect. Haruka does a lot of complicated moves, and Omega somehow keeps her body protected, even while kicking her head to the ground.

"Though she be but little, she is fierce," Mabel says, popping into the room to grab her cigarettes and smoke on the porch.

"If I had half the confidence Haruka has, my entire life would be different," I say as she makes intimidating gestures on the screen.

"Mabel showed me the match when I was nine. The same age Haruka is there." Abigail Rose watches the screen with a look of pure joy.

"What would Haruka do?" I say, and Abigail Rose lights up, grabbing her notebook.

"That's a button!" She chews the top of her pen. "And bracelets. Someday the world will take me seriously as a promoter and an announcer, but first, I have to get my family on board with my ideas."

"Mabel's on board," I say. "So is Silas."

"Mayhem hasn't been represented by a female wrestler since Mabel," Abigail Rose says, "of course she's on board. She's also no help at all. But Silas? Working from the inside for us? That's a new angle to exploit."

"What about the Queen City people? Couldn't you recruit some of their wrestlers?" I ask. "Even if I had fun today, I don't know the first thing about being a wrestler."

"I've tried. Cami's got it all athletically, and her wrestling IQ is off the charts. But she's going to Columbia in the fall." Abigail Rose rubs her temples and closes her eyes.

Columbia? So Cami isn't just the most kickass local indie wrestler; she's Ivy League–bound. I'm not surprised because of Cami—I'd believe it if you told me she could do literally *anything*, that's how impressive she is in the ring—but because it's wrestling. The two worlds, professional wrestling and the Ivy League, seem like alternate universes from one another, and Cami has one foot in each.

"The other Queen City Crew girls are too busy to commit to anything other than a one-off cross-promo. They think we're hicks off in the middle of nowhere. Plus, Frankie's given the family name a shit reputation in the indies because, well I don't know if you've noticed, but he's kind of a dick." I laugh. "The Barn's only an hour north of them, but they act like it's in Canada." Abigail Rose rolls her eyes. "I need a local. Someone who can build this thing with me, here."

"I know it sounds crazy, and probably seems harder than hell, but I promise you," she says, and I'm certain Abigail Rose takes her promises as seriously as her style, "I'll give you all I've got.

I know everything there is to know about wrestling. If being in a match wasn't the equivalent of playing offensive lineman in a football game, I'd be the one in the ring." She says it matter-of-factly, like she has no choice but to concede to reality in this one area. "But sports entertainment is in my blood. It's not getting rid of me that easily."

"What if there's no such thing as destiny?" I have to ask, since I know there isn't.

"I'm not spending my whole life looking for proof of something I know in my bones," Abigail Rose says. "Destiny isn't some passive thing that guides your choices without you having to make any. Destiny is just choosing to be yourself."

I can't bear to tell her what I'm thinking: that this is the same kind of New Age BS that landed my family out here in the boondocks to begin with.

"This is the start of my life's work," Abigail Rose says. "I'm creating the Future of Mayhem, and you're my pick. The one I choose. Why?" she asks, reading my mind. "Because I know what I'm talking about." Then she says, "Your destiny is in your own hands."

I tell her I'll think about it and when Mabel drives me home, she says, "I don't like to put my nose where it doesn't belong. But this means a lot to my granddaughter, and I don't know where she's gonna find another fighter like you."

"That's the thing, Mabel," I say as she pulls down my driveway. "I'm not a fighter."

"Honey, you're a woman." She shifts the Thunderbird into park and looks me straight in the eyes. "You were born fighting."

CHAPTER 8

Dad wakes me at five A.M. with a cup of coffee on my bedside table.

"Cinnamon buns downstairs," he whispers, binoculars slung around his neck, and I rub my eyes in agreement. I'd hike ten miles up a mountain at sunrise if there was a gooey cinnamon bun from the center of the pan at the top.

I wound up further down the wrestling rabbit hole last night after reading more of *Real to Me*. I think I passed out around two in the middle of a "Top 10 Most Underrated Lita Matches" montage on YouTube. My eyes look and feel like they should on three hours' sleep.

Dad's been taking me birding as long as I can remember. When I was too small to object, he'd pack me up on his back and take me. But as I got older, I liked doing it. Not that you're really *doing* anything. Bird-watching is the opposite of doing. You sit there. Listening. Dad taught me how mating calls differ from morning calls, or songs of warning. He basically speaks bird.

I eat a cinnamon bun while finishing my coffee, and grab another for the walk.

We head back toward the woods behind the house, silent as the birdsong rises and falls around us. The early morning air, wet and cold, steadies me.

"Hear that?" Dad stops, holding his ear out. It's a familiar dawn song, followed by a nest alert.

We follow the call, and when I see it, I gasp. Dad looks up to where I'm pointing.

A bald eagle perches on a drooping Douglas fir, slick with dew, a halo of sunrise soft among its needles. The eagle squeaks its high-pitched whistle of a call.

That bald eagle, anointed by the morning light, looks like it straight-up owns this entire forest. I bet it never wonders if it's "too much." That bald eagle doesn't give a crap what I think of it, which kind of makes me jealous as hell.

I wonder what it must be like to really and truly not know how other people see you. To not care. To be the eye that sees, not the thing that is seen. To just . . . exist.

"Mountain bluebird," Dad whispers, and I feel an urge to climb the tree and save the eggs, even though that's not how nature works. The bluebirds probably won't even relocate their nest. They know there are predators, and they've chosen the best hollow inside the best tree they could find to keep their young safe. The rest is up to something like fate.

The bluebirds sound their alarm under the eagle's immovable gaze until, suddenly, it flies off to prey elsewhere, and—impending doom averted—the bluebirds resume their melodic thrum.

We take slow, quiet steps, watching and listening, until we press up against the wetlands. On the other side, a good five miles away, is the Deep Lagoon. We wind along the property's edge and start the trek back as our whispers turn to quiet voices, and we catch up.

Dad says a friend called last week about a documentary—the kind of work he doesn't usually get to do, since there's more lucrative gigs in docusoaps and food shows. About an hour away, in Gilboa, they found fossils from one of the oldest known forests on the planet. Part of the first-ever greening of the earth, when the first creatures crawled out of water and learned to live on land.

"How about that bald eagle?" he asks. We open the door to the smell of cinnamon buns.

Lately, I've felt like bliss was this thing from childhood. Like ZhuZhu Pets, Heelys, and Matchbox cars. You vaguely remember it was kind of awesome, but it's packed away in a closet somewhere, and if you take it out, it might seem not so great after all.

But seeing that bald eagle felt different. I felt different. It's not like I was in some kind of ebullient, ecstatic state.

I was alive.

And for a moment, just like last night at the match, that was enough.

I pick up my phone, Lexie's text about Mo still unanswered.

Apologizing to Mo and taking my spot on the squad would be the sensible choice. I know that.

But it's like the Queen City Crew wrestlers have become the bald eagle themselves.

They aren't the prey, smiling to assure the crowd they aren't a threat to anyone's safety.

They're the predators.

I used to think, *If only I'd stayed small.* But that isn't how I want to live.

Wishing I could morph myself into a cheerleader—some archetypal image of feminine perfection in my mind—won't make me feel real.

I type, *Tell Mo thanks but I'm not coming back*, and I almost can't send it.

If I choose Mayhem over cheerleading, to everyone in this town, I'll be one of the outcasts to whisper about.

But what if it already feels like I am? And what if, despite that, wrestling still seems fun?

You do you, Harley said, like it's that easy.

I press send on the text, and when Lexie replies, *K see you around*, it feels like I'm making a huge mistake.

I'm watching Guy Fieri midhunch, shoving a triple-decker barbecue sandwich into his mouth somewhere in Kansas, when I get a text from Abigail Rose.

> Fashion Emergency!!!!!

I text back *???????*

> Meet at the shop at 11?

"She's not cooler than you," I say, trying on a floppy hat I could never pull off.

"She *is*," Abigail Rose says, "and it's messing with my head." She dips into the dressing room with an armful of clothes. "I'm never going to find the right thing to wear."

I don't let on, but she might be right. She's already dragged me through most of the boutiques and all the good consignment shops on the street. Tabitha's Closet is the last unturned stone, and from the looks of what Abigail Rose just dragged into the dressing room, this stone is looking pretty . . . turned.

"Don't you kind of"—I pause for the right words, holding up a pair of fake leather pants that are way too cool for *me*—"have a style?"

"Yes, but this is Xena," Abigail Rose stresses from behind the curtain. "She's a drummer, and a DJ, and she's . . . *cooler* than me."

"She invited you, remember?" The moment I got to Mostly Bones, before I was even fully out of my car, Abigail Rose exploded with the details.

How she's had a crush on Xena for over a year—since she went to a local David Bowie tribute concert and Xena was the drummer *and* was dressed exactly like Ziggy Stardust, down to the haircut and color—and how Xena invited her to Musical Melee, a DJ battle she's going to be in tonight, and how she has absolutely nothing to wear.

"True," Abigail Rose says, emerging in an outfit that's cute— silver pants with a tube top—but not her. "But after an invitation, the next step is to show up. I want to really show up."

"What about this?" I slide it over the railing.

"Um, that's amazing." When Abigail Rose steps out this time, she's draped in a long black jumpsuit with strips of sheer gray and silver cloth hanging from the waist like knives. There's a V-neck in the front with thin straps, and when she turns to show me the silver skull print on the back, she's beaming. "You'll come with me, right?" Abigail Rose asks as she changes back into her clothes.

"On your date?"

"It's not a date," she says.

"It's a date. And it's weird to bring a friend on your date," I say, and the cashier says, "Mm-hmm," without looking up from his phone.

"Your shoulders probably look amazing in a halter."

She hands me a jumpsuit with a halter top and wide bell-bottom legs, with a sixties swirly pattern.

"I will never pull this off," I say, but try it on just to prove I'm right. "See," I say, stepping back out into the store, expecting Abigail Rose to laugh with me, but the moment I do, Kayleigh and Lexie come in and I freeze.

"That's actually kind of hot," Abigail Rose says, oblivious. "You're giving off Charlotte Flair vibes. And here I pegged you as more of a Becky Lynch."

"Nice spandex," Kayleigh says, without a trace of sarcasm.

"Right?" Abigail Rose says. Then she does a double take when she sees who it is and eyes me like, *You cool?*

Lexie looks at me like I'm some stranger who's replaced her old friend. Maybe I am.

"You should try this on." Kayleigh picks up a purple suit that Janelle Monáe might wear, and holds it out to me.

I almost say something snarky, like, *Why? Will it soften my shoulders?* But I can't. Because she's right. This suit is freaking lit.

"Can we get back to business?" Lexie asks from the counter. "We've got team tanks to order, and I have to get to work." The cashier takes down their order for matching tanks, and I put down the clothes Kayleigh picked out, too embarrassed to try anything else on.

"You need that," Abigail Rose says. She takes it from the rack without pausing for me to argue and heads to the cashier with her jumpsuit.

Lexie and Kayleigh wait to finalize their order as we pay and leave. We're out the door when Lexie sticks her head out.

"So, this is it? You're not doing cheer, and you're, what? A wrestler now?"

Her words hit me in the back like rocks, stopping me in my tracks.

"What if I were?" I ask. Lexie glares at me like I should know better. I promised I wouldn't embarrass her.

"I've got to get to work," she says, and then she leaves me outside with Abigail Rose.

"That's your favorite shirt, right?" Abigail Rose nods toward my polo shirt.

We're wearing the mud mask Mabel sells, while watching the Festival of Friendship: the culminating match in a best-friends-turned-enemies plot between Kevin Owens and Chris Jericho. The mask smells like a riverbed and tightens as it dries. I can feel my pulse in my face.

KO is a gruff Quebecois prizefighter. Jericho's a narcissistic scarf-wearer with the kind of loud mouth that only seems to exist on white guys who have the gall to front bad metal bands, and he's guilty as charged. Abigail Rose's favorite definition of wrestling comes from him: a live-action stunt show, mixed with Shakespearean drama.

"It's comfortable," I say.

"It's your drag," Abigail Rose says, and I arch an eyebrow, which tugs on the mask. "RuPaul says we're born naked. Everything else is drag."

"Like everyone's performing a role whether they know it or not?"

She nods and taps her head in that same *think about it* way she did my first day.

We've already watched the lead-up matches, with Jericho strung above the ring in a shark cage during KO's fights—"like a sexy piñata!" Jericho kept shouting—to solidify their best friendship. Which, in the world of wrestling, somehow makes perfect sense.

The culminating Festival of Friendship, a celebration of the platonic love between two men who fight for a living, is the perfect setup for betrayal. It's called a best-friends-turned-enemies plot for a reason.

On the screen, Jericho unveils his gift to KO: a riff on *The Creation of Adam*, the famous painting where God reaches out to Adam, gifting him with the divine spark of life. In this version, KO is in the place of God, reaching to touch Jericho, who beams at the camera, his scarf draped over his glistening torso, the championship belt slung over his shoulder.

"That painting's getting destroyed tonight," I say.

"You're a quick study," Abigail Rose says. Wrestling is funny like that—for how outlandish the plots and gimmicks are, it's comfortingly predictable. Except for when it isn't.

"In fourth grade, I used to wear this poncho from Mexico that my grandma brought back for me," I say, still thinking about what Abigail Rose said about how we're all in drag. "But my friends called it a dress-up outfit," I say, and at that moment, Jericho realizes that the gift KO has given *him* is in fact a diss. Owens attacks Jericho, who's knocked to the floor and pummeled by someone who was, moments prior, thought to be his best friend.

"Bitches," she says, dead serious.

"They were little."

"They were playing the part of 'girls who tear down other girls for doing anything remotely different from what everyone else does.' We've all played that role once or twice."

I cock an eyebrow at her. "Even you?" Kevin Owens picks up the painting and sends it flying, crashing into pieces outside the ring.

"You don't wake up one day this utterly fabulous," Abigail Rose says. "It's a process."

"I find it hard to believe you were ever anything other than yourself," I say.

"I haven't been. That's, by definition, impossible. Everyone I've ever been was myself," Abigail Rose says, like it's that simple.

We lie on Abigail Rose's princess bed, propped on her decorative pillows, and watch on her laptop while Owens and Jericho smash what remains of their friendship.

"That's the Fabulous Moolah," Abigail Rose says, as we're flipping through one of Mabel's old photo albums. I remember the name from the first night in Mabel's car. The one from the masked match against Wendy Richter. "Probably the only female wrestler from Mabel's era who was as famous as the guys. Held the belt for almost thirty years."

I flip a page to reveal a close-up of Mabel's face, her tattooed brow dripping with sweat, mascara running down her cheeks.

"That must be amazing," I say. "To be at the top for three decades."

Abigail Rose sinks into the pillow, shaking her head.

"The Moolah was bad. Wendi Richter called her evil, and Penny Banner—one of the biggest names from the time—she called the Moolah a pimp. Not like 'Oh, she's the shit.' Like, someone who profited from the exploitation of women."

I flip the page to another spread of Mabel using a series of grapples to dominate a slender woman with huge hair.

"Where'd this whole thing come from? It's so bizarre."

"Same as some of the greatest foods ever invented," Abigail Rose says. "It was carnival sideshow entertainment—feats of strength, that kind of thing. A lot of times the wrestlers would challenge the audience. You pay a price, and if you win, you get a prize. Sometimes they'd fix a match against people pretending to be audience members, so more people would put their money on the line for a chance. But some wrestlers could take on anyone from the audience. Even some of the women did that, and they could kick a guy's ass like that." She snaps.

Definitely not how I imagine women from a bygone era behaving.

"How do you think they got so brave?"

"To take on dudes from the audience?"

"To be the kind of women they were." I flip the page and there's another shot of Mabel, this time holding a guy half her size in a headlock on the mat. "It's not like they grew up in a time when everyone told them, 'Girls can do whatever they want.' But they did it anyway."

"There weren't a lot of jobs back then that offered women adventure, or the chance to travel."

"Does Mabel talk about how she wound up so . . . her?"

Mabel's a walking heel: The whole town loves to hate her, and she doesn't bother to correct their assumptions. It boggles my mind how much she loves and accepts herself. It rubbed off on

Abigail Rose, who doesn't care what anyone thinks of her. Other than, apparently, Xena.

"Mabel says before she was a wrestler, people couldn't get over how big she was, for a woman, and how unusual she was, being from a family of taxidermists. But as a wrestler, she figured out that the stranger she acted, the more people let her be herself. Then she gave herself a permanent reminder of who she is."

"Her tattoo." I asked Mabel about it once, how she chose the symbol for woman, and she told me it's also the astrological symbol for Venus, which rules Taurus, her sun sign. But she said something else, too. *Looking like I do, sometimes hecklers would shout that I wasn't a woman. I'd just point to my tattoo.*

I think of those boys, the ones who would say I'm too fast or too strong to really be a girl.

Mabel didn't get permission to be herself from anyone. She took it.

I flip another page to see a wrestler in the center of the ring, her hair shorn to her scalp and dyed bright red. She wears a sparkly leotard that says BIG RED and stands with her arms raised, one foot triumphantly perched on the back of Mad Mabel.

"I want to dye my hair really red," I say, and Abigail Rose raises an eyebrow. I picture a red so bold it actually looks hot— like the red flame of the fire opal on the talonsman I stole.

"I'm way overdue for dyeing mine. My roots make me feel so exposed." She tugs on her hair. Both the purple and the black have grown out to reveal her natural light brown at the top. "Tomorrow, we transform."

I growl like an animal.

"Ooh, that's good. Scary." Abigail Rose scrunches her face,

cracking the dried mud mask, and pulls off a chunk. "You should growl more often."

"I don't want to just dye it," I say. "I want to cut it all off. Like Big Red." I sound more confident than I feel, but that's OK. I said it.

"Drastic hair changes and wedding proposals," Abigail Rose says, reaching up to wrap her arm around my shoulder. I tuck mine around her waist. "Mabel says you should always sleep on both."

CHAPTER 9

Abigail Rose stands at the door to the basement wearing a plaid skirt, the side fastened with safety pins, over leggings covered in cosmic cats shooting rainbows out of their eyes. And, of course, a wrestling T-shirt—black with simple white letters. THE MAN.

"Killer drag," I say as we head down the creaking stairs into the basement air.

I'm playing it cool, but inside I'm freaking out. I meant it when I said I want to cut my hair off and dye it. But the closer we get to actually doing it, the more I think I should text George so she can talk me out of this madness. Only . . . there's this part of me that doesn't want to wake up tomorrow wondering, *What if I was brave enough to do it?* The part of me that doesn't want to live a life where I always tell myself why I can't do the thing I kind of really want to do.

We have to cut and dye my hair in the basement, because cool as Mabel is—and she's pretty much the coolest—she doesn't want us screwing up the linoleum floor in the bathroom with hair dye.

I'm more than a little scared for such a drastic change, but fear and excitement are sometimes too similar to tell apart. At least that's what I'm telling myself.

Last time I cut off all of my hair, George said I looked like a boy, but we were little kids. She was playing the part of "girl who tears down other girl for doing anything remotely different from what everyone else does."

But I didn't realize until now exactly how much I've caged myself in with these internalized, irrelevant limits, even as I've tried to avoid them.

It's not like I'm trying to break free, really. I'm not even sure that's possible.

I'm just trying to find my lewk. Something that might, somehow, remind me of who I want to be. In case the world says I'm doing me wrong.

Abigail Rose pulls a stool into the middle of the room, from back in a corner amid boxes labeled BONES and KNIVES. On one of the worktables, an antler lamp and a pair of fox-foot knives wait for repair, beside a squirrel carcass in a birdcage. All of which would've weirded me out in the past, but now make me feel oddly at home.

I sit on the stool with that familiar quiver in my heart.

Like there's something buried inside me, trying to work its way to the surface. Only there's another part of me that maybe would rather it doesn't succeed.

"Ready?" she asks. I nod, but then shout, "No!"

"Cold feet?" Abigail Rose puts the scissors down on the table.

"I should text George and ask her before I do this," I say, and Abigail Rose looks at me quizzically.

"How would she know what you want to do with your hair?"

It's such an Abigail Rose question.

"It's just"—I pause, trying not to sound like a little sister who can't do anything without her big sister's approval—"our hair's the same."

Abigail Rose waits for me to say more, but I shake my head.

"You're right," I say, taking a deep breath. "It's just cold feet." I picture myself with short hair, so bright it looks like a burning ember. "Let's do this."

I close my eyes as Abigail Rose lops off huge chunks of my hair.

She steps back to assess, holding the fabric shears she wrangled from Mabel's toolbox to "thin the herd." Having no mirror in sight makes this easier and harder. If I could see what she was doing, I might ask her to try to reattach that hair to my head, *please*.

"Let me see it," I beg, and she holds up a fistful of my hair before dropping it to the floor. "I'd hand it to you to hold, but that'll only make you more attached. Trust. Every time I cut bangs—every single time—I regret it at first. But look at these babies." She makes her shaggy bangs shimmy back and forth. "I'd feel naked without them."

Abigail Rose snips the last chunk and starts straight into buzzing. Smaller chunks of my strawberry-blond hair flutter down and glint in the light from the exposed bulb above us.

"Your hair is so freaking thick." She clicks the buzzer off and then on again.

"Sorry," I say, even though I know what comes next.

"Why the hell would you apologize for that?"

I've grown to love this part of our schtick: me being sorry, her asking why the hell.

And maybe it's because my hair *is* so thick, but I never realized how heavy hair is. I mean, I know the pain of wearing my hair up all day, and how it feels when I let my hair down. But the actual weight of hair is nothing to scoff at. My head feels so much lighter.

When she's done buzzing, I run my hands over it—the tiny strands of hair, soft and prickly at the same time, feel good against my palm. But I don't want to see myself until the color is done, too.

Abigail Rose mixes the Manic Panic Flash Lightning bleach kit, and I inhale the ammonia-like pungency, as foreign to me as this new weightless head. Before she starts to brush the mix over my buzz cut, my eyes and the rim of my nose burn.

"Now can I ask about your date with Xena?" I ask. Abigail Rose had me sleep over last night—I watched old wrestling matches on her laptop while she was at the DJ battle—in case she came home dejected and in need of cheering. Instead, she came home entranced, begging me not to ask her anything about it lest the dream bubble be popped.

"She is breathtakingly cool," Abigail Rose says, now with more awe than intimidation.

The whole process, including rinses—which we do in the sink down here even though it only runs cold water—takes about two hours.

I almost can't believe I've done it, but when I reach my hand up and touch my hair again, it's still true. I thought the biggest change with short hair would be external: how other people see me. But somehow, I feel different in my skin, before I've even seen what I look like.

"I knew this was still down here. Mabel thought she sold it but . . ." Abigail Rose holds up the heavy kind of hand mirror a fancy lady would gaze into right before she fainted from lead poisoning from her powdered makeup. But I squeeze my eyes shut reflexively. Afraid to look.

"You're ridiculous," Abigail Rose says. "Every second you waste not knowing your face under this head of hair is a second you'll always wish you could have back. For real . . ."

I open my eyes when Abigail Rose pauses, and there I am.

My hair is short and not just red but so-rich-it's-almost-purple-*blood*red. Manic Panic Vampire Red, to be precise. And *damn*, in the words of The Man Becky Lynch: It's straight fire.

Suddenly, I'm not the same old me with the same old hair.

Suddenly, I'm brand freaking new.

"I'm in," I say, and Abigail Rose blinks hard, shaking her head.

"You're in?" For a second, she looks afraid. Like she's misunderstood, or I'll change my mind.

"I'm in," I say again, my voice as steady as the first time.

"You're in!" Abigail Rose shouts it. She proclaims it. She yawps it from the cement floor like the basement is a rooftop. She grabs her notebook and starts scribbling furiously.

"We'll tell Frankie to get his fighters ready. I've got to contact Angel and Cami. And buttons! I need to order the button maker!"

"We've got under eight weeks before the match," I say. "We can really do this?"

"Is eight weeks long enough to turn you into a championship wrestler? Hell mother-freaking no," Abigail Rose says. "Eight weeks isn't enough time to turn you into a good wrestler. Or even a safe wrestler." I'm beginning to feel crestfallen when she smiles. "But if we get you in the ring right away and you're willing to train as hard as I imagine you did as a gymnast, eight weeks is enough to get this rumble up and running. As long as we play up gimmick and storyline and de-emphasize the actual wrestling on your end. We'll let the Queen City Crew do the heavy technical lifting. It's not a long-term strategy," she says, shaking her head. "But if you stick with me, if you keep training, we can do so much more. It will take time, but you really could be huge." I wince, still not sure I want to be. "Now that you're in," Abigail Rose says, "we can do everything I've always dreamed." She puts out her dye-stained hand for me to shake, and I do. "You're the face of the Future of Mayhem," she says. "And the future is looking bright." She points to my hair, in case I missed her pun.

"Cheese," I say, but I can't stop cheesing myself. I smile at the person in the mirror. The one I had no reason to imagine I would become when we moved here. The one I had no idea I was going to meet.

Abigail Rose grazes the nearby table, draped in a thick canvas cloth.

"I guess now's a good time to let you in on Mouse-o-Mania," she says with a smile. "Since you really are a part of Mayhem."

She swings her arm behind her, hooks the sheet covering Mabel's table, and pulls it off in one swift motion like a magician.

There's a reason why wrestling fans come in droves to Mostly Bones at the end of the summer, but Mabel and Abigail Rose just keep saying "Mouse-o-Mania" every time I ask.

Under the sheet is a dead mouse. Only, for a dead mouse, it's bursting with life: stuffed, arms bent upward as if flexing her muscles, wearing the same THE MAN T-shirt as Abigail Rose.

"First of the Mouse-o-Mania season," Abigail Rose says. "Of course, she went with Becky Two Belts." Abigail Rose lifts a tuft of bright orange strands lying next to this mouse-ification of Becky Lynch, aka The Man. Her hair. Mabel even put a tiny microphone in her hand. Two miniature championship belts are ready to be slung over her shoulders.

"*This*," I say, pointing at The Man, the mouse, the legend, "is Mouse-o-Mania?" How did I not see it coming? Taxidermy mice dressed as professional wrestlers.

"The tip of the Mouse-o-Mania iceberg." She laughs like the fun's just getting started, then she grabs my shoulders and looks me square in the eyes. "We're going to pull this off. You have no idea how much this means to me."

I hold up the mirror and look into the gray-veined, splotchy antique glass. The ornate frame rims my face and behind me I see the antlers, the fox feet, and Mabel's machete (don't ask) dangling from a wire metal rack. It's like a snapshot from a graphic novel, not my life.

I barely recognize myself, but looking into my eyes, sure enough, I'm me.

"I'm pretty sure I do."

I pick up the dustpan she swept my old hair into and can't bring myself to throw it in with the trash. To send it off to the landfill to fester inside some plastic bag for a century.

"What are you doing with that?" Abigail Rose asks as I start up the stairs.

"Sending it down the creek."

When we get outside, I drop it into the current and watch as it floats downstream. My old hair catches on rocks and twigs; strands stick to tufts of moss and grass. A clump hooks a creek-side sapling, and a sparrow drops from a low-hanging tree branch and grabs it in its beak.

I run my hand over my head and smile.

"You look happy," Abigail Rose says, and I am.

I let go of a weight I didn't even know I was carrying.

I'm afraid of what George will say when she sees my hair. More so even of what she'll be too kind to say. But when I plop on the couch next to her binge-watching *Queer Eye* for at least the fifth time, what I get is, "And whoever said you have no style?"

"You," I say, but inside, I'm so relieved.

"I'm glad you didn't ask me if you should do that," George says. "Because I would've said no, and for the first time ever in recorded history, I would've been wrong."

"Thanks?" I take a sip of her purple Vitaminwater without asking, and she lets me.

I'm used to sitting next to George and feeling small. It's not that she's taller than me—she's an inch shorter—but she's so full. I don't mean to say she's full of herself, even if she probably is, at least a little bit. In a good way, though. Like all filled up.

George might seem like a chameleon changing herself in the right way at the right moment to capitalize on the next great trend—but somehow, every self she steps into is actually her.

"Well, that's different," Mom says from the doorway. I'm almost afraid to see her expression, but when I finally turn, she doesn't look upset, or even disappointed. She looks genuinely surprised. "Different suits you."

"You like it?" For a moment I worry she's doing that mom thing where they try to make you feel good about everything, even your mistakes. She looks like she's taking in a painting.

"Nearly as much as I love you." She smiles—a real smile, so I know she's not just being nice—and I realize: This is where I learned the difference between a real smile and a fake smile. I've seen my mom wear both.

CHAPTER 10

Abigail Rose is out on the stairs, waiting for me. She whistles a catcall.

"That haircut's like a casserole. Even better on the second day."

"Please don't eat my hair."

"Inventory's off for today," she says.

We've spent the last four work days taking pictures and creating product entries. We were supposed to finish loading the rest of the online inventory today. We're done adding all the Bones and now we're into the Mostly: candles, rugs, and wall hangings made from pelts, and the case of Herkimer diamonds mined upstate and set by a jeweler who sells on consignment.

"Mabel closing for Operation Rodent Wrestler again?" I ask, but she shakes her head and narrows her eyebrows to a point.

"We've got non-store-related business to tend to," she says, gritting her teeth. We head out to the street and wait for Silas to swing around in the Suburban. "Mabel gave us permission to head to the Barn. She says you can count it toward your hours."

On the way to the Barn, Abigail Rose and Silas fill me in. The Men of Mayhem—aka Frankie the Chaos Kid, promoter *and* booker, self-proclaimed alpha of the pack—selected the five fighters they'll be entering into the rumble.

For the Future of Mayhem, we have Cami, Drita, and Jimena all committed to the match, but not Petra, the other wrestler we met at School's Out. Petra's from some huge family that owns everything in Poughkeepsie, including the Civic Center, so Abigail Rose's dream of having an in at the most significant local venue in wrestling history is delayed.

We still need a fifth fighter, and now Abigail Rose is dreaming about recruiting Xiuying Liu, an eighteen-year-old trans mixed martial arts fighter who's got her sights set on the UFC but has been meeting some resistance in local circuits.

Call it luck—Abigail Rose assures me it's fate—somehow, I'm not only going to be among them: I'm going to come out on top. At the end of the rumble, one of us will hold the Future of Mayhem championship belt above their head. It's going to be me, and I haven't even started training yet.

"Calling a meeting during work hours," Abigail Rose fumes. "You know they're trying to turn Mabel against me."

"They're just jealous she loves you more," Silas says.

"Who do you think they've scrounged up? The Roller Derby girls?" Abigail Rose has tried to talk the Roller Derby girls into fighting for Mayhem, but like the Queen City Crew, their derby schedules are too packed. "That would grind my gears."

When we head into the Barn, it's empty.

"Typical. Why would he be on time for the meeting *he* set up?"

The sound of tires kicking up dirt in the driveway draws us outside, and I don't know what I expect to see. But then here comes Ted, leading the pack. My stomach sinks.

Frankie, who rounds out the caravan in a Dodge Ram, stacked his side with cheerleaders.

Lexie and Kayleigh get out of Ted and the other girls stand behind them. The synchronized flippers Mo used to show me my way out the door. Lexie eyes my hair and whispers something to Kayleigh.

I haven't seen her since our run-in at the boutique. I try to stand taller.

"Let's get ready to rumble?" Of course, it's Kayleigh who speaks first.

"So, we meet again." Abigail Rose steps up to Kayleigh like she's meeting her archnemesis in a comic book.

Abigail Rose hasn't told me that she used to be friends with Kayleigh. But when I told her about how bad I was at cheerleading practice before the tryout, she asked if they still had the Trampoline Wrestling Foundation set up at Kayleigh's house. That's what Kayleigh and her brothers call their trampoline—the TWF, with signs and everything—named after something these wrestlers the Hardy Boyz had when they were kids.

It's weird to imagine Abigail Rose and Kayleigh as kindergartners, wrestling together on the trampoline. Kayleigh acts like she's way too normal for Abigail Rose, and Abigail Rose acts like she's way too badass for Kayleigh.

"That's the thing about a rivalry in the ring." Kayleigh matches Abigail Rose's bravado. "It doesn't disappear—it hibernates. Saves up its strength for when the time's right."

For someone who claims to think wrestling is for losers, Kayleigh seems to have a raging case of wrestling mouth herself.

"Enough of this back-in-the-day-when-we-used-to-wrestle-the-shit-out-of-each-other crap," Lexie says, her eyes darting to my hair. "What are you, like a Mayhem groupie now?"

"You're looking at the face of the Future of Mayhem," Abigail Rose says, and it sounds so stupid, even to me. I could not be a less convincing wrestling hero. If anyone knows that, maybe even more than I do, it's Lexie.

"You've got to be kidding me," Frankie mutters under his breath, loud enough to be heard.

Lexie laughs, not even a mean laugh, just a full-throttle *that's the funniest thing I've ever heard* kind of laugh.

Silas is completely absorbed in the action, like he's watching a particularly tense moment on one of the docusoaps Dad edits, and I realize: This is the kind of real, natural tension that *could* make for magic in the ring.

"Ladies, ladies, ladies," Frankie says, stepping in between us. "I was going to say meet the opposition"—he pauses to laugh—"but clearly you already have."

"You're going to train them here at the Barn?" Abigail Rose asks.

"I never said I'd train them." Frankie starts back toward his truck and pulls himself up on the door's threshold. "They've got the TWF," he says, even though Kayleigh's family's trampoline hardly counts as a training facility. "That'll get your little match up and running."

Abigail Rose kicks at the dry dirt of the parking lot and then coughs on the dust cloud.

"That's bullshit. You promised me fighters, not cheerleaders on a trampoline."

"I used to kick your ass on that trampoline," Kayleigh says.

Abigail Rose's head swivels back like she's about to kick her ass right here, right now.

"Listen, kid," Frankie says as he starts up his truck. "No one wants to see a bunch of chicks fight in the ring. They'll pay to see a bunch of cheerleaders bounce around in it, though. The classics never go out of style."

The other cousins stand there, looking at the dirt. They're afraid of him, maybe. But they're also embarrassed by him. They wish he'd shut up.

This guy makes my blood boil.

"Now if you'll excuse me," Frankie says, "I've got to go feed Shithead and get back to work."

They peel out in their trucks, except for Silas, and we're left with the opposition.

"Balls!" Abigail Rose cries out to the open country sky.

"Shithead?" I ask.

"His python," Silas says.

"Whatcha got against cheerleaders on a trampoline?" Kayleigh asks.

"Whatever I've got is against Frankie, not you."

"Keep telling yourself that," Kayleigh says, and the cheerleaders start off toward Ted.

Lexie follows but then turns back.

"Who are you, even?" Lexie asks like she really wants to know. I reach my hand up to run it through my hair, but there's nothing there.

"You're the one who made me promise not to wrestle."

"Why'd you do that?" Lexie shakes her head, looking at my hair. "I hate it." It kills me to hear her say it, but I try not to let it show. I *like* my new hair.

"Come on, Lex," Kayleigh says, but hearing her defend me makes it hurt even more. To me, she says, "I think you look, like, super cool."

"You've always been weird, but this is next-level, even for you." Lexie's gaze is unmoved. I guess I've always known she thinks I'm weird, but it's different to hear her say it, like an insult. That all along, I've been a *little much* without even trying. Just by existing.

The tallest of the synchronized flippers says, "This is embarrassing. If I see a single picture online linking me to this freak show before the event"—she takes out her phone and starts to text—"I'll sue." She looks around at the woods like there might be paparazzi lurking.

"Kay," one of the other flippers says, "I would follow you to the end of the earth. You are my cheer captain. But are you *sure* about this?"

I get it. Mayhem's the town freak show. Wrestling is fake and for losers.

People like Kayleigh aren't friends with people like Abigail Rose.

Lexie's words echo in my head. *You've always been weird, but . . .*

"Why are you even doing this?" Abigail Rose asks.

"He's paying us to show up," Lexie says.

"And there's not a whole lot of difference between being a Dallas Cowboys cheerleader and being in the WWE, except that the cheerleaders earn about twenty percent of what even an average female WWE superstar earns," Kayleigh says.

Abigail Rose and I share a look. Lexie eyes her warily.

"My brothers said the word around town is that the scouts have their eye on Mayhem again because of this one." Kayleigh nods toward Silas.

"They might," Abigail Rose says. "What's it to you?"

"If I can get us all on board," Kayleigh says, "I want a

commitment from you. We live in the middle of nowhere, and your weird-ass family is one of the biggest names here." Abigail Rose shrugs like that's a given. "If we agree to give you what we've got in the ring, you agree to promote us to the WWE scouts as a legitimate part of Mayhem."

"Why would we want—" the blond flipper asks, but Kayleigh throws a look her way that shuts her up, quick.

"You can get your squad on board?" Abigail Rose asks, skeptical.

"Of course. I'm cheer captain." Kayleigh says it with such an air of authority, it's like she's the first female president of the United States of America.

"Kayleigh was a wrestling maniac as a kid," Abigail Rose says over the case of Herkimer diamonds. "Her brothers are so into it they started the Trampoline Wrestling Federation in their back-yard, and Kayleigh . . ." Abigail Rose looks off, like she can see her past if she squints. "She was fearless."

"I thought you said cheerleaders, dancers, and models were the old guard of wrestling?"

"I did," Abigail Rose says. "And I'm woman enough to admit when I'm wrong."

On a nearby glass shelf, I spot the talonsman I took. It feels like a lifetime ago when I climbed through the window and almost peed myself at the mouth of Mabel's shotgun. In the glass surface, my red hair glows fierce beside the fire opal.

I pick it up—all $1,200 worth—and grip the leathery talon like a wand in my hand. The light catches the smooth black stone, and a fire-burst of red licks out from within.

"Red's the most sought-after color in opals," Abigail Rose says, her eyes drifting to my hair. "That's why it's so expensive."

"If only I weren't already working it off," I say. "I could buy it for your birthday."

Abigail Rose's birthday is two days from now, and she invited me and Xena to go get tarot readings at the local witch shop. I've never had my cards read before, and I'm excited. But nervous, too. Not that I believe in that kind of thing.

"I'm going to ask how to do a binding spell," she says. "On Frankie."

"So, this lady's like"—I pause, not wanting to sound stupid—"a real witch?"

"Oh, for sure," she says.

"Isn't that . . . dangerous?" I almost say *fake*.

"Witches aren't dangerous themselves. I mean, historically, the fear of witches was dangerous, but mostly for witches. Or powerful women, if you want to be real about it. Mabel tells this story all the time about this guy from the audience who volunteered to fight her and then thought she was possessed by a demon," she says. "She used to carry this box into the ring."

"The Box of Mayhem," I say. "She told me about it."

"It was a rip-off of Pandora. She'd put it in the corner of the ring at the start of the match, and then, when she was nearing the end, she'd make a big display out of opening the box and unleashing Mayhem. It was like she accessed another level of brutality and chaos by opening the box. She unleashed Mayhem, and it possessed her." Abigail Rose spreads the talonsmans out in a fan on the new table. "The guy lost it, though. Started to think Mabel was a powerful witch who had cursed him. All these bad things kept happening to him, so he tracked down her and Grandpa Wyatt, showed up at their house and everything.

They had to call the cops. He was convinced she was out to get him. Meanwhile, she had no clue who he was."

I stare at the talonsman in my hand.

"That'd be a cool gimmick," I say. "Being possessed by something from the store."

"These bones tell stories we can't," Abigail Rose says.

The entire town gossips about Mabel, but they're really talking about the bones. It's a mythology larger than itself. *She eats the animals and sells their bones*, they say.

Mabel comes upstairs from the basement, carrying the Mouse-o-Mania version of Xavier Woods with his trombone, Francesca II.

"How weird are you ready to get?" Abigail Rose asks me, waving a talon. She's smiling, and I can tell her mind is bubbling over with ideas about how to twist this into a new plot.

"I'm friends with you, aren't I?" I say, but according to Lexie, I've always been strange. Weird is my natural state. I guess, if the secret's out, I can stop trying to find my inner normal.

So what if Lexie hates my hair? I'm all in.

"Let's get ready to rumble," Abigail Rose says, waving a talonsman in the air like a magic wand. "With bones."

CHAPTER 11

We're eating gelato-topped fried chicken and waffles in celebration of Abigail Rose's birthday, because it's the one day a year when she eats, and I quote, "whatever the freaking hell [she wants]."

Xena slides closer on the bench seat to kiss Abigail Rose on the cheek. They've only been together for a week, but after their second date (record shopping and bubble tea), Abigail Rose and Xena are a full-on *thing*. With her violet-platinum pixie cut, her olive cheekbones dusted with the most gorgeous glitter I've ever seen, Xena is—just as Abigail Rose said—*breathtakingly* cool. But sitting here with the two of them, I don't feel like a third wheel, the way I would with Lexie and Zeke.

"Are you into anyone right now?" Xena asks me, the way people in relationships always ask, like it's the universal summit we're climbing toward.

I used to be so busy with gymnastics and school that I didn't have time to think about anything else. I barely had friends outside of training. Then I sank so deep into schoolwork, volunteering, internships—whatever would look good on my college applications—that I hardly looked up from my game plan.

Though I do have a recurring dream where I kiss Casey from *Atypical*.

"I fall exclusively for fictional characters and perfect celebrities. That's my sexuality." I spear a bite of waffle and dip it in maple syrup. "On a pedestal. Inaccessible. Most likely a figment of my imagination," I say, and they both laugh. "Is it normal to be kind of terrified before a tarot reading?" I change the subject.

"If you're afraid of the truth," Abigail Rose says.

"Or if you're just afraid of the occult," Xena says with a shrug. "My aunt was convinced some psychic in her town was possessed by the devil. She made the entire family cross the sidewalk every time they passed her porch, until the lady died."

"Quit creeping her out," Abigail Rose says, picking up her fried chicken with her hands and biting into it. "The witch shop is full of sparkly things," she says through a mouthful. "It's common knowledge, sparkles repel evil."

"Science," I say.

The server comes over and drops our check, which Xena and I split despite Abigail Rose's overly dramatic protest.

"You're such a Leo sun," Xena says.

"With a Scorpio rising." Abigail Rose holds the door for us. "Consider yourself forewarned." We barrel onto the street, almost crashing into a guy on a bike, which for some reason sends us into a fit of laughter.

"No wonder," Xena says. "What's your moon?"

"Capricorn," Abigail Rose says, full of pride.

"Of course," Xena says. "That's where you get your intense sense of duty."

"Not to mention my emotional fortitude and tenacious work

ethic." Abigail Rose stops suddenly on the street, transfixed before a telephone pole layered with flyers advertising cover bands, a dog walker, and a world of instrument lessons, including *sitar*.

As Abigail Rose rips down a flyer and crushes it in her fist, I make out Frankie's face. It's for Mayhem's July promotion, Summer Splatter, coming up this weekend.

The door to The Otherworld chimes as we enter.

"I knew you were coming," the woman behind the counter says, cracking a wry smile.

"It's not a premonition if I made an appointment," Abigail Rose says.

"Still."

The Otherworld is a witch shop—it says so on the sign—and inside it's all crystals and herbs, incense and tarot decks. There's a stained-glass window at the front of the store, and a huge wooden fireplace.

Xena heads to the back wall, lined with Reiki-infused candles that remind me of Mom's, and I stop at a marble slab with a coffee table book titled *Crystal Grids for Every Home*.

The shop owner, a tall woman who looks like she might've come to the area for the original Woodstock festival and gotten stuck here, flips the sign on the door to CLOSED FOR READINGS and takes her seat on the other side of the table.

"Since the birthday girl hasn't bothered to introduce us," she says, shooting Abigail Rose a look, "I'm Morgan."

"Cut me some slack, I'm lost in thought," Abigail Rose says. "Morgan's been reading my cards since I was twelve."

Morgan looks like a cross between Janis Joplin and Amy Schumer. Long brown hair, silver streaking through it, with a round face and bright, smiling eyes.

"In this lifetime anyway," Morgan says in a throaty smoker's voice, with a phlegmy gurgle of a laugh.

"How do you know what to ask?" Xena says, and I'm thankful she does.

"You can ask anything you want," Abigail Rose says.

"It helps if you're not looking for a yes-or-no answer," Morgan says, placing her palms on the deck of cards and closing her eyes. She takes a deep breath in and relaxes her shoulders.

"I'd like to know how best to face my adversary," Abigail Rose says, shuffling the deck when Morgan asks her to. Morgan nods and fans out the cards, then Abigail Rose chooses three.

Wheel of Fortune. Ace of Pentacles. The Hanged Man.

"The major arcana pursues you today," Morgan says, touching each card with the tips of her fingers. I zone out as Morgan describes each card, its placement, and how it could relate to Abigail Rose's question.

I don't want to even think about what happens after this summer. I'm finally settling in here, but mostly because I'm not thinking about the future. At all.

Now that I am, even if it's from inside a witch shop, waiting for my tarot reading, it feels like getting back together with an old friend and finding out everything's changed. And I've had enough of that this summer.

I'm lost in thought, staring at the cards, when Morgan sweeps them back into a pile and Abigail Rose stands up, tapping me on the shoulder.

"That wasn't so scary, was it?" she says, but I'm too embarrassed to admit I zoned out and missed her reading. I can see in her eyes that she learned something that feels important. Like a missing piece.

I sit across from Morgan and slouch, attempting to look nonchalant and at ease.

"You look nervous," Morgan says, bursting my delusional bubble. "Try to trust." I take a deep breath in and out and try to sink into the moment. "What's your question for the cards?"

I bite the inside of my lip, thinking. "I want to know how I'm supposed to go forward," I say. "Like, which way?"

It feels like too vague an ask, but Morgan nods like she knows exactly what I mean. Then she fans the cards out again and waves a hand over, gesturing for me to choose.

I move my hand over the cards, hovering a few inches above them, and unlike every time I have ever played with a Ouija board, I swear I feel a tug. Like a magnet drawing the center of my palm toward one particular card, from the inside. First, it pulls toward the third card from the left. Then to the right of the middle. And the final card, almost halfway between those two, is practically jumping off the table to get my attention.

The Fool. The Tower. Seven of Cups.

"Major arcana in the house today," Morgan says.

"The cards must know it's my birthday," Abigail Rose says, peering into the crystal display.

"I don't like the looks of that." I point at The Fool. He wears a mocking smirk. "Is he about to fall off that cliff?"

"That's the thing about The Fool." She taps his foot with her fingernail. "Faced with an uncertain future, there's no way to know if it will all work out."

"Then why leap?" I ask, my eyes drawn to the empty space on the other side of the cliff.

When Morgan picks up The Tower and puts the card in my hand, I actually shudder.

It's an ominous image: a stone tower struck so powerfully by lightning that its top is blown straight off. Flames crawl through the windows and lash the outside walls. Two human bodies ejected from the tower catapult headfirst toward the ground.

"Sometimes you don't get a choice," Morgan says. "The Tower of change comes for you, reduces everything you've ever known to rubble beneath your feet, and makes you start anew. If The Fool leaps in the face of The Tower, she's not such a fool after all." She sits back in her chair and shakes her head. "She's doing what she has to do."

I tap the next card. The Seven of Cups.

"The future contains many possible outcomes—both gifts and curses," she says. "But among the illusions is one shining truth. Stay grounded. The path through *is* you," Morgan says. I wait for her to explain, but she doesn't. It's a riddle, and I can't stand riddles.

The path through is *you* is the kind of whacked-out circular logic that spun my mom off her axis and landed me here. In a witch shop with my wrestling friend, who I met working at the bone store. Concerned about the Future of Mayhem.

This does not sound like real life. It sounds like the plot of a comic book, and according to Morgan, the key to figuring it all out is to leap across the rubble of my former life and hope I find myself somehow, midair. This is why I don't mess with this stuff.

But it's Abigail Rose's birthday, so I keep that to myself.

It's Xena's turn next, and when she sits down, she looks as nervous as I did.

"Don't worry. It's mostly confusing," I say, which makes her laugh.

"Xena, right?" Morgan asks, collecting the cards into a pile.

"That's not my real name, though," she says, and I look at

Abigail Rose, but we're both surprised. "I mean, if that matters or anything, like . . . for the cards."

Morgan smiles at her. "Here, all names are real."

"Do I need to say my question out loud for it to work?" Xena asks, and Morgan shakes her head. "OK," she says. "I'm ready."

Xena selects her three cards, and Morgan takes her through the reading.

"This is perfect!" Abigail Rose pops out of the alcove at the back of the store. "How to Bind the Patriarchy," she reads from a box. "You always know what I'm going to need before I do," she says to Morgan.

As we leave the shop, I thank Morgan in a patchouli-scented daze, my skin alive.

When we moved here, I thought I knew this place. This town. Even Lexie. I thought I knew what to expect, and mostly, I wasn't looking forward to it.

If The Fool leaps in the face of The Tower, she's not such a fool after all.

I wasn't ready for everything to change. But I was even less prepared for this feeling. I've felt it at the Deep Lagoon, and in the woods out behind the house. I've felt it at Mostly Bones, and today, hanging out with Abigail Rose and Xena.

Like . . . not to sound completely delusional . . . but sometimes it feels like maybe all of this might actually *be* meant to be. So many twists and coincidences led to being here: Where, for the first time maybe ever, I feel like I'm in the right place at the right time, with the right people.

If I hadn't let Lexie convince me to try out for cheerleading. If I hadn't gone to that party at the Fort, or if I refused to break into Mabel's. If Mom hadn't quit her job. If we hadn't moved here.

Outside, Abigail Rose rocks back on her heels, facing off

against Xena. Her lips are set in a defiant line, her arms crossed in front of her vintage Crush Gals T-shirt. A gift from Silas, it's a Japanese import from the eighties, of Lioness Asuka with her partner Chigusa Nagayo. Abigail Rose says the Crush Gals were her merchandising heroes before the Bella Twins, because even back when women's wrestling wasn't as popular, they drew ratings that'd make the NFL, never mind the WWE, jealous. The *Wall Street Journal* wrote about them.

"I didn't get all hopped up on inflammatory food and a tarot high to back down now." Abigail Rose pouts, like it's her party and she can cry if she wants to.

Xena looks at her, like she's not trying to fight her girlfriend on her birthday, but also doesn't think whatever she's onto is a good idea. "I'm just saying maybe your birthday should be about you," Xena says, "and not about playing mind games with your egomaniacal cousin."

"Mind games?" Abigail Rose says it like she couldn't be more insulted. "That's what you think this is?"

Xena looks at me, like I should know what to do. But I don't even know what they're talking about.

"She wants to go to the Fort tonight," Xena says. "Because that asshole will be there, and she wants to get a lock of his hair and do the binding spell before the weekend."

"We're not even invited," I say, but Xena and Abigail Rose both laugh at that.

"It's the Fort, Birdie," Xena says. "There's not an evite."

"I want to do something fun," Abigail Rose says. "Out of character."

"Who's the designated driver?" I ask, and Xena raises her hand.

"I'm allergic to alcohol."

"Do I know how to pick 'em or what?" Abigail Rose says, and Xena wraps her arm around her neck.

I stop in front of the overpriced coffee shop. "Bubble tea? On me."

"Now that we have the tools to bind him," Abigail Rose says as we move through the door, prouder together, like a muster of peacocks, "what if we wanted to make him *think* he was hexed. You know"—she plops both hands on the counter, ready to order—"make him think we're witches and shit." Xena rolls her eyes and groans, but I have to admit she might be onto something. "Frankie loathes women. What if we made him fear us, too?"

A quiver runs through me as the image of The Tower flickers in my mind, its flames lashing up.

We pull up the long dirt driveway to the Fort and it doesn't feel at all like it did showing up with Lexie.

We head up the pine needle–strewn path toward the light of the fire. Abigail Rose holds Xena's hand and tries to look confident, but when we break into the clearing where people cluster in groups, we skirt the dark edge and stay hidden.

"I want a beer," Abigail Rose says. I eye her, wary. She already took a two-hour nap back at home because of the day's inflammatory load and joked she's *seventeen going on seventy* when Mabel asked how she was feeling. "I've got Lyme disease, not hepatitis."

"Your body, your choice," I say, bracing myself to venture across to the keg.

When I bring the beers back to where Abigail Rose and

Xena stand in the shadows, they both look even less at home than they did when I left.

"I'm starting to understand why I've never come here," Xena says, eyeing a guy making out with two girls, alternating between them like he's taking licks of two ice cream cones he can't decide between. "If those girls don't kiss each other soon, I'm out of here," she says, and we all laugh, breaking the tension.

"Frankie's not here yet," Abigail Rose says, craning her neck to look around. "But according to his Instagram story, he's *off work with fuck all to do and ready to get white-girl wasted*," she says in her best Frankie imitation. "He should be here any minute."

"Did somebody say white-girl wasted?" A girl I don't recognize crouches down to where we're sitting. She holds out her vape pen.

"Tulsi!" Abigail Rose says, taking the pen from her. "I haven't seen you in so long. Tulsi goes to—"

"The hippie school," Tulsi says, putting her hand out for me to shake. Her light brown skin glistens in the heat, and she's got short, uneven hair that looks like she chopped it off with children's scissors . . . but, like, chic. "I was visiting family in India for a few months."

Abigail Rose takes two puffs and passes it to Xena.

"Hm," she says, exhaling vapor from her nose like a dragon puffing smoke. "You always have the best stuff."

"Medicinal," Tulsi says. "I'm on the spectrum."

Xena looks at the pen, contemplating.

"Just one," she says, choking on it and passing it to me.

When Tulsi finds out it's Abigail Rose's birthday, she gives us the vape pen, tells us she loves us, then disappears into the flow of the party.

The three of us lie on the ground with our heads together, our bodies splayed out like light beams from the same star. Bats swoop above us like tiny satellites.

"Did you guys watch that show *American Dragon: Jake Long*?" Xena asks.

Abigail Rose springs up to seated, and for a second, I think she's spotted Frankie and my breathing stops.

"I *loved* that show," she says, grabbing Xena's arm like it's the most important thing she's ever heard. "Are you thinking what I'm thinking?"

"The Witches of Woodstock?" Xena stares at her, like this moment is bigger than itself. Like it must be a dream, and I have no idea what the big deal is.

"I've never met anyone else who remembers that episode," she says, looking into Xena's eyes like this must mean *something*. Then, to me, "There were these three witches, and they literally said they hailed from an island in the middle of the Hudson River."

"It pretty much made my entire childhood," Xena says. "There was life before the Witches of Woodstock episode, and life after. Because it was also the year we moved here."

Abigail Rose inhales sharply, like she's been struck by a genius thought.

"You are my Witches of Woodstock," she says.

I knock back the last sip of beer. We sit in a circle: a coven of witches beneath a cauldron of bats.

"I'm done with being a girl," Xena says, sinking back to rest on her palms.

"Is that a thing?" I inhale another puff of vape. "'Cause I want in." The words fall from my mouth, slippery when drunk.

"Me too, man," Abigail Rose says. "Half the shit I deal with from Frankie would never happen if I wasn't a girl."

"*Girl*, like, the way people think of that word, is how everyone treats me, not who I am," I say, and for the first time ever saying something like this, I don't worry they won't understand.

"That's what I asked the cards about," Xena says. She looks at us both and takes a deep breath. Xena is so cool, so confident, but right now, her breath rises in short, fast bursts beneath her collarbone. "I'm nonbinary," Xena says. "My pronouns are they/them."

They say it, and it doesn't look easy for them to say: It looks important.

"Fuck yeah," Abigail Rose says, raising her beer.

"That's awesome!" I raise my beer to cheers.

"That felt good," Xena says, breathing in deeply through their nose. Abigail Rose leans forward and their lips press together.

"How are you actually this beautiful?"

Xena smiles, and usually Xena's smile is self-aware. Like they're about to crack a joke you might not get, and they're totally cool with that.

But this smile is the sliver of moon that hangs above us.

An undeniable, natural glow.

We all sigh. Like a collective release, and I almost laugh out loud. I've spent so much time questioning whether or not I'm nonbinary. Whether or not it even matters. But if it doesn't matter, what's that warm feeling in my body when I hear Xena speak their truth? That softness in my heart? Like a portal opening to a future I've been too afraid to admit I want. One based more on possibilities than limitations.

What is that, if not bliss?

And what if Mom's been right all along? That bliss—whatever brings us joy—*matters*.

When Mom's new "outside the box" CEO took the executive

team on a Somatic Leadership Retreat up here, at a place devoted to some guy named Joseph Campbell who thought everyone should "follow their bliss," she came home talking about how she *climbed the ladder only to realize it was against the wrong wall.* It was the beginning of the end of our old life. I don't think any of us, including her, expected this kind of upheaval. And I was so pissed at her for throwing our life away for something so ridiculous as *bliss.*

But what if it's not ridiculous?

"That tarot reading cut through to my actual soul," Xena says. "Morgan said 'spells are words' and it was exactly what I needed to hear. The world has been casting spells on me with its words since I was a fetus," they say, and they're right. "It's my turn to cast a new spell for myself. Like when I changed my name."

"You were always Xena since you moved here, weren't you?" Abigail Rose asks.

Xena cracks a smile. "Literally on the drive to our new house, I saw the word *Zena* on a few signs. I liked it with an X because my cousin used to have a T-shirt from *Xena: Warrior Princess.* My parents were super cool about it," they say. "Enrolled me at school and told them to call me Xena and everything.

"I just want to be the person I am. I don't feel like a girl or a boy. I feel like a person." Xena sighs and then laughs.

"It was all over when I started to learn about how the binary is a colonial construct and part of the Western white supremacist patriarchy," Xena says, and my ears perk up. This is new to me. "I mean, colonial settlers straight up tried to erase revered Indigenous leaders whose gender wasn't binary."

"Colonizers gonna colonize," Abigail Rose says, shaking her head.

"The binary isn't natural if that's how it came to be 'normal.' Nature is fluidity and change, not two rigid categories that we cram ourselves into. That's not natural. Why should I live like it is? Because some closed-minded colonizer says so?"

Xena's words sink into my body, already softened by the beer and weed buzz. I've never related to anything more in my life.

"Being with you guys," Xena says. "Today. I feel like I can be open to what I want the future—my future—to be."

It's like a wave has broken, and it washes over all of us.

But then I see Frankie, picking on someone smaller than him with a crowd watching.

"He's here," I say, nodding in his direction.

"Frankie?" Abigail Rose says, popping up to stand and splashing beer from her cup. "Holy shit. There he is," she says, looking over my head. "Witches of Woodstock, unite!" She draws another hit from the vape pen, and I take it from her. "You have the nail scissors?"

Xena holds up a tiny pair of metal scissors.

"Snip, snip, motherfucker," they say, opening and closing the blades twice.

Abigail Rose springs up and marches over toward Frankie, and I'm wobbly on my feet as Xena and I chase after her.

"Vibe check?" Abigail Rose taps Frankie on the shoulder, and he rips his attention away from his target and stares at her.

"Shit," Frankie says, spitting on the ground, a wad of dip bulging out from his lower lip. "I'd say the vibe is shit."

"I don't know who needs to hear this, but," Abigail Rose starts into the meme, "hanging out with this juicehead may cause secondhand asshole syndrome."

Frankie's audience looks at her like the weird girl who just entered a conversation she wasn't in, and my stomach sinks, the beer in my belly churning.

"Don't mind my cousin," Frankie says, slurring. He's already wasted. "She's showing off in front of her girlfriend." Some guy who looks like he's worried if he stops sucking on his Juul he might die actually laughs at that.

"They're not my . . ." Abigail Rose pauses, looking at Xena.

"I'm actually nonbinary," Xena says, stepping up so their face is just below Frankie's. It's a bold move I'd be scared to make, but as they do, Xena's hand reaches back toward me, holding out the scissors. Frankie backs up with his hands raised.

If Abigail Rose and Xena can be this brave, I need to back them up.

Frankie turns back to the smaller kid he was picking on when we came over, and for the first time, I notice how drunk that kid is, too.

"What were you saying about how you could outdrink me?" Frankie says, and the kid totters where he's standing.

"That's right," the kid says, but it sounds more like *thaz-ri*. He's incoherently drunk.

"For fuck's sake, Francis," Abigail Rose says, "you're already shit-faced and Rusty looks like he's about to fall over." She juts a thumb out at the small kid.

"Then he shouldn't be talking shit," Frankie says. "And I don't need some girl telling me what to do." Frankie spits on the ground when he says it. "Go home and cry about it to Grandma."

I wish with every cell of my being that I could turn around and knock him out. Frankie's not a huge guy, but he's got a good fifteen pounds on me. He's the size I'd be if I never worried about being too big. If I wasn't worried about having *dude arms*, I bet I could kick his ass in a real fight.

But there are other ways to fight powerful forces. Right now, I need to snip a lock of Frankie's hair or this entire night will be a waste. It's Abigail Rose's birthday, goddamn it.

Witches of Woodstock, unite!

Abigail Rose stares at Frankie like she's trying to set fire to his body with her eyes. As I watch her, I swear I can see the actual moment when she physically loses her shit. She convulses—a shake that racks her body in a pumping motion—and then before I can stop her, she's jumped onto Frankie's back, one arm around his neck, the other hand clamped down tightly over his eyes.

Frankie starts to spin, while Abigail Rose's feet slam into anyone who gets too close.

"I'm telling Grandma, you bitch!" Frankie yells.

"I'm telling Mabel you called me a bitch, you fucking prick," Abigail Rose screams back.

Somehow, I have to get a piece of his hair right now. I need to do it for Abigail Rose.

I step into the fray, and when Abigail Rose sees me, she squeezes Frankie's torso hard with her arms and legs. He struggles against the clamp of her body, and when he freezes in place to try to break his arms free, I find the perfect moment to reach up with the scissors and snip his hair, clasping the strands tight in my fist.

"Snip, snip, motherfucker," I hear Abigail Rose whisper into his ear, and when she lets go and drops to the ground, Frankie whips his head around to find me.

"What the fuck was that?" He reaches back, touching his head. He looks at me, his expression wary, like for a moment he's legitimately confused and afraid. But then he steels himself and recovers in front of his audience as I dip away from him, pocketing the scissors and his hair.

"Someone get me another beer," Frankie calls out to his minions, but none of them moves.

"You just got owned by a girl half your size," Juul boy says. "Maybe she's right. *You've had enough, Francis*," the guy says in falsetto, mimicking Abigail Rose.

Suddenly, he's the butt of the joke, and even though he's a total dick who I just watched bully a bunch of different people, including his younger cousin, I almost feel bad for him. Almost.

When he shouts, "String me up on the zip line," I remember how last time I was here, someone mentioned the zip line a bit deeper in the woods.

Frankie's desperate, still, to be in charge, and a desperate wrestler is a dangerous wrestler. Frankie Mayhem the Chaos Kid needs to show everyone that he gives zero fucks. Like a death wish can outshine his embarrassment at being overpowered by his little cousin.

For Frankie, kayfabe isn't a performance. It's life.

"Don't," Abigail Rose says, trying to stop him. "Frankie, what the hell is wrong with you?"

Frankie looks at her with a vicious contempt.

"Why are you here, anyway?" he slurs, and then he takes off into the woods.

"He can shoot himself through the dark like a concussion-craving arrow all he wants," Abigail Rose says, grabbing Xena's hand. "I'm not going to watch."

We find a spot, far from where the zip line is, and this time, it doesn't feel like it did before. I just want to go home.

"Mushroom chocolates?" Some guy I don't know holds out a handful of aluminum foil–wrapped shapes.

We all shake our heads. "We're good," Xena says.

"That was . . ." Abigail Rose looks back to the spot where we just threw down with Frankie. "I'm so sorry I'm related to such a garbage human."

"It's not your fault," Xena and I both say at the same time.

My stomach gurgles, and I wonder if I'm going to throw up or burp. I'm drunker than I thought.

Brrrrrrrrrrrrp.

"This beer is so gross," I say.

"The worst," Abigail Rose says. "But you guys are the best." She looks like she's about to say more.

"They've got him all strung up!" some guy calls out to his friends, running past us toward the zip line. "I gotta film this."

"Can we get out of here before the ambulance comes?" Xena says. "I don't want my car to get blocked in."

I search Abigail Rose's face for resistance. If she wants to stay and make sure her cousin's OK, we will. No matter his character. But she looks away from where the group gathers in the woods.

"That jackass is on his own," she says.

My phone dings a text.

From Mom. *Shit.*

> It's almost 1 AM. Where are you?

I text back *On the way. See you in twenty minutes*, and she doesn't even write back "safe travels." Just *I'll be up. Waiting.*

On the drive home, Abigail Rose says tonight has made her rethink her Intergender Wrestling Manifesto. That it's unintentionally binary.

"It's got blind spots," she says, holding Xena's hand across the gearshift.

"We all do, babe," Xena says.

"Holy shit!" Abigail Rose yells, spinning around to face me. "I completely forgot to ask. Did you get the lock of Frankie's hair?"

I pull it out of my pocket, still stuck between the blades of the scissors, and hold it up, picturing the look of fear on Frankie's face when he realized I cut his hair.

Abigail Rose takes out her wallet and stows away Frankie's hair for later, then pumps her fist in the air.

"Witches of Woodstock, unite!"

CHAPTER 12

Mom is sitting at the kitchen counter waiting for me, and it takes her all of zero seconds to figure out that I'm pretty wasted.

"What's gotten into you, Birdie?" she asks. "Drinking, smoking—"

"I didn't smoke, I vaped," I say. "Plus, I didn't take the mushrooms that were offered to me by the guy I didn't know." That should count for something, but, simultaneously, I can't believe the stuff that's flying out of my mouth right now.

"You're telling me to lighten up because you didn't take hallucinogens from strangers," Mom says. "That's the bar we're setting."

"Can't you see how sweaty I am?" I say. "I think that's punishment enough." I'm hilarious right now. Inside I'm cracking up. But outside? I'm trying to keep a straight face. From the look on Mom's: I. Am. Failing.

"You're grounded," Mom says. I groan and then almost laugh out loud because I sound exactly like George. "Dad gets back from Gilboa tomorrow," she says. He's overnight for a moonlight shoot. "We'll fill you in on your punishment after we discuss. Until then"—she juts out her hand—"your phone."

"Are you *kidding* me?" I give it a kiss and pet the cover before handing it over. "I'll miss you." Mom walks the phone to the cupboard and puts it in the basket where we keep extra keys, shaking her head the entire way.

"Relax, you'll get it back tomorrow when you leave for work. What's gotten into you?" Mom asks, putting her hand against my cheek so I can't look away. "This is so . . . unlike you."

"I know," I say. "George is the fun one. I'm the boring one."

"That's not what I meant, and you know it."

"When The Fool leaps in the face of The Tower, she's just doing what she has to do," I say, and Mom looks even more confused.

"What?" Mom shakes her head. "Who are you even?" It's the irony of it—her asking *me* who *I* am, why suddenly I'm so different—that makes me snap.

"Who am *I*?" I laugh out loud, like her hypocrisy should be self-evident. "Who are you? Beverly McCoy: Bliss Hunter." I don't mean to yell at her, but I am. I might be crying, too.

Mom reaches both hands out and rests them on my shoulders.

"I'm sorry." I look up and see her eyes, pleading. "That was insensitive. I know this move has asked a lot of you, and that it's not how you would've chosen to spend your senior year."

"It couldn't be worse, Mom," I say, trying to still the quiver in my voice. "I have one year left before the rest of my life begins, and if I don't start off in the right place, that will take years to make up for. And—"

"Birdie," Mom says, drawing me in for a hug, "there is no right or wrong place to start from, and the rest of your life isn't some future destination. This is it." Mom waves a hand around the room. "The rest of your life is always happening, and there are infinite futures for you to step into. You can backtrack, change tracks, do whatever you need to find your way in the world. If you thought there was only one right place to start from, I hate to say it, but . . ." Mom pauses, and she cracks a wry smile. "You know I don't love this word, but you sound kind of like a privileged, elitist citiot."

"Mom!" My mouth is so dry. "I kind of feel sick to my stomach," I say, burping.

"I'll bring up some pizza rolls." Mom hands me a ginger ale from the fridge.

"Pizza rolls," I say, like they're the two most beautiful words in the English language. "Thanks, Mom."

I climb the stairs to my room and change into pajamas to slip under the covers and sip my ginger ale. It feels like a sick day, only I'm still drunk and it's two in the morning.

I open my laptop to message George, who's down in Brooklyn planning for an upcoming event with her friend.

Got in trouble with Mom and Dad, I say. *Worth it.*

I picture that moment, the calm before the Chaos Kid, when we were a coven of witches beneath a cauldron of bats. Rays of light from the same star.

My phone buzzes. *That's when you know you're doing it right*, George says. *Tell me everything tomorrow. Proud of you.*

Tonight, I made her proud. And, sure, I don't really want to drink more than four beers ever again in my life—I feel like my intestines are soaking in fermented acid—but I had *fun*.

I pull up the next *Being the Elite* episode in my queue and press play. I wake up to the smell of hot pizza rolls under my nose and Mom's hand rubbing the top of my head, and I sit up just long enough to eat them before falling fast into the deepest of sleeps. I swear, even though they are the food of gods and always delicious, pizza rolls never tasted so good.

I sit up, rubbing the sleep from my eyes and squinting into the light of the room. My alarm sounds like it's ringing inside my skull.

When I get to the kitchen, Dad slides a plate of pancakes down the counter to me, and I am dying to eat. I slather on a layer of butter to melt.

"Why are you home so early?" I sip my coffee and pour maple syrup over my plate.

"We finished the shoot last night." I arch an eyebrow. He was supposed to stay most of the day to go fishing with his old friend. "And Mom and I both thought we should talk to you about this whole new . . ." He pauses. "You know, you."

"This whole new me?" I take a bite and my stomach gurgles in response. I'm never drinking again. "Because I cut my hair and drank more than I usually do—" I burp.

"So you usually drink?" Mom's standing in the doorway to the kitchen in her bathrobe.

"No," I say, not wanting to lie, but not wanting to make a big deal about it. "I just meant that I'd never had so many beers."

"Was that more . . . uh, vape," Dad says, "than you usually use, too?"

"Oh my God," I say, trying not to get defensive. "You guys are making a way bigger deal out of this than you need to. No. That was my first time vaping, and it was medicinal." I look at both of them, pleading.

"Medicinal for who? Not you," Mom says. She looks angry. Like she can't believe I would say something so stupid.

"Can you guys just punish me already?" If I were George, this would be a well-oiled machine by now.

Mom looks at Dad, and they have an entire conversation with their eyes before he talks.

"We're more concerned about how you're doing," he says. "With all of the changes this summer."

"We talked things over—" Mom starts.

"When?"

"Last night, after you came home," Mom says, and I feel really bad. Dad was off on the first assignment he's been genuinely interested in for years, and I had them both distracted and worried.

"We're not going to punish you, Birdie," Dad says, and I heave a sigh of relief.

"But we need to agree on some new boundaries," Mom says. "A curfew, some rules." She hands me my phone, and I press it to my heart. I have a text from Abigail Rose.

"Mom said you're worried about your future," Dad says. "We're here to help. This place has a lot more to offer than you might think."

I've blamed Mom for agreeing to move up here, but Dad has wanted to return home for years. She just finally got on board.

This isn't where I wanted to spend my senior year. We've established that. But maybe Mom's right and I have been kind of acting like an elitist citiot.

I mean, this place made my dad. It made Abigail Rose. It made Mayhem. How bad can it be?

I'm almost to my room when I check Abigail Rose's text.

Sonny Kiss theme song, she wrote. *YouTube it. Thank me later.*

I google Sonny Kiss, and she's a wrestler with AEW. Sonny's preferred pronoun is Babe, though she/her and he/him are acceptable. In her Instagram profile, Babe lovingly calls herself *Your favorite anomaly.* I press play on a fan video of her theme song, "Kiss the Ring," and the lyrics hit straight to my heart. It's like this song was literally written for me, and I imagine what that must be like. To have a song that *is* written for you. Like an audio lewk.

Been battlin' all my life, just to be me
Some stones have broke my bones, but not my wings
And now I'm flying high, for all to see
I'm here to show the world, strength sets me free

The footage of Sonny Kiss in the ring, set to her signature theme, is so beautiful. She sparkles all over the ring with fierce grace. Even in her movements—popping into full splits and then springing into flips—flexibility is Sonny's superpower.

I have no idea why I'm crying right now, but thick hot tears slide down my cheeks.

I google "tomboy or nonbinary" again before texting back to Abigail Rose, *Sonny Kiss? Holy new hero, Batman.*

CHAPTER 13

"Is it OK if Xena comes over after work?" Abigail Rose asks Mabel.

"Of course."

"Can we hang out in the store?" Abigail Rose looks around the room. She's been uneasy all day.

Frankie texted her after the party. He reminded her that if she tells Mabel about what went down between them, Mabel's probably just going to sell the Barn of Mayhem before Abigail Rose even gets to script her first show.

"What's percolating up there?" Mabel asks, tapping her own head. "And don't try to say nothing. I know that face well enough to know when you're scheming."

"Not scheming," Abigail Rose says, putting her hand on Mabel's shoulder. "Planning."

"You should be a politician, kid," Mabel says. "'Cause you're full of shit." Mabel looks at me. "You can hang out down here, but don't go in the basement. I've got everything exactly where I need it." Abigail Rose rolls her eyes. "It's not a mess if you know where everything is," Mabel says with a self-satisfied huff, and then she heads downstairs to her Mouse-o-Mania headquarters.

Abigail Rose pulls the spell box out of her backpack and opens her notebook to a list of needed supplies. It's the midday lull around lunchtime, so the shop is even emptier than usual.

"Do you think it's actually going to work?" I ask.

"Morgan has *never* let me down." Abigail Rose's unshakable faith in things like fate, in people like Morgan—even in me— it's unnerving. But part of me hopes it's contagious.

Xena knocks on the closed shop door exactly at five thirty.

"They're even habitually on time," Abigail Rose says, like she can't believe Xena's real.

"Swooning over punctuality." I spread the tapestry over the table we've pulled into the middle. "That feels more on-brand for me."

"Being reliable is so hot." Abigail Rose opens the door and Xena holds up the lighter we asked them to bring, waving the flame in the air.

"Call me Prometheus, because I just stole this fire for you," Xena says. "Well, not literally. The cashier wouldn't sell it to me because I'm not eighteen, which isn't even a law or anything. *Store* policy. So, I pocketed it and left two dollars on the counter." They shrug.

"My hero." Abigail Rose takes Xena's hand and kisses their knuckles.

"Do you have everything we need for the spell?" Xena shakes their head. "I can't believe I just said that."

"Witches of Woodstock, unite!" Abigail Rose says, pleased with herself for pulling us into her witchy world.

The deep blue tapestry covering the table has one huge star in the middle, with tiny other stars scattered across it like the night sky. In each corner of the table, we put a crystal. Obsidian in the east. Onyx in the west. Labradorite in the south. Clear quartz in the north. We used a compass app to orient the table with the directions.

Abigail Rose puts a bronze bowl in the middle of the table and rests a bundle of sage inside it. There's a leather cord, and a pad of paper with a pen.

"If you're going to call on spirits, you might as well surround yourself with ghosts," Xena says, looking around the shop. It's not their first time here, but they haven't spent much time in Mostly Bones. "What if this doesn't work?" Xena asks, running their fingers over the tapestry and stopping to touch each star.

Abigail Rose takes the talonsman from the display—the one with the red fire opal—and places it in front of the bowl.

"Didn't you see the look on Frankie's face when Birdie cut his hair?" Abigail Rose looks at each of us, like she needs us to understand. "I don't even know what came over me when I jumped on his back." She shakes her head, and Xena breaks out laughing.

"That was *nuts*! I saw you with my own two eyes and still kind of couldn't believe you were actually doing it," they say.

"Witches of Woodstock," Abigail Rose says. "Do you realize how powerful we are?"

"Shall we?" I point to the chairs arranged around the table, and we each take a seat. Soon the walls are flickering with the warm glow of lit candles.

We follow the steps, filling the room with the charred, herbal bouquet of sage.

In this moment, crackling at the edges with magic, we shoot rays of light up from our triangle of souls amid the bones. We send our intention to bind Frankie, our hope for a brighter future for Mayhem. It's only in my mind, I know, but a lot of things were once just a thought. Like electric cars, Alexa, or labradoodles.

We head to the river, carrying Frankie's lock of hair inside the square we bound with leather cord and our intentions, and the fire Xena (kind of) stole.

When Abigail Rose lights the square on fire, the paper is folded so densely it takes a while for the flames to bite in and take hold, but when the fire does, she rests the flaming spell on a flat creek-side rock. We watch as the spell consumes itself, and when it's burned all the way through, Abigail Rose soaks the embers with water from her cupped hand.

"What do we do now?" I ask.

"Morgan says a waning crescent is good for shedding self-doubt and insecurity. Let's burn what's holding us back," Abigail Rose says, like it's just that simple.

So, we do.

We sit by the river, scribbling our doubts and our fears onto sheets of paper and then taking turns burning them and watching the ashes float downstream.

I don't ever feel normal.

I just want to feel OK. Whatever is in the way of that.

Giving an F what people think about me.

All of the F's I apparently still have left to give.

I don't know who I am. I cross it out and write, *I don't know who I want to be* instead.

We don't talk about what we're burning. We pour it out as ashes catch in the wind and drift around us. We offer it up to the waning crescent moon, so that whatever looms large in our heads might shrink into the nothingness of the coming new moon.

We write and burn, until we've scraped the bottom of our barrels of insecurity and sit on rocks, doubtless husks of ourselves, listening to the water as it flows.

But when we get up to leave, I wonder if it's possible to ever let something go—or if, maybe, it's true what they say, and matter in our universe is never created or destroyed.

It's recycled. Redistributed. Rearranged.

When I show up for the lesson Abigail Rose booked with Angel, I feel like I did the day of cheerleading tryouts. Unprepared. Out of my league. Only, somehow, not entirely like I don't belong.

"We can't do much in the ring until your parents sign this." Angel hands me a waiver. "Wrestling can be as dangerous as a real fight."

"How dangerous is it at the level I'll be learning?" I ask.

"Beth Phoenix's jaw broke during her first-ever singles match on *Raw* when Victoria slapped her in the face." Angel's stare dares me to question his warning. "Her mouth was hanging open slightly when it should have been closed," he says. "This is not an F around and you'll find out kind of situation. This is don't F around at all.

"So," he says, bouncing off the rope. "You want to learn how to wrestle?"

"That would be why I'm here," I say.

"Too bad," he says. I scrunch my face in confusion. "Because wrestling is the least important part of being a wrestler. I don't train wrestlers. I train superstars," he says, the same way he did that first night in the alley. "I make entertainers. Performers. And that, more than how to lock-up, or do an arm-drag, or even finish your opponent off with a moonsault, is what you're here to learn."

"You're not going to teach me how to wrestle?" I ask.

"Oh, I'll teach you how to wrestle," Angel says. "But all of the technical skills you'll practice and hopefully master can't turn you into a champion. None of it is worth anything unless you learn the most important thing for the ring. The one thing that will tie it all together."

"Which is?" Even Angel's pauses are dramatic.

"How to be yourself," Angel says, like it's not the most basic cop-out he could possibly come up with.

"I want to play a character," I say. "Isn't that the whole point of kayfabe?"

"You will," Angel explains. "But in order for your character to work, they need to be you. The you that some of your friends would throw a side-eye at because you're maybe a little *much*."

I picture Lexie in the parking lot: *You've always been weird, but . . .*

"The audience wants your different. Your weird. Your quirky. Your courage. Whatever makes you memorable, which is usually whatever makes you think you don't belong.

"Wrestling changes lives. Not because of suplexes," Angel says. I think back to that first day at work when Mabel told the Mickeys she was going to send them to Suplex City and

Abigail Rose had to translate for me. "Wrestling changes lives because of attitudes."

It's true what he's saying. It's meant so much to me to watch the women of the WWE display, in the words of Abigail Rose's hero, John Cena, "ruthless aggression." I've never seen so much physical power thrown around by women. Ever. And have it be *celebrated*.

"But today we're going to talk rage," Angel says. "Specifically, your rage."

I eye him, like *how do you know about that?*

"I'm not angry."

"That's a shame," Angel says. "What with so much to be angry about in the world." He looks at me like I'm either daft or lying. "Everyone gets angry. As a wrestler, you need to access your anger. Amplify it. Let it explode."

I shake my head. "I'm the face," I say. "The good guy."

"Even good guys get angry," Angel says. "When's the last time you felt rage?"

I picture Frankie's sneer and feel a hot surge rise in my body.

"There you go," Angel says as the anger seeps into my face. "How did you feel? What does the rage make you want to do?"

"I felt small," I say. The rage straightens my spine, stretches me.

"And what are you going to do about it?" Angel asks, his tone authoritative, like he expects a good answer.

I don't train wrestlers. I train superstars.

"I'm going to get bigger," I say, picturing Frankie's face when he said I could never be the face of Mayhem. When he said those things about Angel. *His tutus and shit.* About Abigail Rose. "I'm going to get stronger."

I don't want to live in a world where people like Frankie have any power over me.

Over us.

"I'm going to be freaking huge."

CHAPTER 14

It's Saturday, and tonight is Summer Splatter: Mayhem's July event. Abigail Rose texted last night, right before I fell asleep, about a surprise she's planning for the Men of Mayhem. A message from the Future.

Since she won't tell me the details yet—need-to-know basis—I do the only thing I can. I hit the trail through the woods to the rock-climbing training course Dad built with his parents when he was a teenager.

I've never built muscle through external weights. Gymnasts, like rock climbers, train with body weight. I could do one hundred push-ups by the time I was ten and used to beat all the boys in gym class during fitness tests. This is the perfect place for me to train.

I start up the pegs of the first climbing structure, the one Dad calls Tree-vil. As in, *I've got to go climb that evil tree.*

I pull the weight of my body, one peg at a time, pressing up with the power in my legs. I forgot how far from one another Dad set the pegs, to make the climb a real challenge.

From up high, I see the one Dad calls Boulder-dash: a wall built into a mound of earth. You climb it like a boulder and then sprint around a path through the woods.

I go through the circuit, my muscles burning until they have no choice but to become more of themselves. And for the first time in as long as I can remember, I don't worry about getting bigger.

Back in my room, I finish up a match I paused between Asuka and Charlotte. I press play and Asuka, whose face is painted with green slime running from her eyes and down her chin, spits a cloud of green paint into Charlotte's face, blinding her to get the pin.

So far, other than Sonny Kiss, Asuka might be my favorite wrestler. Between the paint spewing and her lightning-quick movements in the ring, she captivates me. But the *artist known as* Shinsuke Nakamura, also from Japan, could edge her out with his long hair half shaved and his shiny red suit, the way he moves his body like a wave, stretching his fingers, shaking his hands like they contain too much energy for him to hold the electric guitar wail of his theme song. Shinsuke is like an electric, writhing, rock star snake.

Rhea Ripley and Bianca Belair both have unbelievable physiques and awesome gimmicks. Rhea's a malcontented heel who sometimes rolls with a crew of guys, and Bianca is a superstrong ray of sunshine who skips into the ring, whipping her braid like a jump rope.

On the AEW side of things, along with Sonny Kiss, I've fallen hard for the face-painted Danhausen whose slogan is "Very nice, very evil." There's vicious Dr. Britt Baker, DMD, an actual legitimate dentist, and Jade Cargill—who really is *that bitch*. The Sloth Style of Orange Cassidy, whose entire gimmick seems to be *moves slowly and barely cares*, reminds me of Kurt's slacker gimmick. And then there's the badass who is Nyla Rose, the first openly transgender wrestler to sign with a major American promotion.

It's funny to me now that Frankie used AEW to back up his argument on why they, the legacy guys, shouldn't share the ring with any outsiders. AEW is the first real competitor against the WWE in twenty years, and they didn't get to where they are by replicating the mold set out by the WWE. AEW got to where they are by breaking that mold. By welcoming athletes who break the mold.

With Mabel as our patron saint of Mayhem, why would we ever try to fit a mold?

Sonny Kiss knows exactly who she is. *Babe/she/he.*

I imagine my future self standing in the Barn, Abigail Rose announcing me.

Weighing in at 155 pounds and ready to fly, their name is Bird of Prey.

Today is George's first upstate event: Styled in the Wild, with her aura photographer friend from Brooklyn. She's worried people won't show up, so I promised her I'll go later this afternoon. The invite describes it as a mountain glam sesh with George of the Wild, including giveaways from her sponsors, live at the Deep Lagoon. She caps it off with a Ralph Waldo Emerson quote, in case it wasn't pretentious enough already:

Introducing a new fashion ethos:
the Era of the Aura Lewk.

"Each age must write its own books;

Or rather, each generation for the next succeeding.

The books of an older period will not fit this."

I laugh out loud. George and I could not be more different. But that Emerson quote sparks an idea.

It reminds me of Abigail Rose's Intergender Wrestling Manifesto. And of what Xena said about how the binary—the idea that everyone is just a man, or just a woman—had to be enforced globally by the Western colonial white supremacist patriarchy.

Had to be enforced because it's just not the way most cultures saw themselves.

No wonder we need to write new books.

Maybe this reclaiming inside, of my lost selves, is one tiny bubble of ancient truth resurfacing.

Like, the singular *they* seems weird to some old people for some reason, but just like the singular and plural pronoun *you* (or the singular royal form of the plural pronoun *we*), it was part of standard English as far back as the 1300s.

I google "colonial construct binary gender" and soon am swimming in tabs with information from nearly every continent, throughout all of history. In India, a third gender is acknowl-edged by the supreme court. Aboriginal brotherboys and sistergirls. The Muxes of Mexico. The Sekrata of Madagascar. The Hawaiian Mahu. The four genders of the Navajo, including masculine/feminine and feminine/masculine.

Gender-diverse people have always been here because gender is just a way for humans to describe what we are: which is nature.

No wonder so many people feel penned in by the Western binary gender construct. It's far more common and natural in the world to have more than two expressions of gender.

I google "gender binary and sports," and I kind of think I know what I'm going to find, but even at first glance, there's way more to the story than I've considered.

Beyond the pay gaps, the way women's sports are treated like a charity, rather than entertainment business—the most high-achieving female athletes are sometimes subjected to even more degrading experiences.

It turns out, female gymnasts who don't fit the aesthetic mold? We're just the tip of the iceberg. Because according to some definitions that have very real consequences in the lives of female athletes, men are limitless; women are limited. It turns out the world *can* decide that you are too fast and too strong to be a woman. *And* they're especially likely to do that if the women in question don't match Western ideals of feminin-ity. Specifically mentioned: If their muscles are too large and sharply defined, or if they're flat-chested.

Depending on how hard I train, I might be guilty on both counts.

But apparently, even when it comes to biological sex—not just gender—nature doesn't draw a clear line between male and female humans. Not when it comes to chromosomes, or hormone levels. Biologically, even, we're a spectrum. And the efforts to police the bodies of female athletes show how cruel humans can be when they won't listen to the science.

The binary isn't just useless: *It doesn't really exist.*

I feel that tingle in my brain. My synapses firing like a plasma ball. This all makes so much *sense.*

Mabel said all women are born fighting. Not because they want to. We have to fight for the right to exist on our own terms. Men are born fighting, too.

Each age must write its own books . . . The books of an older period will not fit this.

The Deep Lagoon has always been the least popular of the local swimming holes, so I've never seen cars spilling out, parking on the side of the road. George was worried there wouldn't be enough people here. It looks now like she should've had a few more worries.

Like whether or not the banks of the river can survive the full weight of the Jeep currently climbing its edge, searching for parking in an area that usually only sees foot traffic.

And how she'll collect all the garbage her followers have left on the ground. In the river itself, pockets of trash have gathered where wind currents swirl and catch on land. The cups—with an apple-shaped logo—are from the local juice shop George did a sponsored post for, with their cleanses. She posted it right after the video of me at the Deep Lagoon. I know because, despite myself, I kept going back to read the comments.

I spot my sister, holding court in front of her followers, as she styles a girl who looks just like her, holding up a Polaroid picture of the girl surrounded by a fuzzy blue halo.

I wait for George to see me. To meet my eyes so I can ask her what the hell is going on. Why she isn't doing anything about this out-of-control scene trashing our sacred paradise.

But George just keeps talking about how the girl can work with her beautiful blue aura, like it doesn't matter that the stage she's on is currently burning all around her.

I almost call the cops before I get in my car and take off, but she's my sister.

I can't heel that hard. I text her instead.

> Ran out of time and can't make event. Sorry.

I'm standing in front of my closet, disappointed with everything I see. I'd wear the purple suit from Tabitha's Closet, but it's going to be hot tonight.

I take out a pair of snakeskin leggings I wore when George and I dressed as Eve and the serpent who tempted Eve (her idea) for the neighborhood Halloween party, and then I head into her room to find her flapper skirt, knee-length and loaded with sequins and tassel trim.

I pull on the snakeskin leggings, and slide the skirt around my waist. I throw my polo shirt on and tuck it. Then I put on my Chuck Taylor high-tops and spin toward the mirror to take it in. From my hair to my shoes, even if it might not seem like it goes together, it fits. On me.

I twist my hips, and the sequins catch the light and scatter dots of it across the wall. Almost perfect. But still . . . missing something.

I grab a Sharpie from my desk and take off the shirt.

I scrawl THE FACE OF THE FUTURE across the front.

I pull it back over my head and spin around in front of the mirror. With my short red hair and this outfit, I think I may have finally found a lewk.

This I could get used to.

I come to the dirt road that leads to the Barn, and there's a sandwich board advertising: SHOW @ 7. I'm early, so the parking lot is mostly empty. But I recognize Silas's Suburban, Mabel's Thunderbird, and Frankie's Dodge Ram.

Abigail Rose and Xena light up when they see me and dash from the bottom of the risers to meet me at the door.

"I was about to text you," Abigail Rose says. "Ahh! Your shirt!" She pulls me in for a tight hug. "I love it."

"That skirt looks so good with those Chucks," Xena says.

Fans stroll in—a group of teenage guys, a young couple maybe in their twenties holding a sign that reads SUMMER SPLATTER OR NO SPLATTER AT ALL. But unlike the Queen City Crew event, the seats aren't even close to being filled.

Suddenly, all the lights except for the spot shut off and the heavy metal music fades out. The crowd murmurs and the bleachers creak. I'm not expecting much of a show, but I'm happy to be back in the Barn, under the lights, in this new world as my new self.

"Ladies and gentlemen!" Frankie Jr.'s voice rings out over the loudspeaker.

"And nonbinary friends," Abigail Rose says to our bench, and a shiver of joy moves through my body.

"The Men of Mayhem are proud to present . . ." Frankie pauses, and the few audience members start to pound the bleachers, so we join in. "Summer Splatter!"

The group in the back row starts a call and response, half of them chanting "Summer!" and the other half responding "Splatter!" I'm starting to think this won't be so boring after all.

But it's all kind of downhill from there. Unlike the Queen City Crew event, where Cami whipped the crowd into a frenzy before the first fighters even locked up, everything falls flat.

Frankie introduces the first fighter as Lyle the Lover. Lyle comes out onstage in trunks, wearing a red satin robe, carrying a silk rose between his teeth.

The guys in the back row boo him like crazy, like they need everyone here to know they're straight. That they do not find this oiled-up hottie attractive at all. He smiles at them and blows air kisses, so they boo louder. Lyle is heeling hard.

"SHUT UP, SIT DOWN!" he shouts at the crowd.

"And his opponent, the one, the only, the Master of Mayhem . . ." Frankie pauses for bleacher pounding, but this time the audience is much less enthused. ". . . the Chaos Kid!"

Frankie puts down the mic and runs into the ring. The audience doesn't boo or cheer. Mabel claps, because what kind of grandmother lets her grandson face dead air like that? And I get it—this is what it means to not be "over" with the crowd. To be neither face nor heel. To garner no reaction at all. This is a wrestling fail. And from the looks of it, one the Men of Mayhem have repeated over and over again, numbing their audience into boredom.

I've watched enough wrestling by now to have a feel for what works and what doesn't, and this just doesn't. They hit some crazy moves but don't give the audience a moment to let them register. They're all over the place with pacing—too fast, then totally lagging—and neither of them look out at the audience at all. No eye contact. No personality. No fun.

It's just two guys no one cares about grappling in the ring, pretending to punch and kick, and then, finally, Lyle pretending to submit.

Next is a match between Kurt and Robbie. Robbie's character, He the People, is an American hero trope. Kurt carries a guitar and goes by Kurt Mo-Pain, and with his shaggy blond hair and thrift-store grandpa cardigan, he looks like a sloppy music teacher. He slides across the floor like he's too apathetic to lift his feet.

I don't know much about the luchador style, but the way Kurt and Robbie flip and roll around one another is precise and mesmerizing.

At the turning point in the match, when Kurt Mo-Pain starts to take over and pummel He the People, the audience actually starts chanting.

"You de-serve that!" *Clap-clap clap-clap-clap.*

"You de-serve that!" *Clap-clap clap-clap-clap.*

When Kurt Mo-Pain climbs to the top of the turnbuckle, he leaps off, drawing his legs and arms toward his body all at once and then extending them in a perfect frog splash, his pilled cardigan sailing above him like a cape, landing his body across He the People.

Robbie mutters through feigned pain, "You may have won the battle, Mo-Pain, but . . ." He pauses, cueing the audience to his coming catchphrase. ". . . this means war!" they chant along with him.

"I thought he was going to smash that guitar for sure," I say to Abigail Rose.

"He can't afford to every time," she says.

Silas retains the Mayhem championship belt, though most of the audience has already left for the rest of their Saturday night plans before next month's Mayhem Moratorium is even announced.

"If a wrestling match happens in the forest and no one's there to see it, does it make a sound?" Abigail Rose says, looking around.

Little Mickey steps into the ring with the microphone as Silas does his victory strut around Billy the Kid, still twitching on the mat with the aftershock of Silas's bizarre closer, the Silent But Deadly: toxic flatulence.

Xena elbows me. "What's she doing?"

Abigail Rose has slipped into the ring and is grabbing a microphone out of Little Mickey's hand to address the crowd. He stares at her, stunned.

"Folks!" she calls out to what's left of the crowd as they get up to leave. "Hold up, everybody! I've got a message for the Men of Mayhem. Signed, sealed, delivered from the Future."

Abigail Rose points at me, and before my brain can even catch up and protest, I stand up in the bleachers. Xena lets out a solo cheer.

I freeze, waiting for her to continue. She can't possibly expect me to deliver this supposed message from the Future.

The few remaining people start to sit back down, thinking it's part of the show.

"Get her off the stage!" Frankie shouts, but none of the cousins move and Mabel gives him a stare that could burn holes through his eyes.

"I've got a message for you, Frankie the Chaos Kid," Abigail Rose says, and I heave a sigh of relief. "Next month, with the first-ever Mayhem women's battle royale, we aren't going to stop there. The Future is coming for you." She raises her hand and sticks her finger out like it's the tip of a blade. Then she draws it across her throat. "And we're out for blood."

The audience doesn't cheer, but they don't look at her like Frankie's friends did that night at the Fort. They don't boo her, either. Which means, as promos go, this was also a fail.

Abigail Rose holds the mic up high and then literally drops it in the middle of the ring, sending an ear-piercing frequency through the PA. The audience is clearly annoyed.

"That shit's expensive!" Frankie shouts.

"She's coming for you!" the guys mock from the back row, and Frankie's face burns red.

Frankie storms past where I'm standing with Xena, and when his eyes meet mine, our mutual disgust is a candle burning at both ends. I stand taller. Make my shoulders as wide as I can. I'm not wrong. With a bit more muscle, I could have the upper hand.

I catch a look of pride as it crosses Mabel's face, but she clears it as fast as it came, to the neutral gaze of a grandmother who would *never* choose a favorite. Not even that firecracker of a grandkid threatening her kin with the impending wave of the Future.

Abigail Rose scans the crowd, and when she finds me and Xena, she shrugs, like it could've gone worse. I would look mortified up there right now, but she looks proud of herself for trying.

We cheer for her—as loud as we possibly can, until people are looking, like there might be something wrong with us—and I point at my T-shirt and then point to her.

But I see Frankie watching us from the shadows, and I imagine what it was like to stand in the ring and face dead air the way Abigail Rose just did. It was awkward enough in the bleachers. She's so much more bulletproof than I am.

What if Frankie's right, that no one is going to want to watch our rumble?

What if Abigail Rose is completely wrong to think I can pull this off?

I look down at my outfit, and suddenly it doesn't look cool or edgy. It looks like I'm trying to be someone I'm not.

I look like a kid in dress-up clothes.

What if all of this crashes and burns, and we make complete fools out of ourselves?

I look at Abigail Rose and Xena, laughing so hard together they're almost falling over, and realize I don't care. At least, I don't want to.

And then I look back down at my outfit and—as if by magic—I love it again.

CHAPTER 15

My room lights up with the platinum glow of lightning.

Cr-aa-aaaa-ck! The thunder feels like it starts in the earth, and I can't sleep.

It's just after three o'clock in the morning—the witching hour, Grandma calls it—and I should be sleeping. Instead, I'm lying awake. Wondering how I got here.

I keep oscillating between feeling like I'm on some new, exciting path, and feeling like a train that's gone off-track.

What if I really am being Rip Van Winkled out of my future? What if wrestling is my gnome liquor, trapping me here for years to come?

I've lived here for almost one month—one full moon cycle—and I haven't even checked out which AP courses I can take next year or started to freak out about how many fewer APs are available at my new school anyway.

I'm telling time by the *moon cycle*.

With the thunder and lightning cracking around me, I feel

like I'm on the brink of something. An edge. And if I let myself fall over it entirely, I might never make my way back.

It's just, I'm not at all sure which side I'm supposed to be pulling for. Pulling toward.

The old, familiar me, or the new self I haven't fully found yet.

The one casting spells alongside her doubts into the river, like maybe there's more inside than she's let on.

We've been downstairs in the basement for most of the morning, putting together the mouse-sized Hell in a Cell replicas Uncle Frank dropped off this morning. He builds miniature models of the ring and cages that snap over the top. He even crafts tiny tables, ladders, and chairs for the TLC scenes Mabel designs from the year's matches.

"Won't that make everyone hate me, though?" I ask.

Since I got here this morning, Abigail Rose has been pitching an idea for the rumble that involves me playing a character named Brooklyn—a citiot who's "here to ruin absolutely everything."

After what Mom said, it hits a little too close to home.

"I feel like you're thinking in terms of reality, and, I mean, it's funny to be the one saying this, but you do know that wrestling isn't real, right?"

"Says the woman whose website is literally titled *Real to Me*."

"Life's full of contradictions," she says. "But it could set up a great plot with you, Lexie, and Kayleigh." She's holding her breath, wondering how I'll react.

"How so?"

"Brooklyn, the citiot outsider, moves to the very mountains

where you've vacationed your entire life, and your one friend—let's call her Local Lexie—is best friends with the *cheer* captain? That setup is rife with conflict." Abigail Rose snaps a cage over a ring.

"Typecast as the outsider, great."

"What's bad about being an outsider?" Abigail Rose asks. She says it like it's so easy, but maybe it's easier to lean into being an outsider when you know you belong.

Abigail Rose was born here. She might be a town weirdo, but she's *this* town's weirdo.

They can't wish she would just go home. She *is* home.

"What about being a witch?" I say. "And making Frankie fear me?"

"Witches are the OG outsiders," Abigail Rose says.

"Birdie! Your mother's here to see you," Mabel calls down the stairs, and I stop dead in my tracks. I'm frozen like the taxidermy Charlotte Flair mouse sitting out on Mabel's worktable, donning her most regal blue velvet cape with silver stitching and a white furry rim.

The training release in my bag—forged with my mother's signature—suddenly feels even more wrong than it did when I signed it.

"Grab another box of that Herkimer jewelry to replenish the stock!" Mabel shouts. Ever since we loaded those to the online inventory, they've been selling like crazy.

I carry the box upstairs, wondering what my mother's face looked like when she saw Mabel. But mostly wondering what she's doing here and how she knew to ask for me.

"There she is," Mabel says, taking the box from my hand, nodding to where Mom stands, holding a spider resin ring with a look of bewildered intrigue.

"Hey, Mom." Mom looks at Mabel, back at the spider in her hand, and then at me, shaking her head as if waking from a confusing dream.

"Oh, I . . ." She trails off, like she forgot why she's here. "I was in town and figured I'd come see where you work." Mom points through the window. "I spotted your car out front."

"This is it," I say, as nonchalant as possible, like I haven't been lying to her all summer.

"I thought it was the place with the felted fairy hats," Mom says with a nervous laugh. She steps deeper into the store, cocking her head as she examines one of the double-headed ducklings. "That's . . . cute."

"Mabel gets them from a farmer in Pennsylvania. They don't live long," I say.

"So sad and yet, adorable." She touches the glass dome over the double-headed duckling. Then she makes a beeline for the back case of Herkimer diamonds.

"I haven't seen these in years. Your sister had one on the other day—a pretty drop pendant. Your dad took me mining up there the summer we started dating." Mom tries on a few rings and finds one she likes. I can't tell what she's making of this whole thing. Me not telling her where I work; me working . . . here. "These earrings would go great with George's necklace. I'll get these, too, for her birthday. Can you ring me up?"

When Mom leaves, she thanks Mabel for giving me a job and says she might come back for the duckling. I can't tell if she's serious or just being nice.

But as she's leaving, Mom leans toward my ear and adds, more tersely than she spoke in front of Mabel, "We'll talk when you get home from work today."

I haven't told my parents about the rumble, or the training I'm about to start, but Mom looks suspicious. Like she's starting to wonder why I've been lying by omission about where I'm working. And if she scratches under that surface, she could unearth the bigger lies: the break-in, the talonsman, the shotgun.

Abigail Rose comes up when Mabel heads downstairs to finish Charlotte. Eventually, I'm going to have to tell her all of this, but I don't know where to start. So, I pivot.

"I bet I know why we're selling so many Herkimer diamonds," I say, taking out my phone. I open George's blog and two posts down, there it is: "Herkimer Diamonds—Perfectly Imperfect" with a snapshot of George's perfect neck, the drop pendant catching just the right amount of sunlight to look magical. I click on her Instagram link and sure enough, George has been rocking that pendant and tagging the Mostly Bones online store.

"That girl has a lot of followers." Abigail Rose points at the screen. Over two hundred thousand now, since she placed second in the Natural Beauty Challenge. "Wait . . . *George* of the Wild. George. *That's* your sister?"

"That's her brand." I try to put the phone back in my pocket, but Abigail Rose grabs it.

"Look at this smorgasbord of upstate clickbait magic!" Abigail Rose scrolls. "I half want to kill her for sharing all these local secrets, but the other half of me wants to be her. She's a social media genius. What an eye." Abigail Rose shakes her head to dislodge her eyes from the magnetic pull of George on the screen. "Why have you kept this from me?"

"You want her to advertise for the store?" It kind of seems like she already is.

"The rumble."

"My sister is not going to cross-promote our rumble," I say.

"Could you do me a solid and at least ask?"

I relent because I know Abigail Rose. She's got an idea and she's not going to let it go.

"If we sell this thing out, Frankie will have no choice but to accept the Future of Mayhem," she says. "With her help, we don't have to be some local secret."

I almost tell her how right she is.

No one can spill a local secret like George of the Wild.

Just ask the Deep Lagoon.

George is watching a cooking show when I get home from dinner at Mabel's.

"You know the pendant necklace you bought?" I ask.

"You want to borrow it?"

"Since you posted about it, we can barely stock the case fast enough," I say. I don't want her to get a big head or anything, but it's true.

The look of pride on her face, you'd think I told her she motivated people to protest injustice and demand world change.

"Seriously?" George feigns disbelief.

"It's unbelievable to me, too," I say. "But it did. Which brings me to my next question. Abigail Rose, she's Mabel's granddaughter—"

"—the girl with the purple bangs?"

"They're blue now. Not the point. Anyway, she has this big match coming up in August. The first-ever all-female revolving-door battle royale in Mayhem history," I say. "And we were wondering if you would promote it on your blog."

"Of course," George says.

"Thanks." I pause. "Better spreading that word than inviting all of Brooklyn to come trash the Deep Lagoon," I say.

George looks at me. "I thought you didn't come." She winces apologetically. "Things got out of control. I didn't know what to do."

Dad pops his head into the room. "Did I just hear Deep Lagoon? Are you talking about how they're shutting it down?"

"They're shutting down the Deep Lagoon?" George asks, aghast, and I can't even speak.

"Marvin told me," Dad says. Marvin's our mail carrier. He knows everything about everyone. "Said some influencer made posts from there and it got overrun with citiots."

I'm watching the driveway from my bedroom, waiting for Mom to get home. Lately, it's started to not feel *that* different from when she was always at work. She's always at the center for a dream circle, a pottery lesson, or a workshop to make wildflower garlands as offerings to some goddess or another. The kinds of things the old Mom would've cracked a snide joke about.

If she can have her whole new secret life, why can't I?

My parents could've grounded me once this week. Sure, I've been lying to them all summer about where I've been and why, but if they trust me, they should trust that I've made the right decisions.

Mom pulls up the driveway and when I hear her downstairs, Dad calls up, "Birdie, Mom's home!"

"How was pottery?" I ask, trying to gauge her mood.

"I went to a psychic intuition seminar," she says, completely serious. "What?" she asks, noticing my reaction. "If my own daughter could keep me in the dark about where she's been working all summer—for who knows *what* reason—clearly I could benefit from some guidance."

"Mom," I start, but Dad picks up where she leaves off.

"Why would you lie to us about where you work?" Dad asks, shaking his head.

I consider twisting the truth. Trying to pin the blame on someone else.

"I didn't want to tell you where I work because"—I take a deep breath—"I broke into Mostly Bones on a dare, the night I went to that party with Lexie and her friends, and I've been working off the cost of the item I stole." I leave out the part about Mabel's shotgun.

My parents look at me like I've morphed into a stranger before their eyes.

"I'm making it right, though," I say. "I didn't want to tell you guys about it because it's not your problem to solve. I didn't want to worry you."

Mom and Dad look at each other, doing that thing where they don't say a word but somehow come to an agreement.

"It's our job to worry about you." Dad looks at me with sad eyes. "We don't want you to deal with things on your own. You're not an adult yet."

If I were an adult, I wouldn't have had to forge my mom's signature on my training waiver for Angel.

I consider coming clean about that, too, and asking them to sign the waiver for real. It's just . . . all summer long, I've had this other world that's been only mine. At Mostly Bones. And now they know.

My new wrestling self isn't even fully formed yet. I don't

want to have to try to explain it all to them before I understand it myself.

Dad says I need to be more open with them about where I'm going and when, and I tell them I will be.

Upstairs, I find George in her room, editing photos.

"That's the biggest book I've ever seen in your possession," I say, picking up a tome on color theory. George barely looks up from her screen as she taps and clicks away imperfections.

"It's how I got this idea," she says. "How color theory and aura photography could be used together as style tools."

"That's actually"—I pause—"a pretty complicated, interesting idea."

"You don't have to sound so surprised," George says.

"Where are you doing the next pop-up?"

"That's the one sticking point," she says. "We want to avoid . . ." She hesitates.

"What happened at the Deep Lagoon," I finish her sentence, not even trying to hide the disappointment on my face. "Why didn't you call the police or something?"

George looks small and ashamed. "I didn't want to get in trouble," she says. "I fucked up, and I haven't figured out what to do about it. How'd it go with the inquisition?"

"OK," I say. "I forged Mom's signature on a waiver for wrestling training, though, and haven't told them about that, either."

George whips her head around, slack-jawed with disbelief.

"You didn't." She presses her hand to her heart. "You're becoming quite the rebel. I'm so proud."

"Rebels don't let other rebels destroy their favorite swimming holes," I say, and George promises, she pinkie-swears, that she will find a way to fix it.

"I swear I don't try to be the most self-centered person on the planet," George says.

"It just comes so naturally." When she looks up and sees that I'm smiling—that I'm at least kind of kidding—she shakes her head and laughs.

"It really does."

CHAPTER 16

I wake an hour earlier to fit in my workout on the climbing course, and my stomach is growling. The funny thing about working out this much and actually eating as much as I need to fuel it? I'm always hungry. Even when I was training twenty hours a week as a gymnast, I was always watching my weight, which—looking back on it—sounds ridiculous.

I'm watching my weight now, but it's different. Every time I see the scale tip higher, I get a jolt of joy. It turns out *you do you*, for my body, means getting bigger.

Finally, I'm letting it.

Thankfully, Dad stocked the freezer with muffin cup omelets and protein pancakes when he noticed how much food I'm going through. I told him I'm going out for crew at school, even though I have no idea if there's a crew team.

Outside, I climb the course, my sore muscles warming and loosening as I go. I push myself harder with each obstacle, stretching myself, so my muscles can become the biggest, strongest version of themselves.

I do mountain climbers, squat jumps, burpees, standing side

hops, broad jumps, and split squats until my legs burn and my body is slick with sweat. I'm already back up to sixty-five push-ups but I've got a ways to go.

When I get back inside, Mom's at the counter with her laptop and a coffee.

"How was your workout?" she asks, handing me a chocolate chip muffin from the basket Dad put out.

Last night at dinner, Mom was talking about some books she's been reading for her new research project, exploring how gender affects leadership hierarchies and access. She was all aflutter with new information on the supposed difference between male and female brains. Spoiler alert: There's not much.

Most of the differences between male and female brains are largely explained by differences in size. Male humans tend, on average, to be larger than females. But also, Mom said, we don't really know how our brains actually *work*. We can observe what they *do*, not how they do it.

"I can't shake something about what you said last night from that book," I say. Mom looks up from her laptop. "So . . . if the biggest differences between men and women are related to size, and the origin of male power in the patriarchy is linked to that size . . . then why are girls and women always trying to lose weight, and only put on lean muscle, while boys bulk up and try to put on as much muscle as they can?" I shake my head, and Mom does, too, like she wishes she had an answer but doesn't. "Gymnastics is a power sport," I say, choking on the words. "Why couldn't I be huge?"

"Oh, you're not huge, honey," Mom says, trying to comfort me, like my voice is cracking because I worry I'm too big. But I shake my head and laugh.

"That's the thing, though. What if I do want to be huge? What if people already treat me like I am, anyway? Why is it a bad thing for me to be huge?"

"I'm sorry," Mom says. "You're right. That was a gut reaction that came from the idea that my daughter calling herself huge was a sign of self-judgment and not self-love. Which is internalized misogyny." Mom sounds like she's reading from a self-help workbook.

"I made it to seventeen years old as a raging feminist raised by raging feminists, and I mean, props for that," I say, "without realizing that this is why girls are only supposed to put on *lean muscle*: so we stay smaller than men. Like, somehow, how our bodies look is more important than what our bodies can do." I shake my head, but Mom sits back and stares at me, listening.

"What do you want to do about it?" Mom asks, not like a dare, but an opening.

I want to be huge. Too big for small minds.

Which would actually be a great tagline for Brooklyn the citiot heel, if I can get over myself and play the role.

"I don't know yet," I say. "Could you do me a favor?" She nods. "Tell me that's OK."

Mom smiles.

"That's more than OK. I'm starting to think it might be the only way forward."

After work, I go straight to The Underwear Factory. Dad's in Gilboa, Mom's at the center, and everyone thinks I'm working overtime for Mouse-o-Mania.

When I step into the factory, Angel stands in the ring, his

hands on his hips, like he's performing a piece called *The World's Most Boring Wait.* The Queen City Crew wrestlers are wrapping up their practice, and Cami's stretching her leg on one of the ropes. Petra, who I met at the School's Out event, and another wrestler I don't recognize are outside the ring.

"Forgive my abrupt tone, but we were expecting you five minutes ago and are desperately in need of your assistance. Cami's so close"—Angel claps when he says it—"to nailing this dive between the ropes."

"It's hard being a star," Cami says.

"You three," Angel says, pointing at the Queen City wrestlers and me, "stand over there."

He points to a line of electrical tape on the ground, about three feet from the rope, with worn mats spread out behind it. We line up, and Angel sits himself down on the bottom rope.

"Our girl here is going to fly through this like Wonder Woman, and you're going to catch her and fall back on the mats."

Petra starts to jog in place, pumped, but I'm shaking my head, not sure. Cami catches my eye from the ring and smiles.

"It's like Red Rover," she says, and somehow, I believe her.

Angel asks, "Ready?"

"Ready," the other two girls say. I nod.

Cami stands in the middle of the ring and pumps herself up.

"I'm too fast, I'm too smart, I'm too pretty!" she calls out, her voice growing louder and more intense until she's shouting. She takes off running for the back rope and turns to bounce herself off it and propel herself forward. She dives between the ropes, and when her body crashes into us, we fall like bowling pins into a pile of deadwood.

It hurts, but like in gymnastics, not in a bad way. In a way that makes me feel tough. Like, yeah, I can handle that. What else ya got? Coach used to say: *Pain is in the brain.*

There's a silence after the grunts of the fall, but then Angel starts clapping. He whistles through his pinkies.

Cami stands up, pumps her fist in the air, and lets out what I now recognize as a Ric Flair "Woo!"

"That was good?" I ask, still on the ground, and Cami shakes her head.

"That was fit for Wrestling Royalty," she says, and when she reaches out her hand to shake mine, I feel a rush of pride.

That was different than gymnastics. That was Cami's moment, but it was only possible because of all of us.

"Can you teach me how to do that?" I ask, but Cami shakes her head.

"I have to go pick up my sisters."

I'm more than a little disappointed. When Cami competed against Best Wes-tern, she almost clinched the win with her closer, the Crown Jewel—her version of a corkscrew moonsault, where not only does she flip backward off the top rope, but she also does a 360-degree twist, landing to pin her opponent.

When you watch Cami wrestle, it's hard *not* to get chills.

"Cami's family has no idea she's wrestling royalty," Angel says. "They think she's off at chess camp, right? Or is it robotics this summer?" I almost blurt out, *I'm lying to my parents, too!* But catch myself in time before I fangirl my way into getting kicked out of here.

"How about minding your business, instead of airing out mine?" she says, and Angel raises his hands in surrender. "You're in luck, though. Angel's the best trainer we've got."

Their practice over, Cami starts toward the door, and the

other girls follow. She takes off in a sprint toward the exit but stops, remembering to swap out her Wrestling Royalty shirt for a chess camp one before disappearing down the hallway.

I hand over the forged waiver to Angel, feeling less guilty now that I know Cami forged hers, too.

I go to put my phone in my bag and see there's a text from Lexie.

> Plz tell me George didn't get the Deep Lagoon shut down

A pit forms in my stomach.

I text George—*Deep Lagoon rumor traveling. Damage control needed*—but I'm about to have my first in-ring session. I push Lexie's text from my mind.

"We'll start with rolls and master those before you even take a bump," Angel says, sitting on the bottom rope and lifting the top one for me to climb into the ring. "If you know your rolls and a move goes wrong, you can hopefully avoid injury."

Angel teaches me the front roll first, keeping both feet straight up and then planting one in front of the other and popping up to a fighting stance. I do it so many times I start to feel my muscles learning the nuance, the alignment, but Angel keeps critiquing my leg placement.

Every time one of my legs windmills out, he shouts, "DANGER! DANGER!

"A botched roll can lead to hooking your leg on your opponent," Angel says. "That could mean a sprained knee or worse. Torn ligaments. Dislocation. We don't want to see anyone's bones popping out of their sockets," he says, and I remember what he told me about the Glamazon Beth Phoenix's jaw. Like in gymnastics, even the basics can be dangerous in the ring.

Still, the repetition works. With every iteration of each roll, it starts to click, more and more. Until the movements become automatic. Certain.

When we finish, I'm breathing heavily and sweating. I've learned: front roll, back roll, and left and right quarter roll—like a front roll with one shoulder leading on the way down—each of which I've done at least twenty times.

"Next session," Angel says in his super-serious trainer voice, "come prepared to leave hurting. We're taking bumps." I must look confused because he adds, "That means smashing your body against the mat. Repeatedly." He smiles when he says it. Like a sadist.

"I thought you were going to teach me how to be myself," I say to Angel. "This looks suspiciously like teaching me how to wrestle."

"Like I said, I'm not just a wrestling trainer," Angel says. "I teach humans to think outside the box, explore different possibilities, challenge them to grow in every aspect of their lives." He pauses. "But, also, a shit ton of flippy moves."

"Have you thought about your gimmick?" he asks when we're out of the ring.

"Abigail Rose has," I say. "But she wants me to be a heel named Brooklyn, who's moved to upstate New York to 'ruin absolutely everything.'"

Angel laughs out loud.

"Your girl's good. I'll give her that. That's a powerhouse gimmick right there."

I groan. "Everyone will hate me," I say. "It's hard enough

being an outsider in real life. I don't need to play one as my fantasy role in the ring, too."

"The thing about heels and faces," Angel says, "is that it's kind of the same thing as insiders and outsiders." He shrugs. "It's all relative. When you're an outsider"—he points at himself with pride—"other outsiders *are* the in-group. Tell me more about the conflict," he says. "Who would be your opponent?"

"Local Lexie and her head cheerleader best friend," I say, and Angel laughs out loud.

"Tell me *those* don't sound like the names of some heel-ass bitches." He looks at me with a seriousness that demands an answer.

I have to laugh. "They do," I say. "They definitely do."

"Heels, faces," Angel says, and then we lock eyes. "It's just another binary to be transcended." He spins his signature pirouette and then puts me in a headlock that I have to actually wrestle out of.

"What if I'm a heel and I want to eventually be a face?" I ask as we're walking out to our cars.

"A heel doesn't get to decide when she turns face," he says. "It all depends on whether or not you can get over with the crowd. All you can do is lean in and hope you're the kind of person who's fun to hate."

I leave the gym looking forward to taking bumps next class. Is it weird that part of me can't wait to smash myself against the mat? Repeatedly.

You do you.

Why should I care if it's weird, when it sounds so freaking fun?

CHAPTER 17

George is on the porch making a video when I get home.

"Lexie asked me if you're the reason they shut down the Deep Lagoon," I say, and George looks like she might cry.

"I'm sorry I didn't respond to your text. I'm in meltdown mode. Tell me I'm not a horrible person," she says. Thankfully she doesn't pause long enough for me to have to say it. "I love the Deep Lagoon. Contrary to those who say otherwise, like . . . Gunkslovr845," she reads from her laptop. "'Wish you loved the Deep Lagoon half as much as you love yourself, you narcissist.'"

"You've been getting comments like that?"

George scoffs. "You wouldn't believe the comments I delete from my site."

"You're not a horrible person," I say, because even if she made a huge mistake, she doesn't deserve the kind of hate the internet piles on. No one does.

"Look at this, though." George turns her screen for me to

see the comments on her most recent post ranking the top five artisanal ice cream shops in the region.

Look everyone! George eats ice cream! She's a normal just like you and me!

You would *pay five bucks for ice cream.*

Go back to the city and bring your expensive-ass ice cream with you

I hate that ice cream place almost as much as I hate you

I stop reading.

"Can't you disable those things?" I ask.

"Reader engagement is one of the reasons my brand is so successful," George says. "I seem unapproachable, but yet I *am* approachable. It's a whole vibe." She presses delete on the batch. "A vibe I fastidiously filter."

I almost tell George about how a heel doesn't get to decide when she turns face. How all she gets to do is lean in and hope she's the kind of person who's fun to hate.

But as much as George's chosen line of work, if you want to call it that (and she does), blurs the line between reality and performance, it's not *really* kayfabe. She's not a heel or a face.

She's out here like everyone else, trying to be her best self.

"Some ten-year-old kid wrote to say I'm the reason they canceled her favorite swimming hole," George says. "What am I supposed to do? Not promote my brand?"

"Why is the Deep Lagoon *your* brand?" I ask.

"It's *such* clickbait." George shakes her head, like she should know better. "I'm sorry," she says. "Just tell Lexie I'm so sorry."

We're on our way to the Mickeys' house, and I pick up a bag of Funyuns because it seems like the most appropriate wrestling snack. I pull up in front of a small house in the middle of the big open field with the curve of the mountain rising behind it. A dog with three legs hops over and barks an assertive hello.

Abigail Rose drops to her knees and the dog—Fancy—licks her face.

"Who's my Fancy girl?" she coos to the dog, but then she chokes and waves her hand in front of her face. "Ugh!" She backs off, wiping her hands on the grass as if she could wipe the smell off her. "She's been skunked!"

"That's why she's outside," Silas says through the screened door, something tiny wriggling on his shoulder. "Mom went to get tomato juice."

When we get close enough to see, Abigail Rose says, "New rescue?"

"Found her next to the dying tree Frankie came and cut down for Mom," Silas says, rubbing his huge index finger under the chin of the tiny squirrel perched on his shoulder. We head inside, squirrel and all, and the house smells sweet, like a county fair.

Little Mickey (who doesn't look like a Walter) and Silas's dad, Mick—the only one of them whose name is actually Mickey—was a professional wrestler who, ironically, wrestled under the name Tommy Mayhem. The name Mick was taken by a more famous wrestler, Mick Foley.

All three of Mabel's sons made it to the pros and had decent careers, Abigail Rose told me, but as jobbers—wrestling lingo for professional losers.

Kurt and Robbie are in the kitchen with Silas and Little Mickey. Kurt's long hair is held back in a ponytail, and he's rocking a THE MAN T-shirt.

"So it's true." Robbie unscrews the top of a two-liter bottle of cola and fills a cup with The Miz's face on one side and his slogan on the other: HATERS LOVE ME CUZ I'M AWESOME. "Frankie finally gave your whole Women of Mayhem promotion a spot?"

"*Future* of Mayhem," Abigail Rose says. "And he didn't give me the spot, so much as I took what's rightfully mine."

"You should've seen the look on Frankie's face when I told him you're sourcing outside training." Kurt fills his own cup, which features Rey Mysterio.

When eight arrives and the familiar theme song blares through the speakers, we're eating corn dogs, Funyuns, pork rinds, and veggie puffs. Silas hands a pumpkin seed to the squirrel on his shoulder.

Just like when I watch the show with Abigail Rose, we crack jokes. We repeat the elevated vocabulary of the announcers, which is the closest I've gotten to SAT talk all summer.

"OBSTREPEROUS!" Kurt yells at the screen.

Unlike at Mabel's house, they don't have wrestling pictures on the walls, just regular family photos. There's one photo of Mabel and Grandpa Wyatt dressed up for New Year's, a clock behind them striking midnight, their faces turned to one another, smiling, about to kiss.

About twenty minutes into *SmackDown!*, Mrs. Mickey comes home with the tomato juice.

"Aunt Gigi!" Abigail Rose springs up and hugs her hello.

"This must be your new protégé I've heard so much about." Gigi smiles at me, but then turns to Silas with Serious Mom Face. "Did you practice your audition piece?"

He nods, embarrassed, and Little Mickey blurts out, "The Pied Piper played that same song on repeat the whole time you were gone." Gigi eyes Little Mickey like he's on thin ice, and heads outside to give poor skunked Fancy girl a tomato bath.

"Aunt Gigi has watched one wrestling match in its entirety.

Ever," Abigail Rose says. "The Hell in a Cell match between Charlotte Flair and Sasha Banks."

"The one where Sasha peeled herself off the stretcher and went back into the cell?" I ask, because we watched it, and Abigail Rose nods.

"Aunt Gigi came in to ask if we could turn it down because she couldn't hear the opera she was streaming, but she wound up sitting next to me, gripped, the entire time." Abigail Rose launches into an impression of Gigi. "'And I thought opera had the lockdown on drama!'"

"So this, uh . . ." Little Mickey says, waving his hand in the air, "whole Future of Mayhem thing. It's . . . not just for girls?"

"Why do the belts need to be divided by gender?" Abigail Rose asks, and Little Mickey groans the loudest, but he's not the only one audibly displeased. "Hear me out. What does Mabel always say? A great wrestler can have a match with a broom. We've all seen Kenny Omega vs. Haruka," she says, and they laugh dismissively.

"That match is a joke." Little Mickey looks incredulous.

"That match is actually amazing," I say, and he eyes me like, *who are you?*

"Chyna used to fight guys," Abigail Rose says. "She was hands down the most talented wrestler of her time, and she had multiple serious Intercontinental Championship runs."

"Chyna was basically a dude," Little Mickey says, and Robbie laughs under his breath.

"Chyna was The Man before the world was ready for a woman to be The Man. If we'd exploded the gender binary in time, Joanie would probably still be alive." She says it accusatorily, and for some reason, it seems to land heavy in the guys' hearts. Like they're understanding something, through what she's saying about Chyna, that they couldn't understand before. "The problem with the binary is most people don't fit it, but yet there it is. Still a thing." Abigail Rose looks at Silas. "Remember our nail-painting parties before these dickwads starting giving you crap about it?" Silas cracks a soft smile.

Little Mickey groans.

"That's where you're going to take this?" he says. "We should let you have at our belt so guys can wear nail polish?" Little Mickey shakes his head. "Hard pass, thanks." The other guys all shift in their seats, uncomfortable.

"What if I like nail polish? Or think it'd be cooler to wear skirts," Silas says, and his cousins eye him like he's being funny. "It's getting hotter every summer."

"See, though?" Little Mickey says. "It feels like you're turning Mayhem into a joke."

"I'm not being funny," Abigail Rose says.

"Neither am I," Silas says.

"You want us to agree to fight girls?" Robbie asks, and I can tell he's *trying* not to look offended. He's really wondering if they're expecting him to *lose* to girls, which a lot of guys can't handle.

"Brother, it's fucking fake," Silas says.

"Do I look like James Ellsworth?" Robbie says. Everyone laughs at that—because of his Intergender Wrestling Champion stunt, Abigail Rose told me about it when she introduced me to her manifesto—and the wave of serious conversations has broken.

"I'm just saying, what if there were two belts, but anyone could hold them," Abigail Rose presses. "The indies are full of intergender matches. Candace LeRae," she says again.

"You're not taking our belt." Kurt shakes his head, like there's no room for debate.

"You sound like a bunch of entitled, spoiled brats. If you get booked for it, you'll drop the damn belt." Silas shakes his head like he can't believe he even has to say this.

"Can Birdie come train with you guys at least?" Abigail Rose begs. "To practice with a group for the rumble? She's training with a guy right now, anyway, Angel—"

Little Mickey laughs. "The tutu guy?"

"So he wrestles in a tutu and calls himself a wrestling choreographer," Abigail Rose says. "His wrestlers can flip circles around all of you in the ring."

The guys recoil in offense.

"Isn't her sister the citiot who got the Deep Lagoon shut down?" Little Mickey asks, sneering, and my face burns with shame. "Let me be the first to go on record saying that if Mayhem ever *did* hand over its title to a girl—and that's what we would have to do, *hand* it over—it's not going to be to her."

When the show's over, Silas walks us outside, the squirrel asleep on his shoulder.

"Are you ready to defect?" Abigail Rose asks him. "After Birdie wins the rumble, let's have her take it all. Birdie Two Belts! She can defeat you in a—"

"No," Silas says, his calm voice extra quiet for the squirrel.

"What do you mean? This is the perfect moment for—"

"You heard them in there." Silas shakes his head. "They'll never forgive me. I can't go rogue." He turns back toward the house. "You've got your belt," he says. "They're right. You don't need to take theirs, too."

"Why is it theirs, though?" Abigail Rose asks, and Silas shrugs.

"It just is." He reaches a hand up to his shoulder, and when he nuzzles the squirrel with it, it climbs into his palm.

Silas heads back inside to join the group, leaving us alone together in the dark driveway.

But above us, the sky is so full of stars, it looks like some might spill over the edge and fall to the ground.

It takes me over an hour to fall asleep.

If Mayhem ever did *hand over its title to a girl, it's not going to be her.*

I'm that citiot girl. The wrong side of both binaries.

The problem with the binary, Abigail Rose said about Chyna, *is most people don't fit it, but it's still a thing.*

Am I a local when my feet are pressed against the pine needles and memories of this land shoot through me like rainbows?

Aren't most of us, locals and citiots alike, settlers or guests on stolen land, anyway?

It's not that I need to be Birdie Two Belts. I don't need to win the Mayhem championship belt. But because of George, I've gone from outsider to actual heel in real life.

It's one thing to feel like you don't belong. It's another to be told you're not wanted.

The darkness out here is different than our old home, with its streetlamps glowing through the windows.

It's dark with eyes open; dark with eyes closed.

Just complete and total darkness, all around.

CHAPTER 18

Lexie's mom Helen pulls me in for a hug the moment she opens the door, and, like always, she smells like food.

"You made my favorite." I sniff the air.

"Potato, onion, bacon varenyky. Kotleta po-kyivsky. And deruny." I could eat two dozen of Helen's varenyky alone. I'm going to have to eat in shifts to get down on those potato pancakes, too. "Thanks for coming." Helen kisses me on the cheek and pulls back, like she needs time to take in my entire face. "Even if you've been a stranger to us all summer." Helen shakes her head like she can't believe something. "Your hair. It's somehow even better than I imagined when Lexie told me how good it looks."

She told *me* she hates it.

"Go get her and bring her down. Meghan"—that's Lexie's little sister—"is dying to annoy her."

I haven't hung out with Lexie since that last time at the bowling alley—and our two unexpected face-offs since then haven't exactly smoothed things over—so I was surprised when she texted about coming over for dinner. I know it was Helen's idea, of course, but Lexie reached out. She hasn't totally written me off.

Lexie's door still has the LEXIE BLVD sign Meghan got her the summer of her thirteenth birthday.

"If you don't leave me alone, I'll take back those old Crocs I gave you," Lexie says through the door.

"It's not Meghan," I say.

"Come in! You have to tell me *everything*," Lexie says when I open the door. "The entire town is talking about how George got the Deep Lagoon shut down."

"She's so sorry," I say, sitting down on her bed. Lexie's watching me like I'm a docusoap, just *living* for the drama, and I pause. "What is this?" I ask, waving a finger between us.

Lexie shrugs. "You coming over for dinner finally?"

"But we haven't been cool, Lex. Like, at all." I wait for her to put up her usual wall. Tell me I'm being too sensitive. That it's no big deal. "Now you show up with your friends, wrestling for that jerk, Frankie. You talk shit about me."

"Look, I don't know what's wrong with me."

"You said I've always been weird, and that this is next-level. You hated my hair."

"I didn't hate it," Lexie says, and even though I already know that from Helen, watching her face contort with reluctant honesty makes me feel like I finally have my friend back. The one I used to tell everything to, every single summer. The one who I used to think told me everything.

"I was jealous," she says, "and I don't even know of what. You changed your hair, and I found out with everyone else, and it just . . . it hurt, OK? And you *are* weird. Irreplaceably weird. There is no one like you. I love you, you freaking weirdo," Lexie says. "I love you so much. All the weird stuff you make me think about. The way no conversation with you ever goes the way it goes with anyone else in my life. Why do you think we're best friends?"

"We're still best friends?" I ask, letting her words wash over me.

"Bitch, always," Lexie says, and it feels so good to laugh. "I'm just sorry my insecure ass got you in trouble to begin with."

"You really were going to break into some girl's house after we broke into the store?" I ask. "I mean, she can't be *that* bad."

Lexie coughs out a dark laugh. "I've thought about nothing but that one fangirl's thirst-trap posts every waking moment since I started hooking up with Zeke," she says. "I think about her when I wake up and get ready. I think about her when I send him a pic. I think about her when I try to fall asleep." Lexie bumps her back against the headboard. "I think about her every second of every day."

"Uh uh." I shake my head. "Not healthy. Are you in a relationship with Zeke or this girl?" I ask, shocked by how obsessed Lexie's been with this girl she barely knows.

Lexie groans. "Exactly. So yeah . . . I'm sorry my chronic insecurity derailed your summer."

My summer best friend—bowler of perfect games, snagger of Hot Guys in Bands, newly anointed cheerleader—worries she's not enough. Or too much. Or both.

"Ironically, you kind of saved it," I say. "And I need you to do it again. For George."

"What happened at the Deep Lagoon is not good. She needs to fix it." Lexie shakes her head. "This is absolutely destructive for your reputation at school."

I'm taken aback. "My reputation?" I look at her like she can't be serious, but she is. And the worst part of it is that, after all this time this summer trying to embrace being a heel and not caring how I'm seen? I give an F. I give like an entire lake full of F's and *that*, more than whatever these people have been saying about me, pisses me off.

"Everyone's calling you my jacked citiot friend with the hot, horrible sister." Lexie winces apologetically.

"You're kidding." I sit with it. "I'm irritated by the word *citiot* and proud of the word *jacked*." I pause, smiling. "Progress."

"Birdie, she got the Deep Lagoon shut down. This is a PR crisis even I can't help you come back from." Lexie crosses her arms in front of her chest, like there's nothing she can do about the entire town talking trash about me and my family. I want to not care. But George? This could ruin her business entirely.

We can't come back from this without Lexie's help.

"Remember when they discontinued Oreo Cakesters?" I ask, and her eyebrows narrow.

"Those shortsighted hacks over at Nabisco heard from me."

"You adapted Helen's whoopie pie recipe into the perfect copycat. Those suckers could've passed a blind taste test." Lexie laughs at the memory. "You dropped the flute when you fell in love with chorus because you loved *Glee*. And then you dropped chorus when you fell in love with bowling and the concert schedule interfered with your team tournaments." I shake my head at her, like her resilience is simply incredulous. "Now you made the cheer squad, not to mention holding down a steady job and buying your own damned car like a *boss*, and you're still bowling like you could legit go pro on the circuit."

"I mean, I could. These are just facts," Lexie says.

"There is nothing you cannot do," I say, and she shrugs like I've got a point. "George wants to make things right. Somehow.

Dare I say she's even learned from her mistake. I need to help her. She's my sister. But I can't do this without your support. You are this town. To me, anyway."

Lexie doesn't even take a moment to think about it. She wraps me in a tight hug.

"Let's save your reputation," Lexie says, like there couldn't be a more urgent need.

"And the Deep Lagoon," I say.

"Of course. That too."

Between Meghan talking my ear off about everything that's happened since last summer, and Helen pushing plate after plate of varenyky and deruny in front of me, dinner is basically the same as always.

"I'm so excited to see you girls in your big wrestling match," Helen says.

"It's not a match, it's a rumble, Mom," Meghan says, like her mother is the most embarrassing person on the planet.

"Sorry," Helen says, hands up. "I haven't seen your parents all summer, either. I should call them so we can plan on going together and catch up."

I almost choke on my butter-soaked bite of crispy chicken. Somehow, I never thought about my parents finding out I'm wrestling from someone they know in town. Like one of their oldest friends.

When I'm leaving, Helen hugs me, and she feels more like an aunt than a friend's parent.

"Please give your parents the biggest hugs for me and tell them I'll be in touch next week about"—she eyes Meghan— "the *rumble*."

I drive the familiar route home from Lexie's with plans swirling in my head.

Mayhem technically means *violent or damaging disorder* and *chaos*. If my parents find out from Helen that I'm leaving them out of the loop *again*, they'll find out about the forged waiver, too. Which means I might not have to worry about the Future of Mayhem at all.

My parents might rain some damaging disorder and chaos down upon my life right in the here and now.

I've already gained about three pounds of muscle, without any concern, and it feels like smashing through the glass ceiling of my own body for the first time ever while training. My muscles are sore, but I feel *good*. For the first time in a long time, dopamine courses through my veins.

I'm lying on my bed, thinking about how and what to tell my parents about the waiver and my training before Helen does, when Abigail Rose texts me.

> The boys won't let you train with them?

> The Future of Mayhem enters squad mode. Kayleigh & co tomorrow w Angel.

A few seconds later, Lexie texts me.

> See you tomorrow?

I've known this moment would come. That Lexie and Kayleigh and the synchronized flippers are just as much a part of this rumble as the Queen City Crew wrestlers. But, training alone with Angel, I haven't had to worry about any of that . . . stuff. What I look like, how I move.

Sometimes it feels like the binary is computer code, running different programs. Only I never got the download. Or the updates. Sometimes, I pretend I did, and I try to be fluent in Girl Code. I do that thing where I slip into the role of Girl. I talk like Girl. I laugh like Girl. I pretend I am Girl. Sometimes it's fun.

But sometimes I can't run the code. Sometimes it just feels too fake.

Part of me thinks this is what it's all like. So-called femininity. So-called masculinity.

All the world's a stage, and all the men and women merely players.

I like the idea of living without a program running. Never feeling pressure to pretend I got the latest download.

That's how I feel when I'm training alone with Angel. But there's this theory in physics called the *observer effect*, which states that observing something inherently alters the thing that's been observed.

Can my inner wrestler survive the gaze of a pyramid full of cheerleaders?

Or will I default to running an old program?

Mimic their mannerisms.

Try to be anyone other than whoever it is I really am.

CHAPTER 19

Kayleigh wasn't wrong when she said she could deliver her squad. They roll up in an SUV, and Freya parks up ahead.

We're meeting at the Queen City Crew ring for our first session, like we'll do once each week until the match. Our second practice each week will be at the Trampoline Wrestling Federation (the TWF, aka Kayleigh's trampoline). I'm going to keep seeing Angel privately, too, to get in as much training as possible before the rumble.

"Let me make sure I have this clear," Tova says. "They chose us because they think we *can't* wrestle, right?"

"They think we're pretty faces who will let this one down," Kayleigh says, pointing at Abigail Rose.

"They figured that because I complain about the WWE using cheerleaders, dancers, and models as female wrestlers," Abigail Rose says, "that they'd really screw—"

"Cheerleaders and dancers are perfect for wrestling," Kayleigh says, looking so disappointed. "You loved Rey Mysterio. He's tiny and he flips a lot. He's basically a flier."

"You're right," Abigail Rose says, and even Kayleigh blinks in surprise at her admission.

"Do you know what we do to jerks who think cheerleaders aren't athletes?" Lexie asks us, pounding her fist into her open palm, and it's so good to see her here after our talk.

"Easy there, Ronda Rousey. You've been a cheerleader for like four seconds," Kayleigh says.

"Some losers want to act like we can't flip around and beat each other up in some corny ring? Because what?" Tova pauses. "We're too ladylike?"

Sofia burps, as if on cue. "I drank that iced coffee so fast."

"Why does everyone think cheerleaders are all prissy, anyway?" Freya says. She points at Kayleigh. "If I had a dollar for every time you farted while I was holding you up."

We burst out laughing.

"You try pulling a needle after being flipped up into a hold," Kayleigh says with a shrug and a smile. "That's a lot of contorting."

I was so worried about them joining practice today. So worried that I'd be the odd one out, like I was at cheerleading tryouts. But so far, these girls are not the archetypes of perfection I made them out to be in my mind. They're flesh and blood. Farts and burps and all.

Freya and Sofia pose for a selfie, and I notice their legs are bruised in multiple places.

Looking around, all the cheerleaders, including Lexie, have bruises and scratches on their arms and legs. They've been kicked and scratched, dropped and grabbed, pulled and missed—they've given what's needed of their bodies, to hold the group together. Like a real team.

"I thought you were all too embarrassed to be seen wrestling," Abigail Rose says. A few days ago, they were mortified to be in the same parking lot as us, and now they're taking selfies outside an independent wrestling gym.

"We just don't want to be seen with—" Sofia cuts herself off, and Freya elbows her.

Freya looks at Abigail Rose. "No offense or anything," she says. These cheerleaders are more embarrassed to be associated with Abigail Rose and her family than anything.

"Shall we?" Kayleigh nods down the alley, and without any argument, we all follow her lead. Even Abigail Rose.

"Did you hear about what happened at the Deep Lagoon?" Sofia asks, and Lexie eyes me. Apparently, word hasn't gotten *all* over town. "People coming up from the city and trashing the place. Must've been on some Instagram list or something."

"No, it was some citiot's website, I heard," Freya says, and my stomach lurches.

The guys already said they wouldn't train with me. If these girls decide I'm a citiot garbage person who's ruined their town, this rumble isn't going to work.

"Citiots ruin everything," Kayleigh says, and when she looks at me, I can't tell if she knows about George. "No offense."

"I'm as upset as you," I say. I want to say more, to come clean about George's role in this whole horrible situation, but I also don't want them to hate me and my entire family any more than they already do.

"I thought you said this was a gym," Freya says. "Why did we just enter this creepy unlit hallway through a propped door in an alley?"

"There's light at the end of the tunnel," Kayleigh says. Enough that it's not *pitch*-black.

"What is this place?" Lexie asks as we enter the cavernous cement room and find Angel warming up by the ring.

"An old factory," Angel says. "My uncle's going to develop it into apartments with some community spaces, but the project's been on hold. He bought the ring, pays the utilities, and insures the place. The dude loves wrestling."

"Your wrestlers are insured?" Abigail Rose asks, but Angel shakes his head. The girls eye the ring and the space, like they can't quite make sense of where they are.

"Waivers and releases. Under New York law, you can train to wrestle at any age. But you need to be over eighteen to wrestle professionally on the independent circuit."

"How do you get around that?" Abigail Rose asks. I didn't know it was illegal.

"The law's meant to protect kids from fighting for money, but this is sports theater. So, we call it a recital." Angel saunters into the middle of the ring and spins around, throwing his arms in the air. "Hence me: your wrestling choreographer."

"Genius." Abigail Rose holds her phone up and snaps a few pictures.

"What," Freya says, Angel's spell broken, "are you doing?"

"Documenting," Abigail Rose says, taking more shots, "for my website."

Tova springs to her feet. "If you post a single picture of me before that stupid rumble, I will . . ." She's fuming, so upset she can't finish her sentence.

Abigail Rose laughs. "What's wrong with you?"

"There's nothing wrong with us," Sofia says. "But . . ." She stands up next to Tova and Freya. "Just being here with you," she says, looking at Abigail Rose like she doesn't want to hurt her feelings, "it's kind of embarrassing. No offense."

Angel rolls his eyes, hard, and then runs into the corner of the ring and climbs the turnbuckle. He's tall above us, his back arched, his arms outstretched like wings. He looks like a youthful god in a fountain statue.

"Aren't you tired of living inside that box?" he asks us. "When you step into the ring, all of that—'Oh no, what will they think of me?'—needs to disappear. Because the moment the audience sniffs out that you don't buy into yourself—that you get your authority from somewhere other than your own instinct—it's over. Well . . . you're done for. Not over. In wrestling, over is a good thing. You need to get over with the crowd," he says.

"Over means they're buying into what you're selling. And what you're selling is always the same: the undefeatable story of *you*." He points at us when he says it. "The you who will never give up. The you who will fight tirelessly for what you know is right. The you who knows that you're the baddest bitch. That the belt belongs to you. *That* you? She gets her guidance from the inside." Angel punches his chest with his fist and screams. "Rah! You gotta find your North Star," he says.

Angel tells us to get into the corners, and Tova and Sofia double up on one. Lexie and Kayleigh take another. And Freya and I each take the opposite remaining corners.

Abigail Rose is in her element in the ring, bossing us around like she's a Hollywood director and we're replaceable talent. I'd be annoyed with her if she wasn't so good at it.

"NO!" she barks at me. She waves her hands in front of her face like she can't bear to see what she's seeing. I tried to climb up on the ropes and then lift both arms above my head like a champion. I kind of felt like I nailed it.

"You look like a ballerina in a music box," Abigail Rose says.

I lift my arms above my head again, and then I wink and blow a kiss the way Mabel does sometimes.

"That's it!" Abigail Rose cries out, waving her hand into a fist of triumph. "Hold that, right there," she says, and I do. Abigail Rose snaps a picture with her phone and waves me down. She holds the picture out for me to see.

There they are. The goddess arms Mabel pointed out the night everything changed.

In Abigail Rose's snapshot, my T-shirt is tight around my biceps, which ripple in anatomical beauty. I look strong, like someone you wouldn't want to F with. And my hair, scorching red, looks like it might burst into flames at any moment.

Angel teaches us how to run the ropes next, which is when you bounce off the rope, run across the ring, and bounce off the opposite rope. It hurts when the rope digs into my back.

We each take five runs, bouncing off the ropes ten times, five on each side.

When it's my turn, I run until the rope hits my hand, cross my step, and pivot. With my body stiff as a plank, I lean back into the rope and bounce. Both feet on the floor. Planted.

On the walk back to our cars, Freya gets a text from a friend.

"Wait, aren't you from New Jersey, Birdie?" she asks, pointing at her phone. "Is your sister . . . oh my God, how did I not put this together?" Freya stops in front of her SUV. "Your sister is George. The influencer."

I freeze. They're all looking at me.

"Birdie has nothing to do with George's brand," Lexie says, defensive, and I almost cry. "She probably wasn't even there."

"I was there," I say, and then I open my mouth to say, *for a few minutes.*

Tova beats me to it. "You were there? The Deep Lagoon was being trashed by a bunch of Brooklyn hipsters and you were there?"

They stare at me like I've betrayed them each personally. Even Abigail Rose.

And it hits me.

I was so mad at George that day, but I didn't call the cops, either. I saw what was going on, and I let the Deep Lagoon get trashed. For the same reason George did. Because I didn't want her to get in trouble.

I *am* a citiot heel.

But what if, like being a powerful girl, it's just who I am.

I might as well lean in and see if I'm the kind of person who's fun to hate.

Mom said sixty-seven percent of Americans feel that *power-ful* is a positive word when ascribed to men. *Ninety-two* percent of Americans feel that *powerful* is negative when ascribed to women. No wonder being raised as a girl and being strong is kind of a bitch.

All this time, I thought it was a choice. That I could shrink myself small enough somehow, and the world would let me be. But no one is going to give me permission to just be.

I have to take it.

"My sister is part of the problem, and maybe I am too," I say. "No, I *am* part of the problem, I'll admit that. I was there. I didn't report it. But I left, and a lot of other people didn't." I shake my head, looking at each of them. "How many times have you gone to a party in the woods and not stuck around to clean up the morning after?" I ask, and their body language shifts as a group. "George is part of the problem. I am part of the problem. We are all part of the problem. But blaming my sister for all of the upstate ills you can think of is scapegoating, and you can do it if you need to. If it makes you feel better about yourselves, like we're the bad people coming in and ruining everything that was perfect, then . . ." I take a deep breath and look at them, my rapt audience. "Then be *my* guest. You don't need to welcome us as yours. Be *my* guest. Treat me like crap. I can take it. I'm stuck here. I have to."

Abigail Rose starts to clap, and the others shoot her confused looks.

"Ladies, that was a masterclass in cutting a promo. You just witnessed raw talent," she says, and I laugh in relief.

I think I finally understand what she means.

CHAPTER 20

We're downstairs in the basement, painting detail on the Mouse-o-Mania rings, the Hell in a Cell cages, and the miniature championship belts.

"I've been thinking about what you said." I dip my paintbrush into the cobalt and run a smooth, thin line around the rim of a *SmackDown!* Women's Championship belt. "About how witches are the OG outsiders, and how well that could work with my Brooklyn gimmick. Maybe Mabel would let me borrow one of the less expensive talonsmans?"

"*Your* Brooklyn gimmick?" Abigail Rose says, excited. "So, it's a go? You'll play the citiot heel, here to ruin everything?"

"I'm thinking about it," I say.

"That rant about your sister was on brand." Abigail Rose holds up the cage she's painting to check her lines in the light. "Silas said the guys haven't stopped talking about how *you're the last person on the planet they'd let hold their belt*, and how *you'd probably do to Mayhem what your sister did to the Deep Lagoon*."

"What's that?"

"You know," Abigail Rose says, like it should be obvious, "ruin it."

"All right, everyone," Abigail Rose says, opening the trampoline net and waving us through. "The first part of our lesson today is on your gimmick. Then I'm going to teach you everything I know about selling it to the back row."

We sit in a ring around Kayleigh's trampoline.

"The Undertaker. Charlotte Flair. The Miz. Asuka. Hangman Adam Page, the Anxious Millennial Cowboy himself." Abigail Rose rattles off the names. "These are just words, but to wrestling fans, they call to mind archetypal characters, larger than mere people. We know them by what they wear, by the catchphrases they say, and by their iconic moves, including their finishers."

"A gimmick is like," Kayleigh says to the newbies, "creating a superhero character for yourself to play."

"Or a supervillain," Abigail Rose says.

"Why are you looking at me?" Tova asks, and Abigail Rose shrugs.

"I see something in you." She means it as a compliment, and Tova takes it as one. "So you've got your good guys—your faces—and your bad guys—your heels—and then there are some classic types of gimmicks. Like the Out of Touch Rich One, the Corporate Yes Guy, the Cult Leader, the Hottie, the Wack-a-doo, the Narcissist. Oh, the Monster. The Hometown Hero. The Evil Outsider."

"That's *so* xenophobic," Freya says.

"Agreed," I say.

"You can base a gimmick on pop culture. One of my cousins does a take on Kurt Cobain from Nirvana."

"So, a gimmick is like a stereotype?" Sofia asks.

"Sometimes," Abigail Rose says. "That's why a lot of gimmicks throughout history have been offensive. A gimmick needs to be so specific and true that it's relatable. Like a part of you, magnified until you're like a character out of a comic book. Or so supernatural and abstract that it transports us. And you have to have that something else. That . . . je ne sais quoi . . ."

"Oh, I have that," I say, and her eyes spark. "It's right here." I twist, like I'm looking for something behind me, and then I spin back around with both middle fingers in the air.

Everyone laughs, which makes the trampoline bounce gently under us.

"All right, tough guy," Abigail Rose says through her smile, "why don't you tell them what your gimmick is going to be?"

"You mean Brooklyn?"

"Who else?"

I shake my head. "OK, so Abigail Rose got this idea that my name is Brooklyn." I look around at the group, waiting for more. "I'm a citiot who's here to ruin absolutely everything."

The group *explodes* with laughter. They laugh so hard, some of them fall over and start to roll. Kayleigh is facedown, pounding the trampoline with her fist as she laughs.

"That's brilliant," Tova says, clapping.

"Perfect, really," Freya says, but her tone is different. Biting.

"Why?" I ask, even though I know exactly what she's implying.

"Because your sister is literally ruining our town." The other girls don't back her up. But they don't call her off, either.

The air between us pops with static.

"I was going to save this idea for later," Abigail Rose says, steering the conversation. "But what do you all say about recording a music video with a dance to our 'Welcome to Mayhem' theme song as a promo for the rumble?"

Every other person on the trampoline looks excited about the idea. Of course, they do. They're a bunch of cheerleaders.

"Like the 'Land of a Thousand Dances' video I sent you in the group text," Abigail Rose says.

"That was *hilarious*," Kayleigh says. "I'm so in."

A *dance* promo. If I wanted to do a freaking dance promo, I'd have crawled back to Mo and would currently be a cheerleader.

I'm here because I want to be a *wrestler*. Not shake my ass in some sexist spectacle to attract attention. Not that the "Land of a Thousand Dances" video was anything like that at all. But these are *cheerleaders*. If they get their hands on the dance, it won't be silly and fun. It will be super serious and sexy. And I can't pull that shit off.

But I don't say that.

I don't say anything at all.

"Now I get to show you guys how to sell your pain to the last row when your opponent is putting the hurt on you," Abigail Rose says, changing the subject. "I want you to think about the best lie you ever told. The most convincing thing you've ever said that wasn't true. And I want you to think: How did I get to a place where I was so convincing, even I almost believed me?

"Making your gimmick and your pain both feel real . . . it comes from learning how to feel like the role you're playing. Not thinking. You don't want to be thinking, 'What would my character do?' If you're not feeling it, the crowd won't, either. If you want to make *them* feel, you have to let yourself feel it. Feel your power. Feel your pain. Feel it all.

"Now let's pretend to hurt each other and try to get the neighbors to call the cops because they think something's wrong," Abigail Rose says, bouncing to her feet.

"You could skin a man alive down here and no one would hear him scream," Kayleigh says. "What? I didn't say I've done it."

"But you didn't say you *didn't*," Sofia says.

"Enough chitchat," Abigail Rose says. "I want to see you destroy each other!" Then she grabs my arm and Freya's and shoves us together.

"I'm sorry," I say. "And if it helps any, my sister is, too."

Freya takes a fighting stance.

"I forgive you," she says. "I'll forgive *her* when the Deep Lagoon reopens."

We lock up, our hands on each other's shoulders.

"I want to hear you scream!" Abigail Rose cries out, and we all shout at the top of our lungs into the open sky.

"Ahhhhhhhh!!!"

We scream like someone is pulling our hair. Or yanking our arms behind our backs. We scream like no one ever asked us to before, and we've been waiting for this our entire lives.

We scream until she asks us to keep screaming, to let the birds hear our pain.

We scream until we start laughing. Our insides soft and shaking. Our heads dizzy with the vibration of it.

We scream.

CHAPTER 21

By the time our Friday session with Angel arrives, I'm excited to get back in the ring. My muscles are sore from a week of morning training on the climbing course, and my brain is zapped from working overtime on Mouse-o-Mania prep.

I still haven't found the right moment to tell Mom and Dad before Helen does.

"The good thing about a rumble is that there isn't too much pressure on any individual wrestler," Angel explains. "There's a lot going on in the ring at once, and instead of getting your opponent to submit on the floor for a three-count, you're all trying to fling each other over the ropes and out of the ring. By the match, you should have solid, basic skills under your belt."

We're running the ropes, our feet pounding across the mat, the ropes tugging on the frame of the ring and then snapping back, like a steady, hypnotic drum cadence. The warehouse echoes the sounds so they're bigger. Louder. The smell of the mats, the metal ring and our sweat in the air is familiar now.

"Soft into the pivot," Angel calls out to Sofia as she shoots herself into the rope too hard, winces, and bounces to the mat.

When it's my turn again, I fall into the rhythm like a familiar routine. I step forward, reach and grab the rope, pivot with my elbow over the rope, body straight as a plank so I don't get whiplash, bounce against the rope—sore and aching at the bruise line—and take off again . . .

There's a grace to it, because if you run full throttle into the rope like Sofia just did, well . . . that's where the darkest bruises come from. I took a few of those last week.

We follow the ropes with our rolls, and I feel like the spinning blade of a deli slicer.

"The most dangerous thing about taking bumps is the risk of whiplash. If I wanted to give you whiplash, I'd grab you by your shoulders and shake your neck until your head fell off."

Angel's eyes burn into ours as he swivels his head around the ring to make sure we get how serious this is. We're all seated on the mat, taking a breather from the warm-up, and I recognize the speech from when I took my first bumps here last week.

"Bumps epitomize a wrestling fundamental. That it looks like you're fighting, but you're working together. When someone shoulder tackles you, they're not knocking you down. You're tripping yourself intentionally. You're throwing yourself to the ground, not taking a hit. You're always working *with* someone. There's no such thing as a solo wrestler," Angel says.

It's like that zen koan: the sound of one hand clapping.

"It's time to learn how to throw yourselves," Angel says, but I'm a gymnast. We *throw* ourselves all the time. We throw moves and routines. That's *our* verb. "A bump requires your total surrender and commitment. Part of your brain will want to protect you, but the best way to protect yourself is to do it correctly. Go hard."

"I know you've all got bruises under your blades from running the ropes," Angel says. "I saw you wincing. Hitting the ropes is the force of a car crash at twenty miles an hour. Hitting the mat is more like a thirty-five-mile-an-hour crash. But it doesn't need to give you whiplash if you do it correctly."

The first time I did it, it felt kind of like when you get off a roller coaster and your brain's a little . . . loose.

"I'm more likely to get whiplash or sprain my neck in a basket toss than I am pretending to fall on a flat surface," Tova says, unfazed, and I get it. Cheerleading and gymnastics are high-impact sports, like snowboarding and skiing, or even boxing or football. These things that seem so dangerous in the ring are the same risks we're used to taking in supposedly daintier sports. The pain isn't new—just concentrated in new places.

The bruises and scratches they wear year-round for their sport make them as fierce as any athletes I've ever known. They're adrenaline junkies, just like me.

Angel shows us how to stand and when to tuck our chins to our chests as we throw ourselves onto our backs on the mat. He shows us how to kick our legs up into the air so we land exactly where we were standing, instead of arcing ourselves back.

"Exhale as you hit the mat," he says. Then he throws himself back, his legs popping out and up into the air at the same time. He tucks his chin and lands, arms out and palms smacking flat against the mat.

"Upper back and shoulders," he says, popping back up to standing. "Not lower back, not middle back. Land where you're standing. Where your feet are. If you don't land where you're standing, if you go back, you can give yourself whiplash. Slap the mat as hard as you can with your palms down flat. And this cannot be emphasized enough: Glue your chin to your chest."

Angel stands facing the other direction, and then throws himself into the back bump.

"Wrestling requires confidence. Indecision gets people hurt."

Angel squares up again to make sure we get it. Then he crosses his arms in front as he bends his knees gently, and then he whips both arms out wide, throwing himself again to the floor with a slap.

"Any questions?" he asks, looking through his raised feet.

"Does it hurt?" Sofia asks.

"Every time, a bit," Angel says. "That's why you want to make your body as broad and flat as possible. It hurts a little bit everywhere instead of a lot in one place."

The girls ahead of me take their turns, but no one slaps that mat harder than Kayleigh. With each turn, she hits the mat like a thunderous clap.

When it's my turn to take a back bump, I replay Angel's instructions in my head like I'm studying a sequence from Coach. Each movement, each adjustment, as important as the next.

I take my stance and play it out in my mind, swinging my arms. Then I cross them in front of me, bend my knees, and I imagine the ground being pulled from under my feet like a rug. I swing my legs up and throw my back down, as broad as I possibly can hold it, tucking my chin to my chest and gluing it there. When I meet the ground, I exhale as my back hits and my palms slam flat into the mat with a satisfying smack.

The pain, though not sharp, is real. An impact, not a warning. I stand up.

"I feel a little . . . fuzzy," I say, touching my head.

"A little fuzz is OK. Dizzy, less OK."

Facing the other side, I focus. I reset. I run through the sequence in my mind. And then I smack the ground like I was thrown to it. Feet up, broad shoulders, palms flat. Smack.

When we've each gotten a few turns to try the back bump, Angel shows us the front face bump and the front flip bump, which both look super fun.

"Normally we'd take a while to get to the flip bump," he says, "but you already know how to flip. So, next week, bring your knee pads." Angel reaches out to Tova and puts her in a head-lock, pretending to pummel her back as she struggles to get free. "We're going to start practicing chops, blows, and blocks the week after that."

Tova throws a punch toward his stomach and stops before hitting him.

"And we're working on finishers, promos, and selling pain for our remaining Wednesday practices." Abigail Rose looks up from her notebook. "I heard from J Flav and Giorgio that they'll have your theme songs done in time for the rumble. And our Future of Mayhem theme for the music video before that."

"I've always felt worthy of a theme song," Freya says.

"Next announcement," Angel says. "Next weekend. All of us. Hanging out." He pauses for dramatic tension. "You decide where and text me the details."

"Thunder Bowl?" Lexie says, and we all groan.

"What about the new rage room?" Tova says, the closest I've ever seen her to having a twinkle in her eye.

"That's my favorite kind of room," Abigail Rose says.

As Angel grabs his bag and heads for the door, he shouts, "Text me the invite!"

"And we *have* to have a sleepover! At my house," Freya says.

As Angel runs out the door, he almost crashes into Cami. She's got the gym booked for rehearsal with Drita, Jimena, and Petra for their final showdown the Friday before Mayhem's rumble. But she's managed to get here early to show us how she organizes her storylines.

"Who's ready for some conflict?" Cami asks us, rolling a white board out from the corner. "Every wrestling event I organize starts with a conflict web." Cami draws ten circles and we gather around. "Each circle is a character—one of us— and the more complex our web, the stronger our storylines. It's like every English teacher you've ever had told you: Stories are conflict, and every wrestler needs at least one strong conflict in the storyline. Usually, I start the show with whoever is going to win the main event in some smaller battle." Abigail Rose smiles at me from across the ring. "Something to give the audience a reason to believe, in the moment when it seems like failure is certain, that our hero can defeat the opposition.

"The rumble," she says, making two columns on the side of the character web, "is to determine the Future of Mayhem champion from the pool of contenders." She pauses for dramatic effect. "That's all of you, plus the Queen City Crew—me, Drita, and Jimena. Rounding out the group is Xiuying Liu." Cami writes Xiuying at the top of the list.

I look at Abigail Rose, like maybe she already knew this. But she looks awestruck.

"The mixed martial artist?" Kayleigh says. "She's from here, right? My brother showed me a video of her knocking out some guy. She's amazing."

Cami smiles like she can hardly believe it herself. "Things

have been complicated in MMA, getting opponents, but she's into the idea of professional wrestling as a side hustle. I told her about the scouts looking at Silas," Cami says, "and gotta say. The clincher was when I shared your blog with her."

"Xiuying Liu read my blog?" Abigail Rose says.

"Called it fun and important," Cami says.

"Don't mind me. Just dying happy over here," Abigail Rose says, fanning herself with her notebook. "Xiuying Liu is going to wrestle for Mayhem." Abigail Rose slaps Cami's leg with her palm. "You're my hero."

Cami winces. "The only thing is, and I know this isn't how we talked about it going," she says, looking at me and then back at the whiteboard. "I promised her the championship."

Even though the outcome is fixed and I shouldn't care, it lands like a punch to the gut.

"It's the reason she agreed. Look, I probably should've run this by you, but the opportunity presented itself. I know how badly you wanted her on the roster. This is what it takes to make that happen."

Abigail Rose looks at me like she knows this wasn't the plan, but also like she can barely believe our luck.

"It's OK with you, right, Birdie?" she asks.

My dad used to call me Cutthroat McCoy. When I quit gymnastics, he was more upset than I was. He tried to convince me that it didn't matter if I could never be the best. He said, *You look happy when you do it, you look proud*, like he thought all that time and energy, all that sacrifice, was worthwhile.

I didn't get it then. But looking around the ring—being here with Cami, with Abigail Rose, Lexie, and all these athletes— I'm happy to be here. I'm proud.

It doesn't matter who wins the rumble. What matters is that we help wrestle control of Mayhem to give it the future Mabel's legacy deserves.

"Of course," I say, and when everyone cheers, I don't even have to fake my smile.

Abigail Rose spends the entire drive back north on her phone, coordinating final details with J Flav and Giorgio, the Queen City Crew's music producers.

When we get back to the apartment, there's a note from Mabel. She's working overtime for Mouse-o-Mania, but there's a veggie pot pie in the slow cooker. In the living room, we watch a cartoon called *Camp WWE* that features the superstars as little kids.

"Are you mad that you're not going to win the rumble?" she asks me.

"I wouldn't say mad," I say. "It's disappointing."

"Disappointment makes me angry as hell," Abigail Rose says.

"I'm not angry," I say again. "I think it's awesome. But I'm having second thoughts about this whole Brooklyn citiot heel thing."

"They all loved the idea." Abigail Rose shrugs.

"Why, though?"

"Because it's funny."

"Do you think of me as a citiot?"

"Not really," Abigail Rose says, like she can't bring herself to say no. "I think of you more as a newcomer."

"A newcomer citiot?" I ask. "What if Freya's right? What if everyone really hates me?"

"Then you'll have done your job?" Abigail Rose says. "I mean, *everyone* hating you is probably an unrealistic standard to set for yourself. If sixty percent of the audience hates you, even, you should be very proud."

Losing the title to Xiuying—a real fighter who could break my face with her bare hands—before I ever even hold it above my head *is* a disappointment. No doubt.

But having everyone in town think I'm a believable citiot villain?

Being someone who, it turns out, people really do love to hate?

That sucks. I still care way too much about what people think to pull that off.

"I don't know if I'm ready to heel that hard."

"Consider for a moment that it's OK if you don't want to fit in and be a local." The way she says it, it doesn't sound quite as horrible. "What's the point of life if you don't let yourself live it?" She taps her head.

She has a point.

But then, an image of a Harvard admissions counselor googling my name and finding videos of a crazed wrestling heel bashing her opponents in an indie circuit barn ring flashes through my mind, and I realize, Lexie was right before. This is next-level weird.

Maybe I *should* rethink this whole thing altogether.

"Do you think I think I'm better than everyone, though?" I'm ready for the answer.

"Do you?" Abigail Rose asks.

You've got to beat the best to be the best. That's what I was thinking the day I got myself cut from Mo's cheerleading squad. I was thinking I could show her that I was better than everyone else there. Because that's what I thought I needed to do to belong. To earn my place.

Mom's right. That does sound like some elitist BS.

We eat the pot pie when it's ready and then bring a plate down to Mabel.

She's hunched over her table in the basement, and under her bright work lamps, her hands move methodically.

"That smells good," Mabel says, without looking up.

"It is," Abigail Rose says. "But I'm not sure if you remember how food works?" She pauses until Mabel looks at her. "You have to take a break from work to actually eat it, in order for it to sustain you." Then she adds, "Mabel turns into a workaholic this time every year."

"Will you take a look at this and tell me if anything's missing?" Mabel asks.

She holds out a mouse Asuka, in her patchwork Technicolor robe, green slime tears dripping from her eyes.

"You should give her a mask to hold in her hand," I say, because Asuka always wears a mask when she enters, though she takes it off when she fights.

"That's right!" Mabel says. "I'll tell ya, this new Asuka does justice to her namesake."

"You met Lioness Asuka once, didn't you, Mabel?" Abigail Rose asks her.

Mabel nods with a look of solemn respect.

"One of the best wrestlers of all time. Nothing like her since."

"Were you a heel, Mabel?" I ask.

"Honey, do you think this"—Mabel waves her hand around her face—"was the babyface of any company?"

"You would be in mine," Abigail Rose says.

"How'd you deal with it?" I ask. "People booing you?"

"It was my job to make them boo," Mabel says, "and I was damn good at it." She shakes her head and laughs. "I made little kids cry, and I loved every second of it. How many women in the history of the world got permission to just be outright awful? I got to let my ugly out, and it led to a pretty spectacular life."

"Let my ugly out, I like that . . ." Abigail Rose jots it down in her notebook. "Anyone who ever did anything worthwhile," she says, "has received their share of boos." An image of George, filtering her own hate mail in the comments, flashes in my mind.

"Probably more than their share," Mabel says. "Might as well develop a callus to it."

Abigail Rose heads upstairs to unwind before bed, and I'm about to take off when Mabel says she'll see me tomorrow and then gasps.

"I completely forgot! I looked at your hour sheet, and as of yesterday, your debt's paid."

For some reason, it's a punch to the gut—my second today—and my first instinct is to hunch over, lie down, and cry. Clearly, it shows on my face.

"Don't look so happy about the good news," Mabel says. "Aw, come on. Don't cry."

Being here became my new normal. I kind of stopped thinking about that ever coming to an end. Still, that doesn't explain the deep ache in my lungs. The way my chest feels like it's going to cave in. Like, if I were to give in to it, I might start sobbing and never stop.

I see it there inside, waiting. A shadow over my heart. Asking me to feel it, so it can be let free. *Recycled. Redistributed. Rearranged.*

"I'll tell you, though," Mabel says, putting her arm around me. I sink into her embrace and take a deep breath. She smells like cigarette smoke and the basement, but somehow, the musk is almost sweet. "I could use help through Mouse-o-Mania. How'd you like to make some actual money?"

I smile and Mabel kisses my forehead, and it makes me miss Grandma so badly.

I thought it was my grandparents who made this place special. The way they told me about it always made it feel so much more alive than where we lived. They're not here anymore, but somehow, I feel that pulse, the heartbeat they taught me to hear—the one Grandma always writes about in her poems—that calls me home, deeper inside myself.

"Could you donate what you'd pay me to Noah's Park instead?"

Mabel's friend Babs runs a wildlife rescue facility called Noah's Park, named after her first-ever rescue over twenty years ago: a groundhog named Noah. Ten percent of every sale at Mostly Bones goes to Noah's Park, except for Mouse-o-Mania, when half of every sale goes to the Johns Hopkins Center for Alternatives to Animal Testing.

Mabel musses my hair the way she does to her grandkids.

"I'm glad you found us, kid," Mabel says. "Anam cara, you two."

"What?" I ask, thinking it must be wrestling lingo I don't know yet.

"Anam cara." Mabel says it again, slowly. "It's Gaelic for soul friend. Your anam cara frees the wild possibilities within you. They're a mirror to reflect your soul."

On the way out the door, I see myself, reflected in the glass panes.

One month ago, I was on the other side of this glass, pressing my face against the window and staring right back at those bones.

I looked and felt completely different before I met a mirror to reflect my soul and she asked me, like she actually wanted to know, *Who do you want to be?*

CHAPTER 22

Rage-o-Rama is in a strip mall, between the Hobby Shop and Dollar Dave's. The windows advertise things you can smash: electronics, furniture, and housewares. A 3D printed bust of Donald Trump.

We gather around Angel like a team in huddle.

"Before we go in, who has ever done a primal scream?" No one has. "You haven't lived." Angel looks at us and lifts both eyebrows. "Ready?"

Then he tilts his chin to the sky and starts to scream. A bloodcurdling, loud-as-he-can-manage, full-throttle wail. He waves his hands for us to join in, and soon we're standing in the parking lot in front of Rage-o-Rama, screaming at the top of our lungs. A balding guy who might be Dollar Dave squints through the glass, concerned, then shakes his head and turns away.

Angel conducts us like a symphony, and with the wave of his hands, we're silent again.

"Inside this room you're going to unleash the person you

would be if there was no such thing as civility. All your life you've been told, be careful. Don't break that. But today? Today you break. Today you destroy." His smile is sharp, like a weapon. "Today I want you to unleash a lifetime of anger. I want you to destroy what you've given up to survive in this world. The parts of yourself you abandoned or shamed, so you can hide in the open without being disturbed. I want you to smash whatever's lurking in your shadow, holding you back."

"My shadow?" Freya asks.

"Your shadow is like . . ." Angel pauses.

"The parts of your browsing history that remind you to delete it so no one knows the questions you're too embarrassed to ask in public," Cami says.

We laugh, nervously, at that.

"Your shadow is the anger you tell yourself you shouldn't feel. The thoughts you think you shouldn't have. The moments that make you wonder if there's something wrong with you. Spoiler alert: There's something wrong with all of us. Humans are a mess."

"I've tried this before," Tova says. "I can't embrace the cringe or whatever."

"Oh no," Angel says, starting toward the building. "Embracing the cringe alone won't set you free. You've got to embrace the *universality* of cringe. The web of life strung together by our boundless awkward."

Tova laughs at that, and her face—almost always sharp, cynical—softens.

"Let's go smash everything that makes us feel like we have to pretend we aren't the awkward messes we know we are," Angel says. "Let's go smash everything that stands between us and our greatness."

"In character," Abigail Rose reminds us. She made the reservation under our ring names.

Someone named Eve checks us in and takes us to our Den of Destruction. We've got a group reservation, which comes with 1) a lot of stuff to break, 2) a baseball bat and a crowbar to break things with, and 3) leather jackets, helmets, and gloves so we don't also get broken.

"Which one of you is the Spiralizer?" Eve asks, after doing a double take at the list.

"Ooh, me first?" Angel asks. He spins so fast he cuts his opponents into ribbons.

"Crowbar or bat?" Eve asks him, and he reaches out with both hands.

"I'm going to need both."

I film through the glass as Angel tosses ceramic plates up and smashes them midair with the crowbar. Abigail Rose asked me to film a bunch today for B-roll footage for the music video, and Freya, Sofia, and Tova even gave me their consent to be filmed.

Angel cranks into an old printer with the baseball bat. He tucks the crowbar inside a vase and smashes it against the wall. Then he stops, and I can see he's breathing hard.

He picks up the printer and starts to scream like he did in the parking lot. He spins around, holding the printer above his head, screaming, and then he faces us, shaking the printer like a deranged John Cusack in *Say Anything*.

Then Angel spins and hurls the printer at the back wall, shattering it into an uncountable mess of pieces.

He comes back outside, pulls off the helmet, and looks positively radiant.

Cami takes the leather jacket and helmet from the bench.

"How can anyone follow that performance?" she says. "Watch me."

Cami's leaving for Columbia at the end of the month, but she's taking Wrestling Royalty with her. It's like Abigail Rose said: *Everyone I've ever been is my real self.*

Cami goes for a rack of test tubes and a box of beakers, lining them up like toy soldiers. Then she smashes them, one at a time, into pieces, like the exploding seeds of jewelweed.

Grandma's favorite wildflower was yellow jewelweed, also known as touch-me-nots. They grow this time of year, at the edge of the wetlands. Soft yellow flowers with orange flecks dotting their mouths like freckles. When a ripe seed capsule is touched, it explodes, projecting the seed up to four feet away.

Sometimes I think of those seeds—like when people grab my arms the way Darren did—and wish that I could also explode when touched.

Cami comes back out after smashing a broken media rack into a pile of sticks, and I put on the protective gear. Everything looks different through the motorcycle helmet.

"I feel like a villain from the future," I say, picking up the crowbar.

"Well, if it isn't Brooklyn, heinous heel from the Future of Mayhem," Lexie says.

I hold the crowbar out menacingly. "Watch it, Local Lexie. Or I just might buy up your precious bowling alley, knock it down, and turn it into a glamping property."

"Hear ye, hear ye!" the Notorious TCB, Tova Chaya Bernstein's homage to Justice Ginsberg—also TCB for Taking Care of Business—calls out, rapping her gavel against the bench. "You're going to need a permit for that!"

I open the door to the Den of Destruction and spin around

to say, "What are you going to do? Fine me?" And they all boo as I step into the room to wreck everything in sight.

Alone in the den, the helmet smells like Lysol, which feels ironic. I look at the wall in front of me, at the mountain of detritus before it, and wonder how many other people have stood where I'm standing, carrying something they don't know how to let go.

I see the pile of glass Cami smashed—her jewelweed seeds—and Angel's printer on top of the pile. My friends brought their pain into here, and when they came back out, they looked cleansed.

There are boxes of things waiting to be smashed lined against the back wall, and I find a stack of old VHS tapes that look like they'll make a satisfying crunch. I put one down on the cement floor and stare at it. I imagine I can pour into it everything I want to release.

Not loving my body.

Trying to keep my muscles lean.

Wanting to be smaller.

Feeling frozen.

Wanting to fit in. Wanting to feel normal.

Caring about what other people think.

Overthinking. Overthinking.

There is something wrong with me.

I take a deep breath and lift the crowbar above my head and then rain down with all of my force on the VHS, cracking the case open. I turn around and Angel's face is pressed against the glass, Lexie next to him. He motions to his bicep, his eyes wide and impressed.

I hook the tape with the crowbar and swing it around, the black tape spilling out like intestines. And then I fling it at the wall in front of me, busting the case.

I don't know what it is—maybe the sound of the plastic case cracking, or the feeling of launching something at a wall and being responsible for its destruction—but I start to laugh.

I find a small, old TV with a crack in its face.

When I break into the TV with the steel bar, I picture Darren's grubby hands and all the others that have grabbed my arms through the years. I crank into it again, shattering the surface into tiny fragments. I picture myself training, gaining muscle, and still trying to lose weight. Coach the time he didn't believe me when I said my muscle felt like it was pulled. Smash. Coach telling me to stay smaller, until finally he just said I was too big. I rip into the last piece of glass clinging to the frame. I picture Frankie and everything he said about me. About Abigail Rose. About Angel.

I picture Mom at her computer and those stupid fucking statistics that show why women don't earn as much as men. Because people don't like powerful women.

I smash that TV like it's possible to smash it all. Not just the patriarchy. The binary that upholds it, too. The idea that anyone's brain or behavior is somehow determined by their sex. That there is a *male* or *female* way to do anything. That who we are—the dominant and the dominated—is imprinted on our birth certificate along with the box checked for sex.

But as I'm launching the husk of the small TV at the wall, as I watch it crash upon impact and explode like a touch-me-not seed, the sound much louder than I imagined it would be: I finally see it.

I bend over, catching my breath as I pull off the helmet, hair sticking to my face.

I see myself. Through all that rage, all that confusion.

Not in a reflection in the glass, but with clarity, in my mind.

My *selves*.

I see all of them, together.

Every version of myself that has ever been.

And they're so, so tired of playing small.

George rolls up to Freya's pool house with her huge-ass suitcase in tow, while we're watching the Gorgeous Ladies of Wrestling documentary and eating the lifetime supply of pizza her parents ordered for us.

"Did someone order lewks to serve up with that pizza?" George asks, opening the case of design tools. She's got a section for hair, a section for makeup, and a section of the case that's filled with notes on our gimmicks and that behemoth color theory book. George is *prepared*. "Who's up first?"

When I explained a gimmick to George—*it's like a part of yourself, amplified, or an archetype you tap into*—she immediately said, *It's like a lewk.*

Freya springs up. She swore she wouldn't forgive George until the Deep Lagoon reopened, but the power of a makeover from George of the Wild—even if she did get your local swimming hole shut down—should not be underestimated. George. Is. That. Good.

"This makes up for the Deep Lagoon partway," Freya says.

George looks at the group, remorse clouding her face, despite her glowing skin.

"I posted an open letter to my followers, telling them what happened, and someone started a change.org petition and the hashtag #savethedeeplagoon," she says.

"That'll fix it," Tova says.

"Who's in charge of the Deep Lagoon?" I ask.

"The town?" Sofia says. "My mom said the town was going to try to issue permits, but then they'd need to put a lifeguard there. And they could be sued."

"A lifeguard, permits, and lawsuits for the Deep Lagoon?" Lexie shakes her head. "Hello citiots, goodbye summer freedom."

"This is my fault," George says. "There's got to be something I can do."

"What if you used your powers for good instead of evil," I say.

"I'm not *evil*," George says.

"Verdict's out on that one." Freya crosses her arms in front of her chest.

"I mean it, though," I say. "What if you created a guerrilla ad campaign to put an end to all these upstate places getting swamped with more tourists than the ecosystem can handle? Like . . ." I pause, thinking. "Couldn't you make it uncool for everyone to go around trashing the planet like oblivious, materialistic selfie-seeking automatons?"

George nods along, like there's something to that. If she can come up with a way to use aura photography and color theory to style someone's essence, she can figure *this* out.

Abigail Rose cracks a smile.

"You know what else could raise a lot of money? If you let locals pay to say that kind of stuff to your face," she says, looking at George. "Tell Off a Citiot for a donation to the Deep Lagoon."

"Mm-hmm," Tova says. "That's like a whole upstate NY meme account *mood*."

"Like a reverse kissing booth," Lexie says.

"A *dissing* booth," George says, covering her mouth like she can't believe it.

We all burst out laughing. It's too perfect.

"Come diss the most hated girl in the most famous small town in the world," Abigail Rose says, like a carnival barker. "Maybe we could get an upstate meme account to spread the word."

While George styles us, we watch the Gorgeous Ladies of Wrestling documentary—the real wrestlers the Netflix show is based on—and come up with more ways to help the Deep Lagoon, including a clean-up day, to be the first of many.

"What about if we made the rumble a fundraiser for the Deep Lagoon, too?" I ask.

"I'll make sure you sell out if you do," George says with conviction, and Abigail Rose beams.

"Deal," she says, sticking her hand out. They shake on it.

"I'll ask Zeke's band to play, if you want," Lexie says. "They've got a big following."

"You guys, you're missing the best parts!" Tova calls us over to the TV. "This lady, Queen Kong—" She points at the screen where a woman who reminds me of Mabel is being interviewed about the time she wanted to wrestle a man, but the gaming commission forbade it.

"I couldn't wrestle a man," Queen Kong says, "but they let me wrestle a bear. And I lasted longer than a lot of the men against that bear."

We look at each other like, *this can't be real life*. But it's a documentary. It is.

"That's how fucking stupid the gender binary is." I say it before I can overthink it, and I stop breathing for a moment. I can't believe I actually said that out loud.

Tova's the first one to start laughing, hard, and then Abigail Rose, and then *everyone* is laughing at my joke about the stupid binary. Not laughing at me because I'm stupid, or because my joke didn't make sense. Laughing because they *get* it.

"Oh my God, it's here!" Abigail Rose holds up her phone. "Our theme song! Holy crap!" She takes a deep breath to steady herself amid the excitement. "So, I got the idea from this thing Mable said the other night to me and Birdie, about how when she was a wrestler, she got to let her ugly out. And I wrote this poem thing and sent it to J Flav and Giorgio and they've sent a few versions, and . . ." Abigail Rose beams, proud.

"Will you play it already?" Kayleigh shouts. "I can't even!"

She presses play.

The song starts with a deep, rumbling bass, and then there's a metal guitar that doesn't feel out of place in the Mayhem world.

"I'm digging up the demons in my front yard." The vocal is fuzzy, a little distorted, like maybe the voice of a ghost itself. "Open up the closets, let the skeletons walk. I lift up all the windows so I can let the ghosts float. I'm tired of hiding inside of my siding." When she launches into the chorus, she's almost screaming. "I let my ugly out. I let my ug-ly ou-ou-out. Ain't got no time to feel haunted, got some flaws to be flaunted, I let my ugly out."

I look at Abigail Rose, and then around at the group, while we listen to our *theme song*. When it's over, Sofia says, "Is it just me or is that amazing?"

"We are going to crush this music video," Lexie says.

They start to dissect how to choreograph the dance for the music video, and I zone out, remembering what a loser I felt like at the tryout when I couldn't keep up with the dance. They don't need me bringing down their perfect cheerleader dance vibe.

Is it too much to ask to have been born at a time when everyone *wasn't* making TikTok dance videos and watching *Dancing with the Stars*?

"What do you think, Birdie?" Kayleigh asks, but I have no idea what they're talking about.

"I'm probably not," I say, "I mean . . ." I take a breath. "Can I just not do the whole dance thing?"

They all look at me like I'm nuts.

"You love dancing," George says, and I fix her with a stare. I love dancing *with George, like a fool, when no one is watching.*

"You're perfect for this," Lexie says. "You can get out of your head and into your body. We were just saying—"

"I mean it," I say. *You can get out of your head and into your body.* Can I? Then why does that sound so hard? "I don't want to."

"She doesn't want to, you guys," Kayleigh says. "Drop it."

"We're still going to make Frankie think I'm possessed by the bones? That I've hexed him?" I ask, changing the subject.

"You saw him tweak when you snipped that lock of his hair in the fight." Everyone looks at me, impressed and a little afraid. But she's right. He looked confused, and then he looked terrified. "We're going to use that one seemingly insignificant moment of paranoia, and amplify it. We're going to make him think you've been plotting this all along," Abigail Rose says, nodding. "We want him to fear you."

"How else could we mess with him, though?" I ask.

We want to show him what he's up against. The Future of Mayhem is here, whether Frankie the Chaos Kid wants us to be or not.

"We could get Silas to defect ahead of schedule," I say, but Abigail Rose shakes her head because she's tried. "Or get Mabel to . . ." I trail off, because even I know Mabel's not interfering in anything. She owns the Barn, but she's been clear she's not involved. If the cousins can't find a way to coexist, Mabel's just as happy to sell it out from under them.

"What are people afraid witches will do?" Kayleigh asks.

"Steal their kids," Lexie says, laughing, and Abigail Rose blurts, "Shithead!"

We all turn to her, confused. But then I remember. Frankie's python.

"His snake. Shithead!" She smiles a devious smile. "He's on a fishing trip with the guys. Let's steal Shithead."

"If you want to mess with his head," George says, "you could also make a social media account and start sending him DMs from some witchy name."

"You should make it W.I.T.C.H." Tova shows us what she means on her phone. It stands for the Women's International Terrorist Conspiracy from Hell, an arm of the women's liberation movement in the 1960s devoted to overthrowing the patriarchy. "My great-aunt was a member," she says.

Abigail Rose looks at me, nodding.

"The W.I.T.C.H. of Mayhem," she says, tapping away with her thumbs on her phone. "Frankie's going to rue the day he messed with the Future."

"Things are about to get ugly," Kayleigh says, pounding her fist into her open hand. Then she smiles. "See what I did there? That's our thing. Getting ugly."

"Play it again," Tova says, nudging Abigail Rose.

We listen to our theme song at least ten times, until we're singing along to every word.

For the rest of the night, we get styled with lewks by George, eat a five-pound bag of Swedish Fish to "soak up the pizza," and watch most of the first season of *GLOW* after we finish the documentary.

At one point, Kayleigh turns to face me.

"I'm serious about the rumble," she says, and I say I know. "I slowed down on the weight lifting with my brothers when my mom kept saying that it was making my arms get too bulky. But I love wrestling. I really want to do this. Can you help me get stronger?"

The way she says it, my heart melts. I reach out and hug her.

"I train every morning at seven," I say, and suddenly, we have a standing plan.

Outside, the dark turns gray, and then blue, as the birds wake up and start to sing.

The sun comes up through the trees past the pool, its warm orange rays reaching through the windows and lulling us all, finally, to sleep.

CHAPTER 23

Kayleigh and I are dripping with sweat from our first morning workout on Dad's course.

Looks like a redneck jungle gym, she said when she saw it, and Kayleigh would know. Her family doesn't even have internet.

"Mark my words, captain," she says, opening the door to her mom's station wagon. "I'm going to put on five pounds of muscle before the rumble."

When I head back inside, Dad is at the kitchen counter, reading the local paper, and finally it feels like the right moment to come clean about the waiver and wrestling in general.

"Did you know your sister was involved with the problem at the Deep Lagoon?" he asks me, and I don't know what to say. I shrug. "You don't know if you knew?"

"Does it say that in the paper?" I ask, and he closes it and puts it down.

"I've heard it from two different people, and first I dismissed it as a rumor but then it started to make sense." Dad shakes his head. "You wouldn't keep us in the dark about that, though."

I head upstairs to take a shower without complicating that thought in his mind.

I knock on George's open door, and she waves me in. She's awake but still in bed, on her phone.

"Dad just asked what you had to do with the Deep Lagoon," I whisper, and she closes her eyes.

"I knew this moment would come," she says.

"Any brilliant ideas so far, for the guerrilla ad campaign? Other than the dissing booth?"

George shakes her head.

"But I swear to you, on my *brand*, I will figure this out."

I get in the shower, and as the hot water warms my sore muscles and steam fills the room, all these different binaries swirl in my head.

Citiot vs. local. Female vs. male. Heel vs. face. Love vs. hate.

The cheerleaders aren't as one-dimensional as I thought they were.

The locals aren't whatever I thought *they* were.

George is universally loved or universally hated, depending on who you ask.

Someone's heel is someone else's face, depending on what they root for.

The water warms me from the outside in. I'm completely uncertain about everything.

"Our lesson today is on your finisher. The most powerful weapon in your arsenal," Abigail Rose says. We're at the Trampoline Wrestling Foundation for our midweek practice.

Lexie's next to me, so we partner up.

"You want to find something that plays to your strengths, and exaggerates them. The most iconic finisher of all time," Abigail Rose says, "is the People's Elbow."

"It's literally just an elbow drop," Kayleigh says, unimpressed. The People's Elbow is The Rock's signature move, outside of the Rock Bottom.

"That's its genius," Abigail Rose says. "The Rock is six and a half feet tall. A mountain of muscle. But what gave him his superhuman power in the ring was his arched eyebrow." Abigail Rose arches her brow dramatically. "Do you smell?" she bellows, her chin jutting up into the air, "what The Rock is cooking? The People's Elbow," Abigail Rose says, "is ninety-nine percent theatrics and one percent wrestling.

"Your signature move doesn't need to be fancy. Or hard," she continues. "It also needs to be a move you can pull off from anywhere, at any time, under any conditions."

Lexie and I face off against each other.

We lock up, hands on each other's shoulders, and start to find our way into the fight.

I cut Lexie's legs out from under her with a swift kick and then cross her chest with my forearm to press her down. Lexie hits the trampoline with a perfect back bump and almost bounces to standing, but I'm stronger than her. I hold her down on the trampoline, and she rolls to the side and slides free. We face off again, hands out in front, but Lexie grabs mine and twirls me around, twisting me up in my own arms.

She crosses my arms in front of my body, down low, and then grabs me in a lock from behind.

Then she lets go of one of my hands and rolls me around with the other until my arm is behind my back. She pretends to put pressure on my shoulder and elbow, and I scream out like Angel made us practice the other day.

"I felt that pain in my *veins*," Abigail Rose says, clapping.

Lexie nods toward Kayleigh, who looks downright vicious as she pretends to bash Tova's head against the metal rim of the trampoline. Tova cries out in agony.

I shove Lexie playfully. "Sorry, didn't mean that." She shoves me back.

"No!" she shouts. "I'm sorry."

We shove each other back and forth, apologizing, but each shove gets harder until we're knocking each other back onto the trampoline and scrambling back up to knock the other one down.

Lexie shoves me, hard, and when I bounce up to standing, I shove her, harder.

"Whoa, that's what I'm talking about!" Abigail Rose says, and I look up to see everyone else has stopped and is watching us.

Lexie shoves me even harder this time, knocking me down.

"Sorry not sorry," she says, her face contorted in a menacing sneer that makes me want to practice mine in a mirror.

"I think you found it," Abigail Rose says to Lexie. "The Sorry Not Sorry Shove."

I'm sweating, breathing heavy, and am lucky I don't have whiplash from that off-guard shove. But I crack a smile. It was fun to lose myself in the fight.

Lexie shoves me, hard, and I fall back onto the trampoline, bouncing and laughing. She launches herself into the air and lands across my body in a flop, and we both laugh so hard spit flies from our mouths.

I grab her arm and pull it behind her back, with her stomach pressed to the trampoline. I pretend to yank it, hard, like Becky Lynch's Disarm-her.

Lexie screams out in fake pain, and Abigail Rose shouts, "Brooklyn has Local Lexie in the Arm Robbery! Watch out, everyone! She's here to steal your real estate and your arms!"

Lexie taps the trampoline with her free hand and I release the hold.

"We're starting in on promos soon," Abigail Rose says, "and I need you all channeling a repugnant level of self-confidence. I want you walking with that I've-been-training-for-a-month-but-I'm-already-the-best-who's-ever-wrestled swagger."

"You want us to be pompous jerks?" Tova asks, like the thought thrills her.

"I want you to have the confidence of a mediocre white dude," Abigail Rose says. "But why stop there? Make yourself a legacy white dude. I want you to have the confidence of Frankie."

"Can I have the confidence of Haruka instead?" I ask.

"That feels way less toxic," Kayleigh says.

"Haruka is my everything," Tova says, completely serious. We watched Omega vs. Haruka at the sleepover, and everyone else fell in love with the match, too.

"OK, let's go with Haruka," Abigail Rose says. "I want you to know you belong. That you are Mayhem. Like anyone who tries to tell you otherwise will get a high kick to the face from the Headless Head Cheerleader. A Sorry Not Sorry Shove or a bowling ball to the brain from Local Lexie. A Touch-Me-Not Explosion from Crystal. A Superwoman Punch or a gavel to the groin from the Notorious TCB. A Wild Stampede from Horse Girl. And"—she looks at me—"will get their arm ripped from their freaking body before they're cursed to a life of misery with Brooklyn's feared talonsman." Abigail Rose looks us each in the eye, one at a time.

"First up? Frankie gets what's coming to him." Abigail Rose looks ready for battle. "The Future of Mayhem has finally arrived, and it belongs to us all."

CHAPTER 24

Shithead smells like he sounds, which is why it's such a surprise that Freya agreed to keep him in her pool house while her parents are away on vacation.

"You have to feed him, and he has to be gone by next weekend," she says as Abigail Rose cracks a raw egg into the feed dish. "And no mice."

Abigail Rose shakes her head. "Nothing live. Promise."

"If this snake gets loose, I will kill you," Freya says, locking the door to the pool house and showing us where she stows the key.

"That snake is my hostage," Abigail Rose says. "I'll be back with overnight supplies, to guard it with my life."

I'm on the way out the door to help out with Mouse-o-Mania prep when Mom stops me.

"I got the strangest call from Helen this afternoon," Mom says, and I almost throw up. Mom shakes her head.

"I wanted to tell you," I say.

"When I didn't know what she was talking about, she mentioned a waiver she signed."

"I was following my bliss?" I say, but she's not buying it.

"Why have you been lying to us all summer? You know what? Go to your room."

"Mabel's counting on me," I say, and Mom shakes her head.

"How do I know if that's even true? What am I supposed to do? Follow you around? Track your every move? Is that what you want?"

"I want to be in this rumble," I say. "This is the first time in my entire life that I have ever felt like I can just be myself, and I wasn't ready to let everyone else in on it. I wanted to figure it out first, for myself."

Mom's face softens. "When have you ever not been yourself?"

"Most of the time," I say, and Mom looks genuinely surprised. "I'm . . ." I pause. "I'm nonbinary," I say, and Mom's eyes widen with curiosity. "My pronouns are they and she."

"Why couldn't you just tell me? About the wrestling, I mean." Mom puts her hands on my shoulders and looks me in the eye. "Thank you for telling me, though." She hugs me.

"The nonbinary part I'm just figuring out," I say. "You're actually the first person I've told." Mom keeps her one arm wrapped around my shoulder, and I breathe in the smell of coffee in her hair.

"I really like wrestling, Mom, and I know I should have asked you and Dad. I definitely shouldn't have forged your signature. I've never done it before, and I'll never do it again. I promise."

Mom sighs deeply and laughs.

"If we tried to stop George from doing what she wanted every time she forged our signature," she says, like someone who knows when she's been defeated by a force greater than she, "she probably would've run away." I laugh at that.

"We're used to you listening to us," Mom says. "You usually do. But you're seventeen. Almost an adult. And as much as we need you to listen to us, you're right that you need to be able to listen to yourself, too." Mom's eyes well up with tears. "It sounds like you are. I'm so proud of you, Birdie."

"I've been thinking," I say, "that maybe you guys could just call me Bird?"

"Of course," Mom says. "I love your name. But instead of lying to us and doing this stuff behind our backs, maybe we can still be a part of your awesome life?"

I launch my arms around her neck and kiss her on the cheek.

"Welcome to Mayhem," I say, wrapping my arm around her shoulder. I feel like Abigail Rose, luring her under the tent of this often-misunderstood pastime. "My name's Brooklyn. I'll be your local guide."

Frankie's home from his trip, and found the note we left in Shithead's tank.

He also got the message we sent from the W.I.T.C.H. of Mayhem account—*First I came for your hair, then your snake. Now, I put a hex on you.*

Abigail Rose sent the screenshot of his reply to the group chat.

Your move. If anything happens to Shithead, you're dead.

We're all back together at Freya's to choreograph the music video promo, and I'd much rather be training at the ring with Angel or messing around on the trampoline.

I'm wearing running shorts and a T-shirt, but all the other girls are basically in their underwear. I mean, dance clothes.

"Did you think about our idea?" Kayleigh asks me. I have no idea what she's talking about.

"I think I'm going to bow out of this whole dance thing," I say. They don't need me messing up their perfect cheerleader flow.

"We need you," Kayleigh says. "You're perfect for this."

"You won't be the star?" Lexie says, visibly disappointed. "We wrote it for you."

"Excuse me?" I'm so confused.

Tova nods. "Like we said at the sleepover, we'll be the demons and the ghosts you're digging up from the front yard, letting out of closets. We'll dance that part. And you can be the main character: digging us up, opening the doors and the windows," she says.

"I don't have to dance?" I say, and they shake their heads.

"Not unless you want to," Sofia says.

"Because I'm so bad at it?" I ask.

"You hate choreographed dancing," Lexie says, like it's fine. Not a problem at all.

"For the record, you can definitely dance as well as if not better than those old wrestlers in the 'Land of a Thousand Dances' video," Kayleigh says. "They just do the dude bounce and make funny faces. You would slay that."

I picture the guys in the video, and realize she's right.

"You're right. I'm in," I say, and the entire group lets out a Ric Flair "Woo!" and then wraps me up in a group hug.

In gymnastics, whatever was possible for me was on my shoulders alone, and that's how I saw my entire future. The whole world, really.

But here in Mayhem, in the world of wrestling, we rise or fall together. My best self is possible because, for the first time ever, I'm not alone. There is no such thing as a solo wrestler.

There's something else I have to say.

"Also, um . . ." I pause, not sure how to say it, so I just do. "I'm nonbinary. My pronouns are they and she."

They don't look surprised. They don't look awkward. They just look like my friends.

"Cool," Tova says. "Thanks for telling us."

"I think this music video is going to be kind of amazing," I say, and then we're all back into planning the aesthetic details.

Lexie puts her arm around me.

"I'm really glad you moved here," she says.

"I wasn't sure at the beginning of the summer."

"Of course, bitch." Lexie blinks. "Is it OK if I still call you bitch, since you're nonbinary?" I nod and laugh.

"Bitch feels great," I say. "Thanks for asking."

"Good. Now, um, excuse me? But why didn't you tell me first, bitch?" Lexie shoves me the way only friends can without consequence, and we both burst out laughing.

My eyes are misty with joy, but the kind that doesn't come from anywhere. The kind of joy that lives somewhere inside you, mostly hiding and waiting until, if you're lucky and the conditions are just right, it blooms without warning.

When the dance is choreographed and everyone's gone home, Abigail Rose and I head back to the pool house to check on Shithead.

Only: Shithead. Is. Gone.

We took Frankie's snake. His *pet*. Sure, he's a jerk, but that snake can't be gone.

But the door is ajar, the aquarium is empty, and Shithead is most definitely gone.

"Freya is going to kill us," I say.

"Hope she does before Frankie finds out."

The next day, Mostly Bones is already transformed into Mouse-o-Mania by the time I get there. Every shelf is full of one-of-a-kind Mabel originals, and the walls are plastered with pictures of Mabel and her sons in the ring.

Mabel has been baking for days, and the refreshments table has tray upon tray stacked full of homemade baked goods.

"Holy wow," I say to Little Mickey as he speeds by me in an orange vest with silver reflecting strips.

"You ain't seen nothing yet," he says, and then he's gone. Silas comes up through the basement stairs holding a Hell in a Cell replica with mouse Charlotte Flair and mouse Sasha Banks inside.

"You should buy that for your mom for Mother's Day," I say.

"Dad bought it for her for her birthday last year," he says, dead serious.

Mabel comes downstairs from the apartment. Her hair's curled and she's wearing one of her velour tracksuits with her signature cape tied around her neck. On her back, embroidered in silver, are four *M*'s connected at the base to form something like an eight-pointed star.

"I need you girls to haul up the rest of the inventory to stock those tables." Mabel points to a display with a wooden sign that says THE WOMEN'S EVOLUTION. Abigail Rose appears from the stairs and waves me down them.

"No sign of Shithead anywhere," she says. "Don't say anything to the Mickeys."

I pick up the Bella Twin Magic piece, with mouse Brie tucked under the flap of the ring with her head sticking out, while mouse Nikki is in the ring rocking her FEARLESS cap backward and facing off against Naomi. I bring the two setups upstairs and put them next to the one of Nikki Cross and Asuka.

People start to arrive, and by ten, when Mouse-o-Mania officially starts, there's a line out the door of people waiting for autographs.

In action with her fans, Mabel is pure magic. They leave with smiles so big they barely fit on their faces. She swoops up little kids in her arms and hugs them, she takes selfies with gruff guys who dissolve into fanboys the moment she looks their way, and she poses with the mouse dioramas as they sell like hotcakes. People tell her how long they traveled to get here, how many years they've wanted to make the trip. She signs everything they put in front of her face, including more than a few body parts.

"Another Mouse-o-Mania on the books!" Mabel exclaims at the close of the day. "And a record-breaking day at that." She's counting the drawer and tallying the credit card totals, smiling as she does. "Mabel needs a new set of tires!"

Little Mickey and Silas head home, and it's just me, Abigail Rose, and Mabel, surrounded by a bunch of wrestling mice.

"How many years have you been doing Mouse-o-Mania?" I ask.

"I opened the shop at the end of the eighties," Mabel says. "At first, I only made them occasionally, and would sign them and sell them. That was before the internet."

"The internet loves Mouse-o-Mania," Abigail Rose says.

"About ten years ago, I got the idea to make a day out of it," Mabel says. "We made a website and advertised it in wrestling forums, and wouldn't you know, they came out in droves."

"Mabel had no idea she was such a big deal."

"A big deal." Mabel laughs. "Look," she says, "I get it. The internet likes weird. And what's weirder than Mad Mabel's Mouse-o-Mania?"

"Oh, I don't know," Abigail Rose says, "the white supremacist ableist capitalist patriarchy?"

"Fair enough," Mabel says.

As Mabel heads upstairs, her cape trails behind her, and I finally understand exactly what George means by a lewk.

Mabel's outfit—her cape, her signature star of *M*'s, her tattoos—is tailored to her essence: one-of-a-kind, pure, unadulterated Mabel.

Mabel's spent her life as a heel—people booed her, spit flying from their mouths like rabid, unhinged misanthropes; she was a release valve for their pent-up emotions. She did that for people, and years later, they *still* show up for her.

Now, once a year on Mouse-o-Mania weekend, Mad Mabel, the Mother of Mayhem, plays the face that runs the place.

The people still want her weird. They want her different.

Only now, they don't come to boo. They come to show her some love.

CHAPTER 25

"I can't do this," George says at precisely the moment we're supposed to be leaving. "That upstate meme account advertised the dissing booth, and people keep tagging me in the comments, saying they're coming from hours away. It's going to be a nightmare."

"That means we could raise a ton of money. Everyone's counting on you," I say. "We're supposed to be there in twenty minutes."

She shakes her head. "I thought I could handle it," she says, "but I just keep imagining myself standing there in the middle of town, in that booth, everyone spewing their hatred at me, and . . ." George's face is apologetic. "I can deal with it on my laptop screen. On my phone. I'm not strong enough to handle it in person."

Part of me can't believe she would let me down like this. But another part of me understands. It's hard to be the heel.

"What if I'm in the booth with you?" I ask, and George's

eyes light up. "I'll show up dressed as Brooklyn, and they can hate us both."

"You'd do that for me?" George asks, and I shrug.

"Haters love me 'cause I'm awesome," I say, quoting The Miz.

George sets up what is her first attempt at a guerrilla marketing campaign: a tie-dye painted selfie frame, propped at the perfect height for people to stand behind. The top reads I HEREBY SOLEMNLY SWEAR NOT TO TRASH YOUR BEAUTIFUL TOWN. The bottom of the frame says #DONTBEACITIOT #SAVETHEDEEP-LAGOON. George posts a sign that reads: $5–10 SUGGESTED DONATION TO SAVE THE DEEP LAGOON.

I'm piloting an outfit George deems *forest grunge witch couture*—a sleeveless sage-green dress with an asymmetrical hemline and a pointed pixie hood. I've got her black Doc Martens laced all the way up my calves, and enough fishnet on my legs and arms that I look like a woodland fairy trapped in a net. Or who wants you to *think* they're trapped in a net, to lure you to your doom. With my deep red buzz cut just slightly grown out, the Violet Fury lipstick, and star-shaped glitter patches on both sides of my face, I could be fronting a dream pop band.

Or I could be exactly what I am. A nonbinary wrestling witch named Brooklyn.

"I picked up some supplies from the store," Abigail Rose says, handing me a pair of earrings. I roll them over in my palm and recognize the shape—Mabel's snake vertebrae earrings from her Spinal Integrity series—and thank her as I put them on. "In case you lose your confidence and need to grow a spine." She shrugs. "Now you have two on backup."

Silas says it always takes a while for anyone to stop and listen to him when he busks. People are funny. We need someone to do something first. Once someone does, others start to, and if a small group forms, it might turn into a large group. Then, if one person offers something for his hat, the others who have stayed are more likely to do so as well.

"Last night before bed, I hit one hundred eleven push-ups for the first time in years," I tell Abigail Rose, psyching myself up. "Not exaggerating when I say I felt like an actual god."

"Good, 'cause we could use a miracle," Abigail Rose says. "Still no sign of Shithead anywhere."

According to Silas, Frankie keeps asking the other guys what they know about me. How long I've been here and where I came from all of a sudden.

"What if Frankie"—I pause, not wanting to worry—"I don't know. Freaks out or something? He wouldn't do something to us, would he?" I look around the street, like he might be hiding nearby. But I see people starting to gather around the town green, like they're here for something. Maybe us.

"Don't worry about him," Abigail Rose says with utter certainty. "If he's a problem, I'll take care of it."

I'm about to ask her what she means when some kid who looks like he's around twelve breaks away from his pack of friends, strutting like he's not afraid to be the first one to ask about our booth.

"What is this?" he asks, picking up a flyer and then looking back at his friends like he's about to crack a joke. Abigail Rose printed up flyers to promote the rumble.

1ST INAUGURAL FUTURE OF MAYHEM
BATTLE ROYALE

FROM THE PEOPLE WHO BROUGHT YOU
THE DISS A CITIOT BOOTH
A FUNDRAISER TO SAVE THE DEEP LAGOON

☆ FEATURING: ☆

FOR THE FIRST TIME EVER OUTSIDE OF THE
OCTAGON AND INSIDE THE SQUARED CIRCLE,

➥ THE INIMITABLE XIUYING LIU. ☚
(YES, THAT XIUYING LIU.)

FROM THE LEGENDARY QUEEN CITY CREW,
☆ FOR THE FIRST TIME EVER: ☆

WRESTLING ROYALTY, THE FIRE CHIEF,
AND MS. MERCY.

FROM THE SOON-TO-BE-LEGENDARY
★ FUTURE OF MAYHEM: ★

THE HEADLESS HEAD CHEERLEADER,
HORSE GIRL, CRYSTAL, LOCAL LEXIE,
THE NOTORIOUS TCB, AND BROOKLYN.

╫╫╫ HOSTED BY THE FUTURE OF MAYHEM ╫╫╫
WITH MUSICAL GUEST: THE BEDWETTERS

"Can't you read?" I point to the sign above the booth: DISS A CITIOT, SAVE THE DEEP LAGOON. "Are you going to pay me for my time, or stand here wasting it?" I tap the clock ticking seconds on my phone. "Time is money, unless you're worthless."

The kid's haughty look shifts to a sneer. "I'm not paying you anything," he says, turning to walk away. But he stops to grab a flyer before he leaves. "I'll come to this," he says to his friends, "to boo the crap out of that bitch."

I stifle a laugh. I don't want to be caught smiling, but I almost can't believe it's this easy.

A Trailways bus pulls up to the stop, and about fifteen people, mostly unhurried tourists, start to meander. Two girls who look like I could have modeled a Brooklyn gimmick after them point at my sign and start toward me. They lift their phones to take my picture.

"Five dollars a picture," I say, stone-faced. They laugh, then realize I'm serious when I point at the SAVE THE DEEP LAGOON sign.

"Do you take credit cards?" the blonde asks, and I point to the card reader Abigail Rose borrowed from Aunt Gigi.

"Gather 'round, one and all, it's the moment you've all been waiting for," Abigail Rose says, and despite the fact that most of the people here had no idea this moment was ever going to arrive, they seem to believe her.

"Forged in the fires of the Future of Mayhem, Brooklyn came here with one mission and one mission only. That's right, folks, Brooklyn is here to ruin absolutely everything, and this fighter will not stop until the Men of Mayhem have submitted to their demands."

A few boos ring out from the periphery.

The audience looks at me. All those eyes. And instead of

shrinking, or collapsing myself to look smaller, I scowl at them and lift my arms like a bodybuilder, making myself as big as possible.

Near the front of the crowd, a little girl, maybe six, smiles at me, and I wink at her before growling. She recoils, looks like she might cry for a moment, and then laughs.

"And Brooklyn's sister, here for the first time ever! Exposer of local secrets! Ruiner of the Deep Lagoon, and of all things pure and good in this world. Here, in the flesh, so *you* can Diss a Citiot, George . . . of . . . the Wild!" Abigail Rose's voice bellows. "All proceeds go to efforts to reopen the Deep Lagoon," she says, and word starts to make its way through the crowd.

"How much does it cost?" some guy shouts from the back. "You ruined my summer!"

"We'll give you that one for free," Abigail Rose says, "but all further insults are a minimum donation of $10. That's not per insult," she explains. "One donation—that's a minimum of $10, but sky's the limit, folks—gets you unlimited insults, until your tank is spent."

The tourists look confused, but the group of boys from earlier has started to catch on. One of them asks a nearby adult, probably his dad, for money, and he saunters up to the booth.

"You're the one who got the Deep Lagoon shut down?" he asks George, and when she says yes, he lets it rip.

Soon people are texting their friends, posting it to social media, and the line for our Diss a Citiot booth wraps around the green, everyone come to let off steam and save the Deep Lagoon. People tell us they saw the post on the meme account and drove from as far as an hour away.

"You wear Carhartt but you never do Carhartt shit," a young guy starts, while his friends film him. "I'm here to tell you that what Sinatra said, it ain't true." His friends goad him on, and the audience enjoys the spectacle. "Just 'cause you can make it there, it don't mean you can make it anywhere. And it sure as hell don't mean you can make it here!"

His friends erupt, and the audience that's gathered laughs along until the guy's had his $10 worth and steps aside for the next in line.

People tell us that even the back roads are clogged with downstate license plate frames. That the restaurants charge NYC prices because we'll pay them.

Twentysomethings blame me for the lack of year-round rentals, and the fact that there aren't any affordable houses.

Someone pays ten dollars to blame us for the invention of the phrase "upstate and chill."

An elderly woman says she blames us for the over-foraging of ramps, mushrooms, and fiddlehead ferns.

I'm behind the booth taking a breather while George takes the barrage of grievances accompanying each donation when someone grabs my arm and I freeze.

I look around, but everyone is watching the dissing booth spectacle, laughing at the town's cathartic release of pent-up rage. No one sees Frankie, his menacing eyes burning into me as he grips my arm.

"What the fuck do you think you're doing?" he says, quiet so no one hears him.

I look for Abigail Rose but can't see her. I want to tell him about Shithead. I want to say I'm sorry. But his face is so full of hate. Frankie doesn't even know me, really, but he hates me.

I try to speak, but he squeezes my arm harder, and I can feel his hot breath as he presses his face close to mine.

"Game's over, bitch."

"What the fuck, Frankie?" Abigail Rose says from near the booth, anger burning in her eyes, but Frankie doesn't let go.

"Where's Shithead, asshole?" he asks, holding my arm like I'm his hostage.

"He's missing right now," Abigail Rose says, "but we're going to find him." It's a lie, and he knows it.

Frankie lets go of my arm and charges at Abigail Rose, but she whips out a knife, the blade mounted on a deer leg bone handle, and brandishes it at him. I almost scream.

"Francis Tully Meyer, what in the name of hell are you doing?"

Mabel's staring at us—at him—at the place where his finger-tips were just digging into my bicep, and at his hands reaching out to grab his cousin. It looks like he's lucky Mabel hasn't already ripped that hand from his wrist.

But then she sees Abigail Rose, holding that knife, and the sight of it breaks her.

"Mabel, I wasn't going to—" Abigail Rose stops herself. "I was trying to scare him."

"Grandma," Frankie says, "they've been harassing me. They kidnapped Shithead."

Mabel looks them both over.

"This all part of your fight over Mayhem?" Mabel asks them both, but they don't answer. My eyes give it away. "Mayhem's supposed to bring the family together, not tear it apart. Look at you. At each other's throats."

Mabel shakes her head. "I'm selling that damn barn." Frankie opens his mouth to protest, but Mabel puts up a hand to stop him.

"It's not my fault," Frankie says, but Mabel waves him off.

"Mabel, I'm sorry," Abigail Rose says, while the audience laughs around the dissing booth. "Things got out of hand."

"Hope you enjoy this month's promotion," she says, like she can't even look at them. "It'll be your first and your last."

Mabel walks away, and Frankie looks at me like this is somehow all my fault, when it was his hand gripping my arm.

"I want my snake back," he says, and then Frankie disappears through the crowd.

CHAPTER 26

The next day at practice with Angel, Abigail Rose looks like she hasn't slept at all.

We should be celebrating how yesterday we had a huge turnout for our dissing booth, and even got interviewed by a reporter for the local paper. We should be celebrating the money we raised for the Deep Lagoon, and what an amazing advertisement it was for our rumble.

But the only text Abigail Rose sent me last night was *It's over and it's all my fault.*

I wrote back that she's wrong. That it's just as much Frankie's fault, just as much all of our fault for getting swept up into this real fight. The one Mabel swore would be the end of the Future of Mayhem altogether.

And now it is.

One and done. That's all we get.

I'm sad, but Abigail Rose? This is all she's ever wanted, and it was just the beginning.

This is her destiny. It might not be mine, but it *is* hers. That path was a lot more sure-footed when her family had a wrestling promotion.

"I once read that snakes can find their way back home when you relocate them. Up to twenty miles," I say, but she doesn't take the optimism bait. "Where's Frankie's apartment?"

"Behind the Barn," Abigail Rose mumbles under her breath. "Don't get your hopes up."

Hearing her say that almost crushes me. *Almost*.

But today we have our final practice with Angel, and then tomorrow we're filming our music video for our theme song. If this is the last time I get to do all of this—I want to enjoy it.

"All right, superstars," Angel says, looking like a proud godparent at graduation. "I told you that with a basic foundation of tools—and if you work together"—Kayleigh catches my eye and smiles—"you'd be ready to pull off this rumble, but that you had to give me all you've got." He puts his hand against his heart. "And based on last week's practice and how all of you absolutely crushed those forward flip bumps and up-and-overs"—we look at each other, as impressed with ourselves as he is—"I think it's fair to say we both delivered on the promise."

We surround him in the middle of the ring, clapping and cheering.

"This is a rumble, so you're going to be using the ropes to work each other, the ropes to move yourself from one point to another in the ring." He looks at us, proud. "Any questions?"

"When I choke slam Tova into a back bump and then Kayleigh comes at me with a Headless High Kick, how long am I supposed to wait before I go Touch-Me-Not on her and fling her out of the ring?"

"OK, so," Angel says, taking a fighting stance. "You want to block her high kick," he says, bringing his hands to his face, "and then hit the ropes." He does it to show her. "And when you get her in a collar tie"—Angel wraps his hand around Kayleigh's neck—"wrestle into that hold. Then she should give you a chop across the chest, or something to knock you back, and when you freeze after *that*, it's finisher time.

"Who's ready to throw some shoulder tackles and take some back bumps?" Angel asks, drumming his fingertips together.

We warm up, facing off against each other, pulling our punches and kicks. We hit each other with loose fists, like a slap, pounding the mat with our feet. And we throw ourselves back—really sell it to the back row—when we're struck. We slap our thighs as we pull our kicks, all to give the illusion of a fight.

"Remember," Angel says, "not enough contact and the audience will laugh and boo. Not in a good way."

Mabel's voice weighs heavy on my mind. *It'll be your first, and your last.* It's hard to believe we've come this far just to have this one match and be done with it forever.

I'm not ready yet, but if I keep training with Angel, maybe someday I could join the Queen City Crew. Or Abigail Rose and I could start the Future of Mayhem in a different venue.

Tova swipes Sofia's legs out from under her and starts to deliver Daniel Bryan "Yes!" kicks to her face, pulling back at the last moment, while Sofia throws her head back.

But their timing doesn't work out, and Tova cranks into Sofia's face, sending her onto her back, clutching her nose, and catching the blood that pours from it into her cupped hands.

"I'm so sorry!" Tova cries out, crouching down to her and taking off her shirt to sop up the blood.

Sofia waves her hand and tilts her head back, slowing the flow of the flood.

"Too much contact," Angel says, pointing at Sofia. She pulls away the bloody T-shirt and shows us her possibly broken nose.

We each have some bruises on our bodies from a hit that connected too hard, or a grapple held too tight. That's the thing about wrestling. People think it's one or the other—it's real, or it's fake—but it's both. It's neither. It's its own thing altogether.

"I think it's broken," Sofia says, dazed with pain.

"I'll get you to the hospital," Freya says, and they start toward the door.

"It's probably not broken, right?" Abigail Rose says to Angel once they're gone.

"It's probably broken," he says.

Abigail Rose looks at the ceiling. "How are we going to replace her before this weekend?"

"Didn't Silas say he was defecting from the Men of Mayhem? That he wants to join the Future?" I say.

Abigail Rose starts to nod, like she sees where I'm going, and in this moment of crisis, the despair that clouded her face earlier lifts. She snaps into action.

It's her intense sense of duty. Her emotional fortitude and tenacious work ethic.

It's her Capricorn moon, back in the sky and lighting her way through the dark.

"I'll text him right now."

"Are we still filming the music video at Freya's?" Kayleigh asks.

"It's what Horse Girl would want," Tova says, in the most sincere voice I've ever heard her use. "But who's going to take her place in the dance?"

Everyone looks at Angel first.

"I can't," he says. "You know I hate to turn down a chance to be on screen, but I'm booked solid."

Lexie looks at me.

"Birdie can do it," she says, but I shake my head.

"I can't replace her," I say. "I can't dance like you guys."

"Neither can I," Abigail Rose says. "But I'm in it."

"You are?" I thought it was just the cheerleaders.

"I'm not missing out on the chance to be in this. Do you think Macho Man Randy Savage was like, 'I can't be in the video. I'm not a good enough dancer'? Plus, what do you know? I could be an awesome dancer."

"You can do it, Bird," Lexie says. "You can get out of your head and into your body."

She says it, and this time, I get it. Of course I can dance in the video. I know how to dance. I'm a human. I just worry that I don't look right. But that's because I've always been comparing myself to some binary vision of how girls dance. You know, like cheerleaders.

But my friends say I can dance like myself.

And that actually sounds pretty fun.

***

We start with the blood, smearing it on our arms and in streaks across our faces. We drip streams of it down our necks. Kayleigh licks what looks like an open, oozing wound on the back of her hand.

"That's some tasty blood," she says with a creepy smile.

"Ew, gross," Tova says. "Maybe you should shove some of that ugly back inside, Kay?"

We're here at Freya's, out on the back of her land by a small lake, getting ready to shoot our video for "Let My Ugly Out." We kept our outfits simple—black leggings with black tops—and our makeup gross.

"Where did you get this stuff?" Lexie asks, adding more fake blood to her forehead.

"We made it with corn syrup," George says, setting up the camera she borrowed from Dad on a tripod. The plan is to have us all in view on that screen and then she'll do close-up footage with each of us on her phone.

"Who's ready to dig up some demons?" Abigail Rose spins around to reveal the blood coating her *entire* face. "What? Freaked out by my crimson mask?" she asks, smiling through the goop on her lips. Crimson mask is wrestling speak for bloody face, and I only know because I watched an AEW episode a little too long and caught sight of some blading gone *really* bad.

"You look disgusting, but I can't stop staring at you." Freya, who's dabbed a bit of blood on her cheeks and rubbed it in like rouge, kept most of the wounding to her limbs.

"That's the idea." Abigail Rose picks up the pitchfork she brought and takes a menacing stance, baring her teeth at us like a bloodied animal. When I agreed to take Sofia's place with the other wrestlers, Abigail Rose stepped into the role written for me. And from the look on her face, she's ready to bring it.

"Let's run through the choreography one more time before we shoot," Tova says through bloodied lips that look partially torn from her face, and we get into formation, laying down on the ground like corpses.

Abigail Rose stands in front of the camera, and George holds the phone up, pressing play on the song. The bass rolls in, and then that soaring metal guitar.

When the distorted vocal starts, Abigail Rose lip syncs into her pitchfork, "I'm digging up the demons in my front yard," before spinning around and dramatically stabbing at the earth by our feet. It probably looks ridiculous, but this is wrestling—it's supposed to.

"Open up the closets, let the skeletons walk." George holds the phone near Abigail Rose's face, which she contorts like she's being tormented.

The ghostlike vocal pipes through the phone. "I lift up all the windows so I can let the ghosts float." I get into a crouching position, ready to spring up.

"I'm tired of hiding inside of my siding," the ghost sings through the phone, and it's my cue.

I jump up, my fingers spread like animal claws, ready to attack. My hands are dripping with thick, syrupy blood, and I know my face looks wretched.

"I let my ugly out," the vocal cries, while we all stomp, and shake and dance. It feels so good, coated in this sticky filth the color of my hair, to move to the pounding drums and lose ourselves in this thing, together. "I let my ug-ly ou-ou-out." I look around at my friends, all bloody and convulsing, and we look so ridiculous I almost break character and laugh.

But I'm a heel, and heels don't smile.

"Ain't got no time to feel haunted, got some flaws to be flaunted, I let my ugly out."

CHAPTER 27

Thanks to our dissing booth stunt and George's social media genius—not to mention our "Let My Ugly Out" music video, which we posted to YouTube *with the comments disabled* as per George's suggestion—tickets for tonight's event are sold out. The local paper ran an article about us, the upstate meme accounts all shared the event, and with the addition of the Bedwetters ("Live from the ring!") as the opening act, we'll probably still be turning people away at the door.

We've raised over a thousand dollars for the Deep Lagoon, and George has reached out to local organizations to collaborate.

This would all be the best news in the world if it weren't eclipsed by the end of it all. We told Abigail Rose to make a hard pitch to Mabel about all the good we're doing, and how the Mayhem name is alive again in the region for the first time in years.

But Mabel doesn't care about any of that. The way she sees it, Abigail Rose says, if her family turning on each other is what it took to get to this place? Good riddance to it all.

I get to the Barn three hours before showtime, and the parking lot is already filling up. We've got so many more fighters on the roster tonight, and Queen City brought a few of their production crew members, too. We rented two extra sets of bleachers because of all the extra tickets we sold.

The Barn buzzes with familiar and new faces: Robbie shows a Queen City Crew guy where he can set up his audio board, while Cami and Silas tend to a ladder setup in the back. I recognize the music piping through the speakers—not the usual Mayhem metal—from the Queen City event, so I know it must be from J Flav and Giorgio, the producers who created our new theme songs.

The Bedwetters are setting up in the ring, and when I pass by, Harley nods and Indigo waves. Zeke plucks his bass, testing the sound, as Luke arranges his kit.

Abigail Rose and Mabel are manning the overflowing merch table. Not only did we print up the first-ever Future of Mayhem T-shirts and stickers, all with Abigail Rose's witchy wrestling logo, but we have a plethora of buttons.

The Future vs. the Patriarchy
Too Big for Small Minds
What Would Haruka Do?
Send the Impossible to Suplex City
The Future Is Female, Male, and Everyone in Between

Abigail Rose has Cami's BOW TO THE QUEEN shirts, and we printed special-edition Xiuying Liu shirts with her headshot under the FUTURE OF MAYHEM FIRST INAUGURAL BATTLE ROYALE.

"Xena's setting up by the audio booth to DJ our theme songs," she says.

"We're so cool I can barely fathom." I plop down the extra box of merch I ordered behind her back.

"I know, right? What's this?" she asks, and I shrug. She opens the box of WWHD—What Would Haruka Do?—bracelets and smiles.

"I needed that. Horse Girl's nose breaking is a sign," Abigail Rose says, when Mabel walks away. "Mabel selling the Barn. Everything. They're all signs, and not good ones. They're signs that the stars are against me. That this isn't my destiny at all." She shakes her head. "Maybe I'm wrong about who I am. I'll become an accountant or something."

I recognize the look on her face. It's like her coach just told her she's outgrown her gymnastics dream. She did everything she could. She gave it her all. And still?

Her vision is on the brink of complete and total annihilation. In the end, it consumed her. She went to battle for her dream. The need for this thing she's so sure is her destiny, it made her arm herself against her own family. Abigail Rose brandished a weapon at her kin. She abducted his pet. I believe she wasn't going to use that knife. That she was just trying to scare him. But she crossed a line in the pursuit of her dream—like George at the out-of-control lagoon—and now she's punishing herself for it. Telling herself she deserves it.

I won't let her make the same mistake I did, and come to the wrong conclusions. About herself. About life.

Abigail Rose is the reason I don't care if people love me or hate me. That I just want to *be* me. She's the reason I feel OK inside my own skin.

Even if there's no barn and no Mayhem. Even if she's wrong about my future in wrestling. I don't care.

"Someone once told me that who you are doesn't matter as much as who you want to be," I say, and she shakes her head at me.

"Destiny isn't some passive thing that guides your choices without you having to make any." I quote her own words back to her. "Destiny didn't put me here in this town, or make me break into Mabel's shop. I just showed up. You turned that random, meaningless fact into magic." I look around at the scene unfolding. The one Abigail Rose dreamed into life. "Because that's what you do. Destiny is just choosing to be yourself." I point at her chest.

"It doesn't have to be in the stars. It's in you."

Abigail Rose nods, remembering.

"Wrestlers win, and wrestlers lose, but never lose their tough," I quote from her poem.

She looks at me, and her eyeliner is so thick, so intimidating, I would probably be scared of her if I didn't know better.

"Wrestlers never ever die," she says, "because wrestlers don't give up."

For the first time since Mabel said she's selling the Barn, Abigail Rose smiles.

"Can you man the merch table for a minute?" she asks, and then she disappears behind the bleachers before I answer.

Little Mickey is setting up the announce table he'll share with Abigail Rose, testing their mics. Silas is still miking a tall ladder in the back corner of the Barn, way off behind the bleachers, and when he finishes, he comes over to the merch table.

Instead of the flannel shirt and work pants he usually performs in, he's in a long black duster and a matching cowboy hat. He's painted black around his eyes and then layered silver glitter over that, like stars in the night sky. He wears bright red lipstick.

"You look amazing!" I say, and he smiles.

"Frankie hates the lipstick," Silas says with pride, and then he starts toward Kurt in the distance.

"This place is packed," Lexie says.

She's not exaggerating. It's standing room only, and pretty soon, there's not going to be much of that.

"How many tickets did we sell?" I ask Abigail Rose when she comes back.

"I lost count," she says.

"You look nervous," I say. "I've never seen you this nervous."

"I've never been this nervous. Holy crap, it's time," Abigail Rose says as the lights dim and a white screen starts to roll our music video. Our new theme song blares through the speakers.

I look into the audience—the bleachers packed with families, people of all ages, tons of them holding up handmade signs—and everyone watches the screen, smiles and laughs at our overblown antics. Little kids mimic the dance moves we make, and for a moment, I'm really glad I'm up there, dancing the way I dance.

This could be the last show ever in the Barn of Mayhem, and—for most of them—this is the first time they've ever been here.

We're not just going to let them cheer and boo. We're going to make them.

Luke smashes his drumsticks together above his head, and when the Bedwetters launch into their rendition of our theme song, the audience is already singing along.

Thankfully, Abigail Rose wrote a few opening skirmishes into tonight's program to give the band time to clear the ring and introduce our characters before the battle royale. To get us over with the audience before the match begins.

Drita and Jimena are up first in a plot against Xiuying. It's the moment when Xiuying, the face of the Future of Mayhem, will give the audience something to believe in when it comes time for the rumble.

"Esteemed guests," Abigail Rose announces in a broadcast voice, "we apologize for the delay. We're experiencing technical difficulties."

Ms. Misery hears her cue, and she runs up onto the stage and starts shouting.

"Would Xiuying Liu please come to the head of the class? I am missing a homework assignment from Xiuying," Ms. Misery says. "If I don't have Xiuying Liu's homework in my hand in the next thirty seconds, it will be detention!" Ms. Misery looks out at the audience, who watch her, rapt. "For ALL OF YOU!" she cries out. "If I don't get that homework assignment," she rages on, "it will be detention, detention, detention!" Some of the audience members start to chant "Detention!" with her.

"Did someone ask for me?"

Xiuying steps out of the darkness, and under the spotlight, her muscles are so defined they cast shadows. She wears simple black MMA ring gear, her hair twisted into intricate braids that zigzag and terminate in a ponytail.

When Xiuying climbs up into the ring and smiles at Ms. Misery, like she's going to enjoy this face-off, I get chills.

"Where is your homework?" Ms. Misery asks, grabbing Xiuying by the back of the neck and squeezing. The audience boos, just like they're supposed to.

Xiuying takes out a piece of paper from her pocket. "You mean this?" She throws it on the mat. But before Ms. Misery reaches down to grab it, the Fire Chief appears, climbs up on the turnbuckle, and flips into the ring, landing on the paper.

"Don't you burn that homework, Fire Chief!" Ms. Misery scolds her, wagging her finger.

The Fire Chief picks up the paper, waves it in Xiuying's face, and as she goes to hand it to Ms. Misery, Abigail Rose turns on a huge fan and it blows the paper out of the ring.

The three fighters look at one another and suddenly, it's on. They're punching and kicking and dragging each other across the ring. The Fire Chief and Ms. Misery team up against Xiuying, who fights back like you'd expect an MMA-trained fighter to, minus the real blows.

The two of them grab Xiuying by the arms and legs, and they lift her up to throw her out of the ring, the way we will to eliminate fighters, but as they heave Xiuying over the side, Xiuying somehow grabs on to the side of the ring, one leg still up on the edge.

The crowd goes wild. They're rooting for our face. Everything is going as planned.

Xiuying faces down Ms. Misery and the Fire Chief, who stand shoulder to shoulder, and then launches a spear that knocks both fighters into the ropes. They bounce and land facedown on the mat, out cold. The audience goes apeshit.

I turn to see Mabel, beaming, and she gives me a thumbs-up.

It's the end of their match, which is my cue. There's one more vignette before the rumble. In the script, Abigail Rose titled this section: BROOKLYN HUNGRY FOR HATERS.

Kayleigh comes out and climbs into the ring as the Headless Head Cheerleader.

The audience cheers like they already know her, because they do. Some just from town, but no doubt at least some of these people saw the promo she cut. They saw all our promos.

"L-O-C-A-L," she chants, with her bleeding throat and sunken eyes. Kayleigh shakes her pom-poms and jumps in the air. "Lexie, Lexie, welcome to hell!"

Local Lexie runs and climbs into the ring, answering the call.

"Where are they?" Lexie asks, and Kayleigh just looks around smiling, creepy. Like maybe her head really is severed. "Where's Brooklyn?"

I suck in a breath and step out into the spotlight as Abigail Rose presses play on my theme song, which cranks out through the Barn of Mayhem, and the audience explodes with boos. I look around the Barn at the enthusiastic thumbs-down, the faces contorted with visible disgust.

These people *hate* me.

I'm about to face my nemesis: Local Lexie and her brainless best friend, the Headless Head Cheerleader.

I'm playing a character, and I'm not. Didn't I kind of think Kayleigh was a mindless cheerleader when I met her? Didn't I act like moving here and being a local was almost the end of the world?

I *am* Brooklyn, and tonight, I get to lean in and hope I'm fun to hate. I get to let my ugly out. How many witches get to do that?

I jump up and down in place, punch my chest with my fist, and scream. Then I run toward the ring to face Local Lexie and her Headless Head Cheerleader best friend, ready to wreck absolutely everything I touch.

The boos are deafening. People are shouting things at me, but it all blends into raucous, angry white noise.

I look to my right, and there is a little kid with a sign that says I'M HERE FOR THE MAYHEM. I know just what to do.

I grab the sign from the kid, whose eyes go wide like they're about to cry, and I rip it in two and throw the pieces on the floor. The audience boos louder than they have all night. I'm giddy.

I don't waste any time. I go right in for Local Lexie, and when we lock up and start the chain—the flow of one move to the next—the crowd grows quiet, absorbed. Lexie has me in a full nelson. When I kick my legs, she rolls me up and over, and we come together in a grapple on the floor.

We give each other chops. Lexie gives me a round of Yes! kicks and the audience chants along.

The Headless Head Cheerleader sits in the corner, on top of the turnbuckle, laughing maniacally. When we're ready to bring the scene to a close, Lexie and I set ourselves up near Kayleigh. We wrestle on the ground, Local Lexie looking like she's going to best Brooklyn. The audience cheers and starts to chant.

"We don't like you!" *Clap-clap clap-clap-clap.* "We don't like you!" *Clap-clap clap-clap-clap.*

But when the Headless Head Cheerleader launches herself off the turnbuckle and crashes into us both with a Cheer Captain's Elbow, her other signature move, the crowd goes absolutely bonkers.

Robbie steps up into the ring in a striped referee shirt to break up the fight.

"For the charge of disorderly conduct here before the rumble," Little Mickey announces, "Mayhem will fine Brooklyn five thousand dollars for attacking our local heroes, Local Lexie and the Headless Head Cheerleader."

The audience cheers.

"You de-serve it!" *Clap-clap clap-clap-clap.* "You de-serve it!" *Clap-clap clap-clap-clap.*

I scowl and shout, "I'm going to buy your house! And your house! And your house!"

I point at them all like I'm Reverse Oprah, taking things away instead of doling them out. Their boos and jeers are deafening.

By the time I'm back behind the bleachers, away from the audience, I'm shaking.

It's *exhilarating*.

We all circle up together in the designated backstage area, also known as "behind the sheet we strung up in the back."

Angel's here. And Sofia, too, her very broken nose in a splint. We all put our hands in the middle. The Queen City Crew, the Future of Mayhem, and the independent artist known as the legend Xiuying Liu. I look around for Silas, who's supposed to be taking Sofia's place, but he's nowhere to be seen.

"'We Are Beasts' on three?" he says.

"One, two, three," we chant. Then we scream, "We Are Beasts!" and get ready to rumble.

"And now, esteemed members of our audience, please put your hands together for the first-ever Future of Mayhem Battle Royale!"

The first fighters to enter the rumble are the Notorious TCB and Crystal, and they start off like royal jesters. Tova chases Freya with her gavel, claiming she's been making statements about the healing properties of crystals that aren't approved by the FDA.

TCB wastes no time and launches Crystal headfirst across the ring, and the audience explodes with cheers. But when Crystal goes on the attack, they wrestle each other to the mat and put the hurt on each other.

One after another, each fighter is announced, her theme song plays, and she comes and joins the fray. The Headless Head Cheerleader, her face painted a ghastly gray-white with a bloody slit across her neck, and Local Lexie—clad in her Stewart's uniform and toting a bowling ball—team up against TCB and use her robe to tie her into the corner.

When it's my turn, the audience boos as intensely as they did the first time they saw me.

"This rumble is brought to you by ..." I shout at them. "AIRBNB!!"

Local Lexie and the Headless Head Cheerleader take me on together, giving me chops and kicks. They use the ropes to work my arms. At one point, all four of the other competitors each take one of my limbs as they try to draw and quarter me, and I scream out in agony.

Since we only have ten fighters, we don't send anyone out of the ring at the beginning.

The Notorious TCB has Crystal over the ropes and almost out, but the goddess clings to the rope and saves herself.

In the corner of the ring with a moment to breathe, I look around the audience.

I scan for Silas, who seems so big I shouldn't be able to miss him, but don't see him anywhere. Part of me wonders if the audience will even bat an eye when this huge guy enters the field of competitors.

Then it's Horse Girl's cue, and Silas should enter, but instead there's a much smaller, masked opponent running from the back, climbing into the ring.

"We're about to see carnage the likes of which we've never seen," Abigail Rose announces. "This is what the Future of Mayhem is all about."

The masked fighter dives at me. He grabs my shoulders and throws me to the ground, and I land a perfect back bump.

"Where's Silas?"

"Forty seconds of fighting," he says to me, his voice familiar, and I think maybe something happened to Silas. "Then throw me out of the ring."

"Kurt?" I ask, but there's no time to find out. We go hard at one another, and then, when we get close to the rope and the masked fighter says, "Now," I lift him up and throw him out of the ring.

The audience boos, because I make them.

"Haters gonna hate, folks," Abigail Rose says, "but Brooklyn is here to ruin everything, and even the Men of Mayhem can't stand in their way."

Kayleigh shoots her high kick up at Lexie's face, and Lexie gives a perfect block, as TCB and Crystal struggle to lift me out of the ring. Lexie grabs Kayleigh's shoulders and lifts her up by her bleeding throat, slamming her down into a back bump.

Kayleigh has to wipe the smile from her face to sell some pain, as the audience fills the Barn with deafening applause.

When I fear it's getting repetitive, Ms. Misery enters, followed shortly by the Fire Chief, and the two of them put on a clinic like only they can do. The audience is absorbed, screaming and booing, and when Local Lexie is launched out of the ring and out of the match, the place erupts.

And that's when Xiuying makes her entrance. Her theme song is epic. When she bursts into the ring, it's obvious Xiuying is here to dominate.

Little Mickey and Abigail Rose commentate, rapid-fire and clever.

"She's incensed!" Little Mickey says of no one in particular. "She's absolutely livid!"

The match wears on, fighters are flung out of the ring, and the audience is with us every step of the way.

There're three of us left. Brooklyn, Xiuying Liu, and the Fire Chief. Which is Cami's cue.

Cami's theme song pipes through the speakers as she races toward the ring. The crowd goes out of their minds, jumping and hugging one another. Cami's QCC fans are here, and their queen has finally arrived.

Cami climbs up on the top rope and launches herself at the Fire Chief, bringing double-knees to her face, one of Sasha Banks's moves. They collapse onto one another with expert grace.

I'm the first one Cami throws out of the ring, and as my body flies over the top rope and crashes against the floor, I feel that familiar certainty of purpose that used to follow a stuck landing.

The audience boos like they hadn't even gotten started before. The entire Barn of Mayhem is thrilled that I've finally been thrown out.

When Xiuying and Cami both pick up the Fire Chief and throw her out of the ring, all is right in Mayhem.

I know what's supposed to happen next. I know that Cami is supposed to wrestle Xiuying to the edge, and flip her out. Xiuying is supposed to hang on for dear life, and when the Queen tries to force her to the floor, it's Xiuying who's supposed to retaliate and pull the Queen up and over the rope. It's Xiuying who's supposed to stand victorious and hold the belt above her head because Xiuying Liu is supposed to be the first-ever Future of Mayhem champion.

But this is wrestling, and wrestling is real life. Sometimes thing don't go as planned.

Cami bear-hugs Xiuying around the waist like she's going to suplex her, and she lifts Xiuying up and out of the ring. Instead of grabbing the rope like she's supposed to, Xiuying reaches out and misses it. From the look on her face, Xiuying is as surprised as we are.

But no one is as surprised as Cami. Xiuying's feet, both of them, touch the floor outside the ring, and the crowd loses their freaking minds.

Cami falls to her knees and she alternates between shock, pure joy, and tears of relief. All real. Natural reaction.

Abigail Rose screams into the mic, "The Queen of Queen City has won the rumble! The Queen of Queen City is the First Inaugural Future of Mayhem Battle Royale Champion! All bow to the Queen of Queen City, the new face of Mayhem! THE FUTURE OF MAYHEM HAS ARRIVED AND SHE LOOKS LIKE WRESTLING ROYALTY!"

"Bow to the Queen! Bow to the Queen!" The audience's chant fills the Barn with an even more electric energy.

I look around, shocked, and people are actually crying, but no one harder than Angel, who I spot in the audience. His face is soaked and he's standing up, throwing his arms in the air toward her, screaming and crying and jumping up and down. I search for Xiuying, and she's shaking her head, laughing at the mistake.

Silas nudges me and points toward the WWE talent scouts hanging in the back with his dad and uncles, and they're all nodding, knowing they just witnessed greatness.

"Who was—" I try to ask him what happened, about the masked wrestler, but the audience is too loud.

"Ladies and ... Ladies ... esteemed audience, please ..." Abigail Rose tries to quiet the audience over the microphone, but the cheers take a while to subside. "This historic moment will be available to stream on RealtoMe.com, in addition to the Queen City Crew YouTube page. Be sure to follow the Future of Mayhem on social media and sign up for our newsletter."

Mabel steps forward holding the new Future of Mayhem championship belt, and it looks downright regal in her hands. The audience still cheers, but some watch Mabel in silent awe. She climbs up into the ring, between the ropes, and when Cami stays down on her knees as the belt is handed to her, it looks like she's being knighted. Cami rises to her feet, crying, and as she presses the belt high above her head, the crowd erupts again.

I feel a warm hand against my back and turn to find the masked wrestler. My opponent and my partner.

He peels off the mask, and Frankie looks different. He looks happy. Maybe even impressed.

I remember the Spider Lady, the masked Fabulous Moolah facing off against Wendi Richter in that first video I watched the night I met Mabel. The Spider Lady represented the old guard—the past and those who wish to cling to it, no matter who they're hurting in the present and how they're limiting the future—but tonight, this masked wrestler was pulled into the Future of Mayhem.

"It was Abigail Rose's idea. To prove to Mabel that we can work together and stop her from selling the Barn," Frankie says. "You weren't bad out there. All of you." He says it like a real compliment.

I eye him, suspicious, and from the look in his eyes, he understands why.

"It's adapt or die, right?" he says. "I get it. I can adapt."

"Clearly," I say. I don't trust him yet, but he doesn't look like he's mocking Abigail Rose as he quotes her. Mabel told him he needed to get on board a thousand times, but Frankie wasn't ever going to concede unless pushed. Abigail Rose *made him* wave the white flag.

"Tonight! Putting his belt on the line in an open challenge that will end in one fall," Abigail Rose pauses.

"One fall!" the audience calls back.

"I introduce to you, Silence and Sorrow."

A spot lights the rafters—where Silas was miking the

ladder—and I see his black hat, his head dipped low so we can't see his face.

He starts to play, deeper and darker than what he played that day in town. His flute wafts through the Barn, the crowd hushed to a silence that moments before would've seemed impossible.

Silence and Sorrow finishes his song, and when he lifts his head, the glittering black around his eyes looks like a thick mask, his bright red lips like they're dripping with blood. He descends the ladder, and the audience barely breathes, never mind speaks.

As he walks to the ring, he plays the eerie tune. He takes off his hat when he gets to Abigail Rose and puts it on her head before stepping into the ring.

He removes his big black overcoat and takes the belt from around his waist and hands it to Billy, the referee. Billy holds it above his head, eyeing Silas with a look of disturbed awe.

And then we wait. We look around the room and wonder where the contenders will come from. We wonder how many guys will take Silas on, and who will emerge victorious.

Lyle the Lover is the first to challenge, but he's not the last. One by one the Men of Mayhem come out of the woods and into the ring. They attack Silence and Sorrow all together. They try to tear him down, but not even their power united is strong enough to overcome him.

When Frankie finally enters the ring—this time without his mask—I figure this is it. Somehow, he'll tear through them all like he's better than he is, and then it'll be him and Silas. And, somehow, we're supposed to buy that this guy can beat Silence and Sorrow?

I'm groaning when the guys flip the script.

Lyle the Lover, Kurt Mo-Pain, He the People, Billy the

Kid—they turn on Frankie, surrounding him, as they join together to pick him up. And then they haul Frankie's ass out of the ring, kicking and screaming. If he's in on it, then *damn*, Frankie is a hell of an actor.

Abigail Rose and I look at one another like this can't be happening, but they keep walking him until he's through those big open barn doors, the audience cheering as he screams.

"You can't do this to me, you losers! You'll never replace me!" Then he cackles like a villain in a Marvel movie. It's kind of magical.

With the Men of Mayhem all out of the ring and nowhere to be seen, there are only two contenders left on the regular roster. Little Mickey and Big Mickey. Walter and Silas.

Little Mickey stands up from his place at the announce table and he calls to Silence and Sorrow, bringing the audience's cheers to a crystal quiet. Abigail Rose stands up and gets out of the way. This wasn't in the plot, and if they do something crazy right now, she could get hurt.

"Twin against twin," Little Mickey says. "We always knew it would come to this, didn't we, Silence and Sorrow?"

It's improbable. Their size difference alone doesn't make this a believable battle, but that's the thing about wrestling. Believable isn't the game. They're *bringing* it right now. They're selling the story so well, and the crowd is eating out of their hands.

Walter stands up on the announce table, and Silas goes to the corner of the ring nearest his twin and climbs up on the post, to the top rope. I watch them make eye contact and Silas nods slightly.

Then Silas launches himself out of the ring, straight at his twin brother, crashing into him and taking the entire table down with them. The crash is loud, but the audience is even louder. The cheers are deafening.

"THIS IS AWESOME!" *Clap-clap clap-clap-clap.* "THIS IS AWESOME!" *Clap-clap clap-clap-clap.*

Billy the referee is back in the ring and he's waving dramatically at the collapsed cousins like, *Oh no, what're we gonna do now?* They're both out cold. He waves in their faces, shakes their shoulders, but they're unresponsive.

Out of nowhere, Abigail Rose, wearing the hat Silas put on her head, steps up to the pile of her cousins. She looks down at them, passed out on one another, the entire crowd watching her, and she knows exactly what to do.

Abigail Rose lays her body across Silas's, and before I really know what's going on, Billy pounds three times, the bell sounds, and he's holding the belt high above his head, waving at Abigail Rose, declaring her the winner of the Mayhem championship belt.

The cousins are all back inside the Barn now, cheering and screaming for Abigail Rose. The audience doesn't really know what's going on, but even they feel the vibes. Cami's crying. I'm crying. Even Kayleigh and Lexie are crying.

Abigail's not, though. Abigail's smiling like she's living her destiny. Abigail's beaming like she's her own North Star. She climbs up into the ring and holds the belt above her head.

"THE FUTURE IS OURS!" she screams, shaking the belt, and the whole crowd screams it back. People hold up their phones to take pictures of the show that is Abigail Rose, and she soaks up every drop of their love. She closes her eyes and starts the chant.

"We Are Mayhem! We Are Mayhem!" Abigail Rose punches the air with the heavyweight belt, as the entire audience joins in.

"We Are Mayhem!"

I *finally* spot my family, cheering and laughing, like they have no idea what might happen next.

But then something happens that none of us could have predicted. Or written. Or even made happen.

A young kid near the entrance shrieks as Frankie comes back inside the Barn, a huge snake strung over his shoulders, tears of joy streaming down his face. I look at Abigail Rose, and we both shake our heads like it can't be, and then laugh in relief. Because it's him.

Shithead found his way home.

"Holy crap, folks, if it isn't Shithead the snake."

People in the audience scream, the entire front row jumps up onto their seats to get their feet off the ground, and more than a few children start to cry.

But when Frankie climbs into the ring holding his snake and he puts his hand out to shake Abigail Rose's, it's Mabel's turn to let the tears fall.

Abigail Rose reminds everyone there is still merch available, and to make sure they check out *Real to Me*, as well as our forthcoming vlog, *We Are Mayhem*.

When they say we'll be back again next month for another spectacular showdown, the audience cheers in a way that tells us they'll be here, too. Mabel doesn't say a word about selling the Barn, but when she takes Abigail Rose and Frankie in her arms at the same time and hugs them, making them hug each other, we all know she isn't going to.

After the house lights come up and the audience starts to filter to the merch table, the Barn begins to empty.

My parents tell me how proud they are of me, and Dad was clearly crying. George grabs me in a headlock and tells me she wants to train with Angel, too.

We thank Drita, Jimena, and Xiuying, and fangirl over how amazing they were in the ring. They're happy to come back and fight again, and we're lucky to have them.

"I'm coming for that title," Xiuying says to Cami, and then they start to plan how to squeeze in one more title match before Cami heads off to college.

Abigail Rose calls me over to the merch table, where fans are buying the TOO BIG FOR SMALL MINDS pins and want Brooklyn to autograph them. We pose for pictures with people who tell us how much fun they had. What an amazing show it was. That they can't wait to come back for more.

When the place is quiet and we aren't swarmed by adoring fans who want our autographs, I sit next to Cami, Silas, and Abigail Rose on the bench.

"We did it," Cami says. "This was fun."

Mabel comes over from where she was talking to the scouts, and she says, "I'm real proud of you kids. Real, real proud."

And that's when Abigail Rose finally cries.

CHAPTER 28

I wake up early, still vibrating with the energy from inside the Barn last night, and I open my window to let the birdsong in. I breathe in the forest air—the pine and late summer flowers, the early hint of decaying fallen leaves—and feel like I'm exactly where I belong.

I've been thinking about the difference between pockets of woods and wilderness. Where we used to live? We had pockets of woods. The kind you can walk through and make it to the other side, always. Without a doubt. The kind of woods you can't really get lost in. You know what it will bring, as much as you can be relatively sure of what it won't bring.

Wilderness is expansive, though. It feels like it goes on forever. Like it would take lifetimes to know it all. The way they discover new species of animals all the time, all over the world. How the remnants of the Devonian forest in Gilboa—the oldest known fossil forest on the planet—were there all along, even though no one could see them.

Being here in the mountains—when I can't tell where I

end and the river begins—makes me feel infinite. *The divine pulse beneath the veneer of time*, Grandma calls it in one of her poems.

The wilderness asks me, "Who do you want to be?"

I want to be open. I want to be free.

There's a difference between being Bird and being little Birdie. Birdie is the girl I was raised as. Bird is the person I am. It turns out I don't have to dress different, or wear makeup, or move my body in a different way to grow up. I can just be me. Only . . . older.

Someone I can't ever grow out of, or apart from.

As expansive as the wilderness itself.

Today we're all together to soak our muscles from yesterday's fight in the lake that abuts Freya's property. We can't go to the Deep Lagoon. It's still closed, but they're holding a meeting in town next month to figure out a way to keep it open and protected going forward.

The sun beats down from the perfect sky, and Xena plays music that I've never heard but can only describe as being the soundtrack to a perfect day.

When we slip into the lake, it washes away the sweat and dirt from the day, but it washes away more than that. I feel the sand and silt against my bare feet, taste the fresh water that creeps into the corners of my mouth.

The lake washes everything away until, suddenly: Here I am.

Bird. The eye that sees, not the thing that is seen. Just . . . existing.

I watch as a frog skips across the water like a stone, and the sunlight catches the cobwebs at the lake's edge, glazing early fallen leaves and the low-lying flora of the forest floor.

I look at my friends and think, *This is what it feels like to be home.*

And for once, I don't care if I'm Rip Van Winkled.

CHAPTER 29

The party at the Fort is nothing like it's ever been before. For one, people keep stopping to talk to me on the walk in.

"Well, if it isn't Brooklyn!" Harley calls out from the fire. "Come to ruin everything?"

"It's kind of my MO," I say, joining the circle of familiar faces. There's Harley and Indigo hanging out with Lexie and Kayleigh. I spot Tova and Freya through the woods by the keg, and Sofia's with them.

"I was so right about that suit," Kayleigh says, eyeing the purple suit she swore was perfect for me. And she *was* right.

"You were all unreal in that ring," Indigo says, raising her cup to cheers us. "Local legends in the making."

"Who you calling local?" Abigail Rose says, the championship belt slung over her shoulder, with her other arm around Xena. "We're taking this brand global."

"Especially if Silas's and Cami's auditions go well," I say. Both Silas and Cami got offers to try out for NXT. Kayleigh was pretty bummed she didn't, but we're all going to keep training with Angel, so who knows? The Future of Mayhem knows no bounds.

Darren and his friends saunter over to us.

"What do you want, Darren?" Lexie asks. "To get your ass whooped?"

"Laugh all you want," Darren says. "I'm not the one who's celebrating that the entire town hates me."

"Oh, Darren," I say. "Hate and love are two sides of the same coin." He looks at me, confused. "Like citiot and local. Heel and face. Man and woman. This world is way too complicated to neatly divide into two categories, Darren." I say his name again for added emphasis.

"Also, Darren," Abigail Rose says, picking up on my pattern. "You do know wrestling's not *actually* real, right?" Everyone laughs as the guys walk off.

Harley sits down next to me on a log by the fire.

"I thought you'd be kind of badass in the ring," they say, like that day on the sidewalk when we first met, and I want to ask how they knew. How they saw in me something I didn't see in myself.

Only now, I see it, too.

Later on, when we're standing by the keg waiting for Lexie to fill her beer, some guy I don't know stops and looks at me. My suit coat is off, and I'm in a black muscle tank.

He reaches a hand out toward my arm.

"Look at the guns on that one," he says, but instead of freezing and letting him wrap his hand around my arm, I grab his wrist, twist his arm around his back, and then press him to the ground as he tries to resist and shouts, "What the hell!"

The guy barely knows what's hit him before I've got him twisted in the Arm Robbery. Brooklyn's version of The Man's Disarm-her.

"What was that?" the guy asks, rubbing his arm after I release him.

I'm walking out of the cage, to feel feral. To feel free.

"My finisher," I say, joining the rest of my friends by the fire.

And as the guy walks away, confused, we chant after him.

"You de-serve it." *Clap-clap clap-clap-clap.* "You de-serve it." *Clap-clap clap-clap-clap.*

BIRD'S SUMMER
OF MAYHEM PLAYLIST

FEATHERS—FLORIST

I LIKE GIANTS—KIMYA DAWSON

BIRDS—KAT CUNNING

YOUR BEST AMERICAN GIRL—MITSKI

NIGHTMARE—HALSEY

LETTER TO THE PAST—BRANDI CARLILE

HEALING—FLETCHER

AMPERSAND—AMANDA PALMER

FOR MY FRIENDS—KING PRINCESS

SPRING IN HOURS—FLORIST

CAPTAIN LOU—KIMYA DAWSON FEAT. AESOP ROCK

KYLE (I FOUND YOU)—FRED AGAIN

WASTED YOUTH—FLETCHER

Q.U.E.E.N.—JANELLE MONÁE FEAT. ERYKAH BADU

HOT TOPIC—LE TIGRE

KISS THE RING—SONNY KISS AEW ENTRANCE THEME FEAT. KEYZ

MY FUTURE—BILLIE EILISH

LOVE ME MORE—SAM SMITH

ABOUT DAMN TIME—LIZZO

BLUE MOUNTAIN ROAD—FLORIST

ADDITIONAL SUGGESTED READING

The Backyard Birdsong Guide: Eastern and Central North America, Donald Kroodsma

Beyond the Gender Binary, Alok Vaid-Menon

Bitch: On the Female of the Species, Lucy Cooke

Dear Andy Kaufman, I Hate Your Guts!, Lynne Margulies and Bob Zmuda

Fine: A Comic About Gender, Rhea Ewing

Gender and Our Brains: How New Neuroscience Explodes the Myths of the Male and Female Minds, Gina Rippon

Gender Mosaic: Beyond the Myth of the Male and Female Brain, Daphna Joel and Luba Vikhanski

Good and Mad: The Revolutionary Power of Women's Anger, Rebecca Traister

"How to Queer Ecology: One Goose at a Time" by Alex Johnson, *Orion* magazine

Orlando, Virginia Woolf

Raising Them: Our Adventures in Gender Creative Parenting, Kyl Myers

Reflections on the Art of Living: A Joseph Campbell Companion, Joseph Campbell and Diane K. Osbon

Sisterhood of the Squared Circle: The History and Rise of Women's Wrestling, Pat Laprade and Dan Murphy

Testosterone Rex: Myths of Sex, Science, and Society, Cordelia Fine

Tomboy: the Surprising History and Future of Girls Who Dare to Be Different, Lisa Selin Davis

ACKNOWLEDGMENTS

Bird's story would not have become this book without the help of so many people. My heartfelt thanks go to:

Kat Brzozowski: Thank you for believing in Mayhem, for shaping this story into the one Bird deserves, and for being so much fun. I gave some of your optimism and unwavering faith to Abigail Rose, so thank you also for making my favorite character who she is. You are the cross-stitching feminist editor of my dreams, and thank you for introducing me to Lauren.

Lauren MacLeod: When you said you had an affinity for stores like Mostly Bones and were familiar with the world of indie wrestling, I thought you were the right agent. But when you swooped in at the last moment like a legit fairy godparent who enjoys cutting thousands of words and is wildly talented at it, I learned you are in fact a godsend. Thank you for answering every question I have, no matter how small, and for bringing so much story wisdom to Mayhem. It is such a joy to work with you.

Jean Feiwel and the entire team at Feiwel & Friends: I'm so grateful for your brilliance and expertise. Thank you for gracing this story with your immense talents. Special thanks to Arik Hardin and Kim Waymer, as well as Julia Bianchi for the beyond gorgeous design.

Sarah Maxwell (whose depiction of Bird on the cover gave

me goose bumps). Books are our friends, and you turned Bird into the coolest friend I could ever imagine.

Ethan Case, the original wrestling bodhisattva. I'm so thankful for the time you took to answer my questions, for the direct quotes you allowed Angel to say, and for the world you've built with the Palmetto Wrestling Championship and school. You make the world a better place. Thanks for being you.

Calli Lombard, Miss Hiss, wrestling announcer and multi-hyphenate creative badass, for sharing what it's like to get in the ring and for being a generally inspiring human.

Gina Schaeffer, for your vlog and the portal into what it's like to train with Ethan, and for answering my questions about training. For reading the book and for your notes: You're amazing.

Randy from Bones and Stones in Tannersville, for inspiring Mostly Bones and for telling me about the two-headed ducklings. Also, for the snake vertebrae earrings.

Dana Cooper, local witch and owner of Ritualist in New Paltz, for the magic you shared that helped Bird cast a new spell.

Nicole Brinkley, for saying "I want to read that book!" when I described the story at Oblong Books years ago. For your insightful notes, and for being the local wrestling fan reader of my dreams. But also for your essays and contributing so much to the kids' lit and bookselling world. You're the coolest.

Merisue Pozniak, for reading, and for your thoughtful notes that made the story stronger.

My writing group, the Story Whisperers: Jen Doll, Pamela Hoh, Alisa Kwitney, Trish Malone, Kerry McQuaide, and Andrea Pyros. Special thanks to Pam, for the ferret book so many years ago; to Andrea, for introducing me to Calli and loving Stewarts as much as I do; to Alisa, whose class I first wrote the haircut scene for; to Jen, for suggesting Abigail Rose's dream could be bigger; to Kerry, for drawing me out of my writing cave many years ago and saying, "You need people." To Trish, for loving stories about kickass girls, and for being one of my people. Writing comes with many ups and downs; I can't imagine navigating them without you all.

Kelly Hoolihan, for mentioning I should write a book about tomboys and having no idea how prescient you were. For introducing me to Jen. For being the best.

To authors I met along the way who shared something that mattered to me or to the book: especially Emma Kress, for that one perfect piece of advice, and Aminah Mae Safi, for sharing, among other wisdom, your grandmother's recipe for cranberry fluff.

The SCBWI Eastern New York chapter, for answering every publishing question, every step of the way. Special thanks to Jalissa Corrie, Lisa Koosis, and Kimberly Sabatini for your guidance.

The Children's Writers of the Hudson Valley, for putting together local conferences that made it possible to connect with editors (and meet Kat!) so close to home. To the librarians: especially Lucy Miller, whose library is where I first fell in love with YA novels, and Aida Merriweather, for your friendship and love.

LeeAnna Guido: one of the first readers to see parts of Bird's story and ask for more. Thank you for always having a bevy of Hallmark movie ideas on hand, for being the best at pop culture banter, and for being my friend.

My Fraggle Rocks: Jenn Jordan and Kaitlin Torp. We're stuck with each other. Forever. Thanks for letting me talk about everything, always, and for being the funniest. You are my Witches of Woodstock. Unite!

Amanda Starfield: The moon and you, too good to be true. So glad your animal past lives led to this human one in time for us to be friends. Thanks for telling me to save all of those text messages for blog posts, and for understanding me. Always.

Lee Pacheco: for giving me the costumed taxidermy mice (and all of the bad taxidermy pics), for having the best music recommendations when I need them most. For answering all of my questions about working remotely as a TV editor, for that Macho Man video about the cream, and for being my friend since before we could drive. Carene Rundlett: For your friendship, the magic you bring, and the photo shoot. Sue LaRocca: For the RuPaul quote. And for being subversive.

Tin Buenavista: "There is no purpose of friendship save the deepening of the soul" (and laughing so hard you pee a little). That's a me x Khalil Gibran collab for you, because I could not love you more. Thank you for the near twenty years of long-distance friendship, and shout out to DeviantArt for entwining our paths and creating a forever connection.

The DeviantArt friends who fanned the writing flame through my early teaching years. Mickey Quinn, for helping me find a writing community after college. Melissa Sheehan, for introducing me to Joseph Campbell and so many others. Jess X Snow, for your tender courage, for being the "unreasonable man," and for telling me to never stop writing so many years ago.

Kelly Going, writing teacher/mentor extraordinaire, your

insights into the art of the YA novel have shaped every story I've ever written.

I wrote this book over a five-year span, from nearly ten different home bases. This mayhem would not have been survived without support. Thank you to Tosha Silver, your teachings have been my lifeline, and my favorite flower magician, Katie Hess at Lotus Wei, for your healing and the amazing care package. Kelli Gilmore, thank you for your compassionate, wise presence, and for reminding me to breathe.

To the writers and teachers I've been lucky to learn from: Martha Frankel, Cara Benson, Jordan Smith, Ed Pavlic. Thanks to Lori Marso for recommended reading, for treating me like a real writer and scholar years ago, and for introducing me to feminist and gender theory. To anupama jain for introducing me to postcolonial studies and forever changing my worldview, and to Hugh Jenkins for making old, dead texts come to life. To Tracy Butler, who taught me to do "less, better," which turns out to apply to writing—and everything—too. To Mr. Curt, for teaching me how sentences work, and to Mrs. Day, for telling me I would regret quitting Honors English. You were right.

The Catskill Mountains, the town of Woodstock. The city of Poughkeepsie: Your storied wrestling history made it easy to imagine the Queen City Crew. Aquidneck Island—thanks for playing the role of home for a while, particularly the intersection of Paradise Drive and Purgatory Road.

To my students at Brown School, Arlington Middle School, and Poughkeepsie Day School. You shaped my adult self as much as any teacher I ever had. Thank you. Thanks to Zaire Malik, for the inspiration and creative camaraderie, to Serena

Pryor, for your friendship and all the memes and to Calder Mansfield, for answering my questions about the "cool kids."

To the music that got me through: the three F's. Fred Again. Florist. Fletcher. Special thanks to Emily A. Sprague for *Hill, Flower, Fog,* the official soundtrack of my office space.

To Sophie Strand, Perdita Finn, and Clark Strand—for your books, all of which have lit my path through the unknowable dark. To Harper Cowan: for capturing my silliness and joy in photo form.

Huge, overflowing thanks to Kimya Dawson for writing "I Like Giants," which was the first working title of this book and is one of my top ten favorite songs of all time. Thank you for reading the book, for loving wrestling, for sharing funny "growing up in the Hudson Valley" stories, and for being such a bright light in this world. Extra thanks for writing "Captain Lou" and for your permission to use the epigraph.

To the authors of the books in the Additional Recommended Reading section. This story was shaped by all of you. To Molly Langmuir for her wonderful *ELLE* Magazine article on Becky Lynch.

To the wrestlers who inspired this book—there are too many to name, and I wish I could have put you all into the book itself. Thank you for putting your bodies on the line to tell great stories week after week. To the original Gorgeous Ladies of Wrestling: I hope everyone who has seen *GLOW* watches the documentary to meet the real women behind the Netflix series.

I have a huge family (too many to name), and am thankful to you all. Special thank-you to my cousins Emily Travis, for responding to my questions when Bird was going to be tall, and to Tayler Travis, for being so funny. Thanks to

Gregory Rourke, for inspiring me to stay in the boat and keep paddling toward this dream. To Karla for making me a better storyteller/liar as a kid. And to Syd, for the books. Walker's right: You're the books.

To Kim and Kinsley, for being you, and for choosing my author photo. To Chloe for our pop song singalongs, and for sharing your story with me. Let's make this author thing a family tradition?

To Kate, Nick, Walker, and Skylar Wilson. To Erin, Owen, and Bailey Phipps. To Maria and Taylor Vidoli.

To Aunt Deena and Uncle George Yachymiak, for everything.

I'm so lucky to have four amazing parents: Cindy and John Rourke, and Celia and Vinny Mooney. The last stretch of years was only survivable because of your love and support. Thank you for your unconditional love.

Finally, and most importantly: to Chris. For loving my strength, and for seeing me. For introducing me to the Catskills, Poughkeepsie, and to wrestling. For being my co-pilot on every adventure, desirable or otherwise. Thank you for the support: every cup of tea made, every meal prepped (and every subsequent reminder to actually eat the meal), every lawn mowed. Thank you for surviving, and for making it home. Thank you for being home. The future belongs to us.